HERO

The
WOODCUTTER SISTERS, BOOK II

HERO

ALETHEA KONTIS

HARCOURT
Houghton Mifflin Harcourt
Boston | New York

11/13

Harcourt is an imprint of
Houghton Mifflin Harcourt Publishing Company.

www.hmhbooks.com

Text set in 12.5 pt. Perpetua Std
Designed by Christine Kettner

LIBRARY OF CONGRESS CATALOGING-IN-PUBLICATION DATA
Kontis, Alethea.
Hero / Alethea Kontis.
pages cm.—(Woodcutter sisters ; book 2)
Companion volume to Enchanted.
Summary: Saturday Woodcutter accidentally conjures an ocean in the backyard and,
with sword in tow, sets sail on a pirate ship, only to find herself kidnapped and held
captive by a mountain witch with the power to destroy the world.
ISBN 978-0-544-05677-0 (hardback)
[1. Fairy tales. 2. Witches—Fiction. 3. Characters in literature—Fiction.] I. Title.
PZ8.K833Her 2013
[Fic]—dc23
2013003895

Manufactured in the United States of America
DOC 10 9 8 7 6 5 4 3 2 1
4500428113

For my beloved grandmothers,

Helen E. Kontis

&

Madeleine DeRonde,

who taught me to be

a singer, a dancer, a chef, an artist,

a poet, a dreamer, a world traveler,

a reader, a storyteller, a tea drinker,

a lover of life,

and a woman of strength

Thief

H, HOORAY! It's you!"

The airy voice burbled like the brook, but there were no women in Peregrine's traveling party save the one he currently pursued, the bright-eyed temptress who haunted his every thought. Peregrine scanned the streambed and the tree line, squinting into the twilight.

"Hello?" Was it a naiad? A sylph? A fairy collecting milkweed and thistledown? It might have been the wind rustling the colorful autumn leaves, or his own mind tricking him, as his dearly departed father's had for so long. "Hello?"

"Please tell me it's you," she said. "The Earl of Starburn? Son of George and Marcella?"

Peregrine's fresh grief turned his confusion to wariness. No one could be so specific as to his identity unless she'd been following him since the funeral. Like a thief. Slowly, the newly orphaned Earl of Starburn backed against a tree and unsheathed the dagger at his waist. It was an ornamental piece, but Peregrine figured it had at least one good jab in it before he'd need to find a sturdier weapon, such as the sizeable fallen branch on his left.

"I am Peregrine of Starburn," he announced loudly to the creek, in case any of his servants stood within earshot. "Show yourself."

She manifested out of fog wisps, falling leaves, and leftover fireflies. Her hair was long, longer than his, and dark as the night but for a streak that bisected her ebon locks with a flash of silver-blue. Her eyes were black as well, sprinkled with starlight, and the sparse leaves of the grove brought out an olive hue in her slightly dusky complexion. The air around them suddenly filled with the stench of burned cinnamon.

Like every other child raised in Arilland, Peregrine knew what happened when one encountered a fairy. In the next few minutes, his life would change for the better or worse, and drastically so. Strangely enough, he was not afraid. He thought this new development rather wonderful. Whatever challenge she saw fit to give him, he was up to it.

"I am Leila," she said. "I am late. And I am so, so sorry."

Peregrine recalled no fairy story that started this way. "I . . . accept your apology?"

"You are too kind. I will now grant you one wish." She

raised her hands in the air and flapped them about like drunken butterflies. Peregrine clumsily caught them and stopped her.

"Thank you," he said, "I think. But I'm very confused."

Leila covered her smiling mouth with long, slender fingers. Her giggle popped like bubbles in the stream. "Your father did not tell you about me?"

"Ah," said Peregrine. "No. He didn't."

In truth, it was very possible that his father *had* spoken about this Leila, but any mention of fairies, real or otherwise, would have been dismissed as the earl's further mental deterioration. Peregrine placed a hand over his chest, felt the lump of his father's wedding ring beneath his tunic, and silently asked a ghost's forgiveness.

The fairy got a faraway look in her eyes, and straightened. For all her affected daintiness, Peregrine noted that she was almost as tall as he was. "Your father was a wonderful man," she whispered.

"I tend to agree," said Peregrine.

"But of course you would. You're a smart boy." Her tone slipped into condescension, but quickly righted back into dreaminess. "He came to my defense once, when I was helpless."

"He did that quite a lot." Peregrine hoped one day to be half the man his father was, before his father had become half a man.

"He was an honorable man, and for his good deeds I promised a boon."

Peregrine frowned. A fairy wish might have helped his father's debilitating state. Why had this idiot vanished before keeping her word?

"But I was captured by an evil witch," she said before he could ask. "I was forced to be her slave in a cave so high in the White Mountains that time itself did not reach the summit. Only now am I free from her spell, and so I came immediately to repay my debt."

"My father is dead."

"Which is why I sought your forgiveness."

"Once again, your apology is accepted."

"And once again, I offer you the wish that should have been his."

The cinnamon in the air dried Peregrine's throat and made him yearn for a brimming cupful of that cool, clear stream.

The fairy sensed his discomfort. "Let me fetch you some water." His golden cup appeared in her olive hands, though he didn't remember giving it to her. She bent down to the brook to fill it. Her dark hair and the folds of her cloak eddied about her.

Every man has one true wish in his heart. Peregrine paid Leila the courtesy of waiting for her to stand and offer him the goblet of water before saying: "I want to live a long and fruitful life. But in the event that I begin to lose my mind, or any other vital organ"—men often perished of less specific lingering ailments—"I wish to die swiftly and in peace."

The statement could possibly be seen as two separate wishes. Peregrine hoped this particular fairy wasn't one to argue semantics.

The sky was dark now. Distant thunder warned of an approaching storm. "Drink," she said, "and your wish will be granted."

Peregrine gulped down every bit of the water. He wiped his mouth with the back of his hand and smiled at the fairy. She smiled back. She was still smiling when the water began to freeze him from the inside out. The hand that held the golden goblet shook, slowly graying from frost. A pressure burst like icicles in his brain again and again, bringing him to his knees. He grabbed at his head and tore his neatly coiffed hair out of its queue, screaming for the pain to stop with a throat that could no longer speak.

She picked up the goblet from where he'd dropped it, and he watched as the silver-blue streak vanished from her dark hair . . . and reappeared in his own long locks. "Thank you, my dear," she said as she removed her cloak. "Do enjoy your long and fruitful life."

She tossed the cloak over his head, and the icy darkness consumed him.

1

Swords and Sisters

ATURDAY DIED for the fifth time that morning. Her shallow breath gently stirred the dust of the practice field. She got to her feet, shook back the strands of hair that had come loose from her braid, and pushed a larger chunk behind her ear, mixing the sweat and soil there into mud. The one clean thing on her person was the thin band of blue-green fabric wrapped around the wrist of her sword arm, a remnant of the only dress Saturday had ever worn. No matter how disgusting she got, it seemed this magic bracelet was as immune to filth as Saturday was immune to injury.

Shoulders squared, feet apart, and tailbone centered, Saturday lifted the wooden practice sword before her. "Again."

Velius laughed at her.

Saturday scowled. There wasn't a speck of dirt on her instructor; no dirt would be brave enough to mar his perfect fey beauty. Nor did he seem fatigued. She hated him a little more for that.

"Let's take a break," he said.

"I don't need a break."

"I do."

Lies. He was calling her *weak*. The insult only made her angrier. "No, you don't."

Velius lifted his head to the sky and prayed to yet another god. Temperance, maybe, or Patience. Was there a God of Arguments You've Lost Twenty Times Before and Were About to Have Again? If so, Saturday bet on that one.

"If you don't stop, you're going to hurt yourself."

"You can't hurt me," she reminded him. Humans with preordained destinies tended to be impervious to danger. She'd demonstrated this quality in the spring, when she'd miraculously recovered from an ax blade to the leg. Half a year later, Saturday was beyond ready to stop playing with toy swords and get on with her fate, whatever that may be.

"I *can* hurt you, though you might heal more quickly than the average human. Exhaustion will still lay you low."

"If that's what it takes, then." Could he please just shut up and come at her already?

"You're just mad I won't let you use that damned sword."

"Not just that, but yes." Her eyes stung with sweat, her

tongue was dry with dust, and her stomach growled more from anger than hunger.

"You need to learn," said Velius. "You may have chopped down a hundred trees, but you don't know the first thing about sword fighting."

"I do when I have 'that damned sword.'"

"Do you hear yourself? It's a crutch. That sword is like an addiction with you."

"It's not an addiction; it's a *gift,*" she shot back. She would have her fight, whether he wanted one or not. "What do you know? You can't turn your power off, or leave it behind."

"There are times when I wish I could." His shoulders fell a little, and Saturday knew she had defeated him. "Fine. Get the sword."

Her legs took off running at the first word, launching her over the fence and outside the practice area before he'd finished his sentence. She threw open the door to the armory, tossed the silly wooden sword back into place, and buckled on her sword-belt with a triumphant grin.

Erik entered the armory after her and made his way to the shelves of daggers and throwing knives. The king's personal guardsman scratched his bushy red beard, as if he were taking inventory. He noticed Saturday's presence out of the corner of his eye.

As soon as the belt buckle was flat into place, Saturday could feel her muscles singing. Her breath came easier. The pain of her bruises lessened. A happy energy flooded her body from head to toe and she felt . . . awake. "I wore him down again," she boasted to Erik.

"I noticed."

"You disapprove."

"Yep." He picked up a dagger, tested its balance, and then selected another one.

Suddenly Saturday didn't feel so victorious. Velius may have been the oldest and most talented of her teachers, but Erik was the one she loathed to disappoint. He'd been the childhood friend of her eldest brother, Jack; they'd been sword brothers in the Royal Guard, before Jack had been cursed into the body of a dog and never seen again.

Since her little sister's recent marriage to the now King of Arilland, Erik had become very much a surrogate eldest brother to Saturday. Of all her siblings, he was the most like Saturday: normal.

Normal.

Saturday had come to hate that word.

All of her other, fey-blessed siblings had been given name-day gifts that complemented their magical powers, which they'd inherited from a grandfather who'd been the Fairy Queen's consort for a time. Sunday's journal was a vessel for writing things that came true. Peter's carving knife could breathe life into his whittlings. Friday's needle could sew any material known to man. Thursday's spyglass let her see into the past, present, and future from wherever in the world she happened to be.

But Saturday's gift from Fairy Godmother Joy? An ax.

A ridiculous present for a baby, Saturday's gift was nothing more than a plain old ax, a boring tool that lightened Papa's load in the Wood. And yet, that same ax had chopped down a monstrous, giant-bearing beanstalk and turned into "that damned sword" Velius despised so much.

He might as well have despised Saturday outright. Without her gift, Saturday was just an overly tall girl with overly large hands and an overly loud mouth. She wasn't even as useful anymore. Since Friday's needle had healed a goose that laid golden eggs, Papa didn't have to go into the Wood as often, which meant Saturday and Peter now had days off. Who had ever heard of days off? Saturday used this idle time to come to the Royal Guards' training grounds to be yelled at and told how lazy she was. It's not like she had anything else to do.

Blessedly, Erik said nothing more, so Saturday hurried back to the practice area, where Velius stood waiting for her. His dark, lithe form leaned against the fence as he chatted to someone in a very large hat and pile of white skirts who had no business muddying herself in the red clay and muck of the training grounds.

Monday. Of course.

Saturday's estranged eldest sister had visited the palace in Arilland for the series of balls held by the royal family and then stayed to witness the marriage of their youngest sister, Sunday, to Prince Rumbold. But instead of returning to some faraway castle in some faraway land the moment the bouquet was thrown, Monday had chosen to stay in residence with Sunday.

Personally, Saturday felt that Arilland had lately suffered

from an abundance of royalty. (As Saturday suffered from an abundance of sisters, she knew what that was like.) Queens turning into geese, giant kings falling from the sky, frog princes, and princess-sisters. Saturday's goal was swordsmanship decent enough to get her hired on the first caravan out of this magic-drenched insanity.

"Good afternoon, sister." Monday's voice was butter and honey on warm bread.

"What are you doing here?" asked Saturday. Monday held one of the wooden practice swords, more as a walking stick than a weapon.

"I've come to see my sister's infamous sparring," Monday answered politely.

"Verbal sparring or physical sparring?" asked Velius.

The corner of Monday's lips turned up, revealing a slight dimple. "Whichever upsets you more, cousin."

Saturday was suddenly very pleased to see her sister.

"Gentlemen, might I have a word with my sister in private?"

Velius bowed to Monday, as did Erik, who had magically appeared in the practice area to bask in Monday's glow. He wasn't the only one. Saturday looked around the field. Every guard, to a man, was staring at the princess.

Monday tilted the brim of her hat up and slowly let her gaze drift across the field. As if released from a spell, each pair of eyes she met reluctantly turned away. Velius and Erik wandered in the direction of the well. Monday indicated a bench at the edge of the practice area and moved to sit. Saturday leapt over the fence and plopped down beside her sister in a cloud of dust.

"How are you faring?" asked Monday.

"Get to the point," said Saturday.

"As you wish."

Saturday wondered if anything ruffled her sister's feathers. She shuddered a little, remembering the brief time their sister Wednesday actually had *had* feathers.

"They tell me you rely too heavily on your gift."

It didn't matter if "they" were Erik, or Velius, or both. "They" were a big rat. Saturday rolled her eyes.

"I'm not here to chide you," said Monday. "I'm here to tell you a story."

"Like Papa." Saturday missed being in the Wood with Papa and Peter, telling stories, playing games, and being useful. Stupid, gold-laying goose.

Monday smiled and Saturday beamed back at her, though she had no idea why. "Yes, like Papa." Monday's face turned thoughtful. "Saturday, who am I?"

"You're beautiful," Saturday answered immediately.

"That's what I look like. Who *am* I?"

Saturday wrinkled her nose. What type of person *was* Monday? She'd gone off and married a prince after surviving a hailstorm and sleeping on a pea. Saturday knew nothing of Monday's life beyond that tale. For the most part, she had grown up without her eldest sister. What had Monday accomplished?

What was she like? Saturday had no idea. This was already the longest conversation the two of them had ever had.

"You're a storyteller?" she guessed.

"Sunday's the storyteller," said Monday. "What about me?"

"I don't know." Saturday felt bad, and not just because she couldn't answer the question.

"Neither do I." Monday removed a tiny, ornate mirror from her skirt pocket. "This was my nameday gift from Fairy Godmother Joy."

Saturday snorted. "A mirror?" Surely Aunt Joy could have done better. As gifts went, a mirror was pretty useless, even if you were the most beautiful girl in the land.

"A looking glass," Monday corrected. "It's for looking."

"To see what?" asked Saturday.

"Right now, I see the most beautiful face in all of Arilland."

"That's got to count for something." Not to her, of course, but Saturday felt sure that beauty was very important to some people.

"Perhaps. But behind that face, inside the woman, all I see is nothing," said Monday. "The beauty has only ever brought me pain."

Saturday wasn't very good at polite conversation, but she was very good at arguing. "That beauty won you all sorts of prizes when you were younger. It got you a prince. It got us a house." The tower that supported the ramshackle cottage in which Saturday and her parents currently lived had been given to Monday by her royal in-laws as a bride gift.

"What help was beauty the day my twin sister danced

herself to death? It snared me a prince who never loved me and then cast me aside for another woman, a witch who killed my daughter."

"What?" Saturday's grip on her sword's hilt tingled. Monday had said it all so casually, as if it had happened to someone else. Saturday hated all their horrid family secrets. She felt bad that she was not closer to Monday, that she had not been able to rescue her eldest sister in her time of need. She wanted to kill the woman who'd hurt Monday and dared harm a niece she'd never known.

"I'm sorry." The words were useless, but Papa had taught Saturday to say them anyway.

Monday cupped her soft, alabaster hand around Saturday's dirty cheek. "Don't worry," she said brightly.

"You're not sad," Saturday realized. "Why?"

Monday held up the mirror again, turning it so that Saturday might see herself in the glass as well. "Look deeper," Monday said. And then with her honeyed voice, she rhymed:

"Mirror, Mirror, true and clearest,
Please show us our mother dearest."

Inside the small oval surrounded by jewels, Saturday watched the image of her dusty hair blur before resolving into that of her mother. Mama was in the kitchen, as ever, kneading dough as if she were scolding it for keeping supper waiting. Saturday could almost smell the smoke from the oven fires, almost feel their heat as Mama mopped her brow with a sleeve.

"Thank you, Mirror," said Monday, and the vision vanished.

"Huh," Saturday snorted again. "Not so useless after all."

"It is the reason I do not believe my daughter is dead."

"You've seen her?"

"Bits and pieces, yes. She's not using the name I gave her at birth, so she's been difficult to find, but I have the sense that she is there. The mirror has shown me the world from a young girl's eyes. I believe my daughter is that girl. I believe she still lives." Heedless of her iridescent white overskirt, Monday took her sister's mud-covered hand in hers. "Saturday. When you leave this place, if you ever find my daughter, please tell her that I love her. And that I've never stopped looking for her."

Saturday nodded, interested that Monday had said "when" and not "if." "What does she look like?"

"Hair as black as night, skin as white as snow, lips as red as blood," said Monday, as if reading from a recipe book. "She is the fairest of us all."

Every mother thought her daughter the fairest of all, but coming from Monday, this was undoubtedly more truth than compliment. "Okay. I mean, I will."

"Thank you." Monday released Saturday's hands. "It may not tell me who I am, but at least it's given me hope."

A thought occurred to Saturday, so she blurted it out, as she did with most of her thoughts. "You are a butterfly," she said. "You are beautiful and light and airy, and you make people happy just by being present."

"Ever at the whim of the wind and fated to die young?"

Monday laughed, and a murmuration of starlings flocked to the fence posts to listen. "I may be beautiful, but I don't think I've blossomed yet. I feel more like a caterpillar: atop a leaf, admiring the view." She stood to receive Erik and Velius, who had returned from the well. But before she greeted them she turned back to Saturday and asked, "But tell me, sister, who are *you?*"

It was a good question. Without swords and sisters, who was Saturday Woodcutter? Besides a clumsy giantess with a big mouth and a never-ending supply of energy?

The mirror exploded with bright colors as the earth cracked and spewed forth geysers of water. Storms raged and towns flooded. Families were swept away from each other, their cries out-howled by the wind and their bodies drowned in the rain. The mirror flashed one horrible scene after another at them, and then went still. Even Monday's lovely reflection couldn't allay Saturday's sense of dread after what she'd just witnessed.

"What was that?" asked Velius.

"I don't know," said Monday. "It doesn't normally do that." She graciously accepted the cup of water Velius had brought her as if nothing out of the ordinary had happened. Erik likewise thrust a mug into Saturday's hands. His eyes never left Monday.

"Velius, would you mind escorting me back to my rooms?"

Velius gave a small bow. "Of course, milady." He turned and bent his elbow so that Monday could rest her hand upon his arm.

"Good day, Erik," Monday said to the guard.

"Good day, Highness." Erik might have been blushing under his beard, but as both blush and beard covered his cheeks in red, it was hard to tell.

"Good day, sister," Monday said to Saturday.

"See ya, Monday." Saturday let Erik watch them walk away for a while before punching him in the arm. "You're in love with my sister," she teased.

"Have been my whole life," said the guard. "So have the rest of these men. In fact, the only bachelor in Arilland *not* in love with your sister is the one whose arm she's on." Erik swung the wooden sword Velius had handed him in wide circles, stretching out his muscles and warming up to spar. "So, what did you ladies talk about? Girl secrets?"

Saturday didn't know the first thing about girls, or their secrets. "She asked me who I was."

"What did you tell her?"

"Nothing." She thought about it again briefly, but those thoughts were instantly swept under storm winds and rains and the cries of the doomed from the magical glass of Monday's mirror. Saturday shook it off. Who was she? She knew who she wanted to be: an adventurer. Someone about whom stories were told, like her brother Jack. But right now, she was neither of those things. "Yeah, I got nothing."

Erik settled into an attack position. "I beg to differ. You got a sword and a destiny. That's more than most people get."

"I guess so." That damned sword again. It was time to find out who she was without it, before she was Monday's age and still had no idea. Saturday unbuckled the swordbelt with difficulty and tossed it in the dust by the fence. The vigor she'd been feeling immediately left her limbs, and her muscles began to ache. She picked up the wooden sword that Monday had left behind and prepared to die once more.

"Let's go," she said.

2

Distraction

THE MESSENGER came as Mama was making dinner. It was a proper messenger this time, not the usual itinerant troubadour curious about the family of legendary Jack Woodcutter and willing to trade dubious ditties of derring-do for a crust of bread and a dry patch of hay for the night. Saturday was the first to dash for the door. Whoever answered the door got out of doing ridiculous household chores for as long as it took to deal with the company.

The boy on the stoop looked about Trix's age, or at least the age Trix appeared to be. With his strong fey blood, Trix would always appear younger than his foster siblings, and it would be his fate to outlive them all. But this messenger boy—assuming he was human—could have been no more than thirteen or four-teen. He had no pony, and his skinny bones stuck out at sharp angles from underneath his tattered clothing. Over those bones was skin of a hue that Saturday knew from experience was due more to birth than to long hours under the unforgiving summer sun. When the boy took his hands off his knees and straightened, skinny chest still heaving with breath, he looked up at her with kaleidoscope eyes of green, blue, and yellow. Straight black hair stuck out from under his dusty cap like the bristles of a horse brush. He was from the south, then, somewhere beyond the perilous desert sands. Had he run all the way from there? Judging by his ragged shoes, it was entirely possible.

The boy eyed her as if he expected something. Money? No one in his right mind would approach a shack like this with dreams of riches, however great or small. He put a hand to his chest and coughed dryly into one bony elbow. "Water," he managed to croak, at the same time it occurred to Saturday. She barreled through the empty living room and the full kitchen to the pump in the backyard, her sword sheath banging against her calf as she ran. She heard Mama call, "Who's that at the door?" before telling Papa to go and see. Papa slowly rose from his usual resting place by the kitchen fire and dutifully obeyed.

Everyone obeyed Mama. They didn't have a choice. That was her gift. Everything Mama said came true, so Mama didn't talk much except to bark orders to her husband and children. Aunt Joy said Mama didn't speak because she was lazy. Mama said it was the only way she knew how to live a normal life.

Saturday thought they were both full of beans. As the only normal member of the family, Saturday knew good and well that Mama was nothing like normal at all.

Saturday worked the hand pump until the water ran clear, then rinsed out a dry bucket before filling it and toting it back into the kitchen. "Come in, son." Papa's booming voice echoed through the house. He led the boy into the kitchen and sat him at the table between Peter and Trix. Saturday handed the boy a dipper full of cool water and he drank greedily. He wiped his mouth on the back of an unclean hand and said without ceremony, "I come to Seven Woodcutter from the abbess."

The statement meant nothing to Saturday, so she looked to Peter for guidance. Peter looked at Papa. Papa looked at Mama. The hand with which she'd been stirring the stew had gone still. "Rose Red" was all she said.

"The very one," said the boy.

"My sister," Mama reminded the rest of them. "Youngest but for me."

"Six," said Peter. Mama nodded.

As if naming your children after a day of the week wasn't silly enough, Granny Mouton had numbered her daughters One through Seven. Over the years, they had all taken other names: Sorrow, Joy, Teresa, Tesera, Snow White, and Rose Red. Only Seven had remained Seven.

"I come from one sister with news of another," the boy said eloquently, as if he were reading a letter. "Tesera is dead."

Tesera. The fourth sister. Trix's wayward actress mother.

Papa walked over to where Mama stood by the fire and eased her into a chair. Trix hurried over, took the spoon from her hand, and resumed stirring the stew. Mama's face was wistful and sad. Trix's face was turned to the fire. Saturday could only guess how her foundling brother felt about the death of the woman who'd handed him off as a baby to be raised by someone else.

"The abbess asks that you come to her," the messenger boy said to Mama.

"Yes," Mama said automatically. Her voice sounded far away. "Of course. Right away."

"Where is the abbey?" asked Peter.

"To the east and north," said Mama. "On the plains between the mountains and the sea." It sounded far. Very, very far. Mama rarely even left the yard. Her sister was asking her to leave the kingdom altogether.

"How will you get there?" asked Saturday. Surely Mama wasn't expected to run in the footsteps of this scrawny boy.

"Sunday," said Papa. Clever Papa. His youngest daughter was Queen of Arilland now, with her bright and generous nature intact. She would happily give Mama a carriage and horses and whatever else she needed to make the trip north. Sunday would also be distraught on behalf of her favorite brother . . . far more distraught, it seemed, than Trix himself.

Saturday didn't understand Trix's lack of reaction. Happy or sad or otherwise, Trix always felt something, and plenty of it. Now his face was turned to the fire, his back to the room. "Don't you want to go?" she asked him.

"No," Trix said quietly to the stewpot.

"Probably for the best," said Mama. "I must ready my things."

"What's your name, son?" Papa asked after the boy had drained another dipper full of water.

"Conrad, sir."

"Conrad. I would have you run one more errand today if your legs can manage it. You will be well rewarded."

Conrad's grimace at the mention of another run melted away at the word "reward," but he still seemed skeptical. He twisted his grubby hat in his grubby hands and nodded at Papa.

"Do you know how to get to the castle near here?"

The boy's dark hair flopped as he nodded. "I saw a tower on the horizon that scraped the clouds. Most of the roads lead there."

"Yes. Go there and say you have an urgent message for my daughter the queen."

Conrad sat up straighter. Smart boy. He was in the presence of the royal family, after all. Not that it made Saturday feel any different.

"Tell her what you told us, and ask her to please send a carriage. She will see you properly recompensed."

Conrad popped out of the chair and snapped to attention like a jumpy summer insect. "Right away, sir!"

Papa chuckled. "Now, now. Not so hasty. Won't you stay for a bit of supper?"

"No, thank you, sir. I'll be on my way. If you please, sir."

"Very well, then." Papa clapped the boy on his scrawny back. "Off with you."

Conrad bowed quickly, wiggled his toes in the holes of his ragged shoes, and ran out the still-open front door. Papa, Peter, and Saturday watched him from the doorway, kicking up dust as he made his way back down the hill to the main road.

"I admire that boy's energy," said Papa.

"He has almost as much as Saturday," said Peter.

"That he does," said Papa as he shut the door. "If she were younger, I might marry her off to him."

Saturday scowled. She was excessively good at scowling. Papa just laughed. "Peter, you go finish up outside. Saturday, please help Trix with dinner. I'll see to Mama."

Saturday paused before heading back to the kitchen. She wasn't sure what to say to Trix; she wasn't even sure yet how she felt about the situation herself. Peter and Papa were so much easier to talk to. They chatted and argued and laughed every day in the Wood. Trix was just so . . . Trix. Sometimes what came out of his mouth was as regular as the sunrise, and sometimes it was more cryptic than Wednesday's poetry.

Now that Wednesday was off in the land of Faerie, Friday had been apprenticed to an esteemed seamstress, and Sunday was a queen, Trix spent more of his time talking to animals than humans. As the last sister remaining in the Woodcutter household, Saturday supposed that it was her responsibility to comfort her cousin-brother. But she couldn't very well talk to him directly about what had just happened . . .

Saturday snapped her fingers and raced up the stairs to her bedroom to fetch the one thing she knew Trix prized above all else: distraction.

When she returned to the kitchen, Trix was just as she'd left him, silently bowed over the fire. Trix usually wasn't allowed to stir the pot, or milk the cow, or churn the butter, or spend time around anything else that might spoil in the presence of his strong fairy nature. Chances were Mama's taste buds would be too coated with remorse to care what passed her lips tonight. Saturday hoped for her own sake that the stew was palatable.

"So I was thinking," Saturday said to Trix's back. She'd learned from the years of working with Papa and Peter to start a sentence like this, with little pertinent information. If whomever Saturday addressed was wrapped up in his own thoughts, she could garner attention without having to repeat herself. Clearing one's throat also worked. Or yelling.

"What," Trix said into the fire, not at all his joyfully optimistic self. His voice was deep and apathetic. He sounded like Peter, thought Saturday, and that was strange enough.

"I was at the guards' training grounds today," she began again. Sunday always chided Saturday for never starting her stories in the right place. When Papa told stories, he engaged his listeners like this, encouraging them to ask questions. At the moment, however, this tactic did not seem to be working for Saturday.

"You're supposed to ask me what I was doing there," she prompted.

"You're always at the guards' training grounds," said Trix.

"Only on my days off."

"Which is almost every other day now," said Trix.

"I know. It's annoying." Saturday shook her head. "But that's not the point! Monday came to see me today."

Trix banked the fire and covered the pot with a lid. "You should have started the story there." He sat down across the table from her.

Saturday stuck out her tongue.

"Gee, Saturday, whatever was Monday doing at the guards' training grounds today?" The humor in Trix's voice relaxed her a bit, even if it was at her expense.

"Monday showed me her nameday gift."

"She did? What was it?" This time, Trix's intrigue was in earnest.

"It was a beautiful little hand mirror," said Saturday.

"How beautiful?"

"As beautiful as anything the fairies could make."

Trix grimaced. "You need to work on your descriptions."

"Almost as beautiful as Monday herself," said Saturday.

"Ooh, that's much better."

"Better still — it's a magic mirror. A looking glass."

"Really?"

Saturday nodded.

"How does it work?"

"She holds it in her hand, says a little rhyming verse, and the mirror shows her whomever she's asking to see."

"That's a pretty clever gift."

"I thought so too," said Saturday.

"Almost as clever as yours."

It was Saturday's turn to grimace.

"Hey, nobody else got a gift that changes with her destiny."

"That's because everybody else got magical powers," said Saturday.

Trix tilted his head and sighed in defeat. "So why does Monday's mirror suddenly fascinate you?"

"Do you remember the trunk Thursday sent this spring?"

"No fair answering a question with a question," said Trix. "Of course I remember."

Saturday knew he would. He'd spent hours killing an army of trees with the bow and arrows Thursday had included for him inside that trunk. Trix hadn't aimed for any animals — on the contrary, the squirrels, birds, and chipmunks made up his arrow-retrieval team. In that trunk had been the miles of material Friday had used to make dresses for all those ridiculous balls Sunday's true love had forced them to attend. Saturday twisted the blue-green bracelet around her wrist, briefly reliving that torture.

"Do you remember what Thursday gave me?" asked Saturday.

The answer took him a moment; he had been too busy testing out his new toys at the time to give much notice to anyone. Then his eyes widened. "You got a mirror."

Saturday nodded and pulled the silver-backed mirror from her swordbelt. There'd been an ebony-handled brush in the silk purse along with the mirror, but Saturday had left it up in her room.

This mirror was larger than Monday's; the silver framing it made it unwieldy, top-heavy, with no balance whatsoever. Saturday had no idea why Thursday had given her the fool thing; she had more use for it as a club than as an instrument of vanity. Roses stood out in relief all over it; the embellished thorns around the handle made it incredibly difficult to hold.

"What's it say on the back?" asked Trix.

He was right; there was a word faintly etched between the petals. "'Very'?" Saturday guessed. "Or . . . 'Merry'?"

"I think it's French," said Trix.

"How would you know?"

"Wednesday," said Trix.

Until her recent emigration to Faerie, Wednesday had often spouted impromptu poetry in foreign languages. They only knew it was poetry because Wednesday used her lofty poetry voice during the recitations, but Saturday wouldn't have been able to tell French from Cymbalese or Trollish. Papa couldn't tell the difference either — he'd told Saturday as much once — but he always applauded Wednesday's performances. Animals talked to Trix; maybe some of them had French cousins. "I think it means 'glass.' Or 'water.'"

"Or 'flamboyant useless object'?" suggested Saturday. Trix made a face. "Well, that's what *I* would have written. Want to see if it works?"

In a flash, Trix leapt over the table and landed in the chair beside Saturday, much like she had vaulted the fence earlier to sit with Monday. As impressive as the move was, it was a good thing Mama hadn't been around to witness it. "Do you know what to say?"

"I'll make something up." Saturday and Peter often played rhyming games while they worked in the Wood — games that Saturday won more often than not. She could easily come up with something that might coax a smile out of her brother. She straightened again in her chair and held the great gaudy thing before them. She and Trix looked back at themselves over her outstretched arm, fascinated by their humble reflections.

"Mirror, Mirror, gift of doom,
Show us Mama in her room."

Trix giggled. Saturday waited for the image to blur and resolve into a picture of Mama rummaging through her wardrobe, but the mirror did nothing. She wished to see something so hard, her eyes began to hurt. It took her a moment to notice that Trix was no longer interested in the mirror, and another moment to realize what an incredible fool she'd been. She'd said "Mama," and Trix's mother was currently dead. It would have been just as easy to say "Papa." Why hadn't she done that instead? But it was too late. She almost wished the glass had shown those terrifying floodwaters. Anything but this.

"Gods," she sputtered, "I'm such an ass."

Trix left her glaring at herself in the mirror and went back to minding the stewpot. "You tried," he said. "I appreciate the effort."

"I only wanted to —"

"Just set the table, Saturday. Please?"

"Okay." Saturday shoved the offending mirror back into her swordbelt and went to put her stupid, idle hands to work. As she set the bowls and spoons clattering upon the table, she said, "I'm sorry," before she forgot.

"So am I," he answered.

Peter returned to the kitchen. Saturday gave him the rest of the spoons and the cloth napkins and a look that explained exactly how far she'd shoved her big foot into her big mouth. He took them all from her without a word and finished setting the table. Saturday and Peter didn't need words to communicate, but for Trix's benefit she said, "I'm going to fetch . . ."

She stopped before saying "Mama" and reopening the wound she'd just kicked with her boot. She thought about switching it to "Papa," and then wondered if Trix knew who his father was . . . or if his father was even human. As there was just no good way to finish the sentence, she fled the room.

She didn't bother knocking; her parents would have heard her footsteps echoing through the living room and down the small hall. Everything about Saturday was large and loud. Trying to pretend otherwise was a waste of time.

"Dinner's ready," she called.

The door opened a crack to reveal Papa's face. "We're coming, m'girl. Thank you."

"Is there anything I can do?"

"No," said Mama, thus effectively tying Saturday's hands.

The look Saturday gave her father said, *There she goes opening her mouth again without thinking. You can't say I didn't try.*

I know, Papa's wrinkled forehead said in return. *At this point, there's really nothing any of us can do.* "Come now, Seven," he said to his wife. "I won't ship that stubborn mouth off in a carriage without kissing it first, and I refuse to do that until it's been properly fed."

Mama granted Papa a smirk, only slightly less rare than an actual smile. She tossed whatever garment she was holding onto the bed next to her carpetbag and pushed past him. He patted her shoulder, and then smacked her playfully on the rump. Making Mama smile in earnest was a knack only Papa had. And Thursday . . . not that she'd stuck around long enough to take advantage of it, or teach it to any of her younger siblings. With no other course of action at her disposal, Saturday followed her parents into the kitchen.

The smell hit them before they'd reached the table. Saturday closed her eyes and took a deep breath. Mama's cooking skills were none too shabby, and the palace cook had presented a scrumptious feast in celebration of Sunday and Rumbold's royal wedding, but this aroma left those dinners all behind.

Peter was already at the stewpot, helping himself to a generous bowlful. The divine dish was a result of Trix's stirring, for sure. Saturday snuck a glance at Mama before snatching up her own bowl and following Peter's suit.

"Go on, girl," said Mama. "I'm not going to scold your

rascal brother. It seems the gods decided we've had enough misery for one day."

At Mama's blessing, Saturday shamelessly filled her bowl. Mama had always been stingy with ingredients and kept an eye toward portion control, but she'd mothered ten children in her life. The current population of the Woodcutter household was half what it had been in the spring, so the stewpot was nowhere near as overflowing as it once needed to be, but there was still enough inside for each of them to have seconds, if they so desired. Saturday anticipated that desire this evening, and happily.

Only . . . when Saturday sat down at the table her appetite left her, fully and completely.

She waited politely for the rest of her family to serve themselves and sit, though Peter had forgone manners and dug deep into his bowl, as if he'd felled a dozen trees that day and toted them all the way back from the Wood barehanded. The rest of them similarly devoured their bowls, as if they'd been starved for a fortnight.

Saturday filled her spoon with the delectable stew and brought it to her lips, forcing herself to chew and swallow. The tender bits of roast melted on her tongue. There was a hint of wine and cream in the sauce, and the potatoes and onions were cooked to perfection. Saturday didn't normally like onions, but this was one of the most delicious meals she'd ever eaten. She only wished her body would stop whatever it was doing and behave. Her muscles were tense from her head to her toes, and her face felt flushed; the only cool spot on her skin lay under her sister's bracelet. When she swallowed the spoonful, it felt like swallowing a rock. Her stomach tightened, and a cold sweat broke out behind her ears. Perhaps she was coming down with something. Couldn't it wait until she was done with supper?

Mama noticed Saturday playing with her food. "Eat up, girl," she said. "I'm not going to—"

Papa laid a hand on Mama's arm before she could finish her sentence, in a subtle effort to force her to think before she spoke. It was obvious that she did not appreciate the gesture.

"Do you think I will be less sad if you starve yourself?" Mama said, turning the second phrase into a question instead of an order. But she had still commanded that Saturday eat, so eat she did, slowly and reluctantly, bit by stony bit, until her spoon scraped the bottom of her bowl.

Papa and Peter quickly jumped up for seconds, but Mama had her elbow on the table and her head in her hand before she came to the end. She set down her spoon and closed her eyes. Papa patted her arm again, but said nothing and continued to eat.

Peter was the second one to fall asleep. He pushed the bowl aside, cradled his head in his elbow, and began to snore. Papa only had time to glance quickly at Saturday and Trix before his own head hit the table. Saturday winced at the sound. Papa's empty bowl spun around and clattered to the floor.

Saturday's eyelids drooped. Her stomach spasmed and clenched. The heat spread down from her ears and cheeks. She wanted to move, to leave the table and run, but her body felt like a sack of the rocks she'd just swallowed. Slowly, she turned her head to Trix.

Trix stood and snatched up the rest of their uneaten bread into a small sack.

"What've you done?" Saturday managed to say without moving her teeth.

"It's a sleeping spell, that's all. You'll be rested and fine in the morning. Or possibly sooner, thanks to that sword of yours. I'll be long gone by then."

"You said you didn't want to go," mumbled Saturday.

"If I'd told Mama I wanted to go, she would have ordered me to stay here, and I would have had to obey her," Trix said. Curse him. Saturday had never been half so clever. "I can't do that, Saturday. I have to go. Tesera was my mother."

He certainly didn't need to explain himself to her. She understood all too well the desire to leave this place, and would have for far less important a reason. "I . . . come too," she managed to say. She may have failed at keeping his spirits up, but she could protect him on his journey.

Trix kissed her hot, stiff cheek. "And you would make a fine traveling companion. But I will move faster on my own. I may already be too late."

Too late? Too late for what? His mother wasn't getting any deader. But the words weren't coming anymore.

"Goodbye, Saturday," he said to her from the door. "I love you. And good luck."

Anger made her skin even hotter, and she growled louder than her stomach. With a hand on her sword, she forced herself to rise from her chair, much as she had forced herself to eat that bowl of stew. With each slow step up the tower, Saturday cursed

Mama. She cursed Trix. She cursed her Aunt Joy and every med-dling fairy she'd ever known, and all the ones she hadn't met yet to boot.

By the time she'd made it to the aerie and crossed to the window, Trix was a dot on the far side of the meadow. Saturday growled again, this time parting her teeth enough to let out a full-fledged scream from her tight belly. She wished she had enough strength to pound the walls or unsheathe her sword, but it took all she had to stand and look helplessly out at the disap-pearing form of her foundling brother. She adjusted her grip on her sword hilt. Her thumb brushed against cool metal thorns.

The mirror. Stupid, useless thing. As useless as Saturday herself, frozen in place at the casement. With the last of her energy she pulled the mirror from her swordbelt and threw it out the window with a roar. She tilted back on her heels. Her eyes rolled up into her head, and her eyelids drooped again. She did not hear the mirror hit the ground below, nor did she hear it break. She lost her footing as the world began to shake and tilt around her.

3

Godstuff

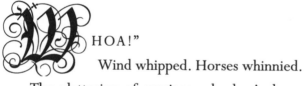HOA!"

Wind whipped. Horses whinnied.

The clattering of carriage wheels. A door opening and slamming.

"Mama?! Papa?!" A woman's voice like an angel. Frightened.

Monday.

"Here. In the kitchen." A deep voice with a common accent, trying to stay calm.

Erik.

"Are they . . . ?" asked the angel.

The rumbling answer was too low to be understood.

Saturday tried to open her eyes. The light that slipped between her heavy lids stabbed mercilessly at her brain.

Painpainpain.

She closed her eyes and concentrated instead on sounds. The two voices swam in and out of clarity, both strange and familiar. She tried to make sense of them through the pounding of a heartbeat that crashed like waves in her ears. The squealing birds outside the window made a horrible high-pitched racket.

Erik and Monday would be looking for her. Saturday had no strength to cry out. She slid a tongue between dry lips and tasted salt there. Was she bleeding? Had she hit the stones when she fell? She opened her mouth to scream, but all she managed was a wheezy moan. *Try harder.* She must tell them what had happened, tell them about Trix. She had to make sure Papa and Mama and Peter were all right.

First, she needed to figure out a way to get down all those stairs. The thought alone exhausted her, but concern for her family urged her onward. She leaned against the sheathed sword at her belt and used it to stand, but it tangled in her legs as she tried to walk. After stumbling twice, Saturday unfastened the swordbelt and removed it.

The moment her body stopped making contact with the sword, she felt a thousand times worse. Her stomach clenched, spasmed, and threatened to rebel. Daylight blinded her as it bounced off the cloud cover framed by the casement. One by one, her disobeying limbs began to shut down. Before she completely passed out again, she forced a hand out and grasped the hilt. Energy and relief flooded through her. Trix was right: the sword's magic actively fought off the sleeping spell.

"Aren't you handy," she muttered. With the sword no longer attached to her person but still sheathed, Saturday used it to stumble and crawl down the many steps from the aerie. Oh, if Velius could see her now, forced to use her gift as a literal crutch. He would laugh himself silly.

Erik must have heard her less-than-graceful descent, and met her on the last flight of stairs. Careful not to knock the sword away, he slipped an arm beneath her shoulder and encouraged her to lean her weight on him. She reluctantly obliged.

"Not going to carry me to safety, Hero?" Saturday teased him, but her words slurred together as if she'd been swilling Grinny Tram's honey mead. The lack of control frustrated her.

Still, Erik seemed to understand her. He'd no doubt helped more than one mumbledy-mouthed guard back from a tavern in a similar fashion. "And throw my fine back out, Giantess? You must be joking." But his arm did tighten around her waist, and she felt a few pounds lighter as they crossed the living area. When they reached the kitchen, he announced, "I found her," and lowered her into Papa's chair by the fire.

Saturday's face was immediately filled with Monday's hair as her eldest sister embraced her. Saturday would have reciprocated, had her limbs not been still full of rocks. But her strength was slowly returning. She patted Monday's voluminous skirts and repeated, "Really, I'm all right," in response to her sister's cooing. Over her sister's shoulder, Saturday could see Mama,

Papa, and Peter, heads down on the dinner table, as she'd left them the night before.

The night before. It was daytime now. She'd slept the whole night through. Trix was half a day ahead of them now, assuming he hadn't stopped to rest. But he probably *had* stopped to rest, so he couldn't have gone that far. If Monday and Erik let her have one of those horses she'd heard, she'd be able to cross the meadow and catch up with—

Saturday's gasp died as she choked on Monday's mass of golden curls. Monday backed up to let her sister breathe, allowing Saturday to see Erik standing at the open back door. Wild gusts of wind whipped at his hair and sleeves; the fabric danced like the exiting storm clouds and the waves crashing on the impossible ocean beyond him.

Saturday slowly raised a hand to her mouth. The salt on her lips hadn't been blood. That hadn't been her heartbeat pulsating in her ears upon waking like waves on the ocean—it had actually *been* waves on the ocean. Above those waves cried a cacophony of gulls and shorebirds, fishing and flirting with some very confused cousins from the Wood. The Woodcutters' little towerhouse was leagues from the nearest shoreline. Or at least it had been.

"I'm dreaming," whispered Saturday, for that was the only sound explanation. The cries of the gulls mixed with the cries in her mind of the drowning people she'd seen in Monday's mirror. Now she knew how Thursday felt when she saw the future. Her stomach rebelled again, but not from spelled stew.

"It is no dream," said Erik.

"What happened?" asked Saturday.

"There was a wicked storm, the air rumbled, and the earth broke," said Erik. "It was like nothing I'd ever seen before. It still isn't."

"Rumbold and Sunday are trying to assess the damage and keep everyone calm," Monday explained. "The palace is in chaos. They could not get away, but we came as soon as we could."

"I felt the rumbling," Saturday said. "Right before I fell . . . asleep." She wasn't sure what else to call it. Trix had poisoned them all and run away. Had he done this, too, so they couldn't follow him? Was this some sort of wild animal magic?

"Perhaps you should tell us what happened here first," said Monday.

Saturday was starting her story in the wrong place again. She persuaded her fuzzy brain to remember. "A messenger came."

"Conrad," said Erik. "Yes, he brought us the same message." Monday tried to interject something, but Erik stopped her, urging Saturday to continue.

"Mama was upset." It took Saturday an incredible amount of energy to open her mouth wide, work her tongue properly, and make her words understood, but she managed it slowly and surely. "Trix got quiet. Papa sent the messenger to the palace. Mama went to pack. Trix said he didn't want to go with her. Peter and I set the table."

"Trix said he didn't want to go?" asked Monday.

"If he'd stated his intentions, Mama would have forbidden him, and then he would have been compelled to stay. He planned it that way. He told me so as I was falling asleep. Right before he ran off."

Erik chuckled. "Clever little bugger."

The anxiety that came with retelling the tale woke Saturday up even more. "He stirred the pot, Monday. He took over stirring the pot when Mama got the message, and we were all so tied in knots over the news that no one bothered to tell him to stop. And when the stew tasted so good"—she could still smell the cold leavings in the bowls on the table and the burned remnants in the stewpot long boiled dry—"Mama didn't even scold him. But she made me eat, even though the sword didn't want me to, because she can't ever keep her mouth shut."

It wasn't fair of her to say that about Mama, but Saturday got swept up in the telling and she wanted to get it all out of her. Besides, Mama was still snoring softly on the table. "Trix poisoned us. He poisoned us, and he didn't care, not one bit. Did he make the ocean too?"

"This is no fey magic, wild or otherwise," said Erik, nodding to the view outside the door. "This is godstuff."

"Why would the gods make an ocean?" Saturday asked.

Monday turned her gaze from the watery horizon and shrugged. "Why not? The gods are responsible for miracles and misery alike."

Erik and Monday shared a look across the room that spoke volumes, much like Saturday and Peter did, only Saturday didn't understand this secret language. Erik bowed his head and resumed his interrogation. "Did Trix take something from the library? Is that why you were up in the tower?"

Saturday shook a head that felt considerably lighter. "I wanted to see which way he ran," she said. "I thought I could call him back. But he was already too far, and the sleep was taking over my body. I was so angry! I screamed at him and I—" The room lost focus as Saturday recalled what she had thrown from the window of the aerie, and the tremors she had felt right before she'd surrendered to the fairy-poisoned stew.

She'd killed him. In a fit of rage, Saturday had killed her little brother.

Peter stirred at the table. Mama and Papa had stopped snoring. Saturday white-knuckled the sword's pommel to give her strength, physically and mentally. She sat up in the chair, ramrod-straight. "It was me," she confessed to the kitchen. "I called the ocean."

This was what Monday's looking glass had shown them: the flooding, the terror, the storm. Wind and rain and death. Monday had asked Saturday who she was, and only then had the mirror sprung to life. Perhaps it didn't know what Saturday was, but it knew who she would be: a chaos dealer. A murderer.

Why hadn't she paid more attention? Why hadn't Monday said anything? But Saturday didn't bother chasing after futile answers. Peter had told her often enough that she was as unstoppable as a runaway horse. The visions in the looking glass had been as inevitable as day after the dawn.

Even the sword couldn't lend her enough courage to voice the rest of her crime. Silence was the only immediate comment, and that was lost to the task of tending to Peter and Papa and Mama's waking. One by one, Monday and Erik checked to make sure they were each all right, ignoring specific questions until Mama said, "Someone had better explain what is going on, right now!" So Saturday's tale waited that much longer for the telling.

"Slowly," Erik advised Mama, who, wincing, put her hand to her head. "One step at a time," he said softly.

"Trix," said Papa. "Gods bless that boy."

"He magicked the stew," Peter deduced, wincing like Mama had at the sound of his own voice.

"Yes," said Erik. "And he ran . . ." He looked to Saturday for help.

"North," said Saturday. "Across the meadow, alongside and away from the Wood."

"Fool child," said Mama, but with care instead of anger. "He's gone to the abbey by himself."

"I agree with you," said Erik. Saturday stopped herself from chuckling — the soldier was a quick study. A good way to keep Mama happy was to constantly remind her how right she was. "Do you have any idea why he would have gone to such lengths to travel alone?"

"No."

Erik tried to be reassuring. "He can't have gone far on foot."

"He won't need to," said Peter. "The animals will help him."

Guilt burst from Saturday's lips. "But the ocean! *I've killed him!*"

Any other sister might have warranted hugs and petting. For Saturday, Peter harrumphed and put a hand on her shoulder.

"Trix is fine. He can travel three times as fast as any of us. He just asks the animals."

"But you don't know for sure," said Saturday.

"Yes, we do," said Monday. "The animals aid him whenever they can." She rubbed her arms briskly against the cold bite of the breeze in the warm, salt-aired kitchen. "They will also protect him. Wherever he is, he'll be fine."

Saturday felt sick in her bones. Her siblings' reassuring words bounced off her thick skin. There was a dread in the pit of her stomach she could not ignore, and it nagged at her. The only way to know for sure that she hadn't killed her brother was to see for herself.

Mama wisely said nothing and simply nodded. She knew too well what it was like to doom one of her children to death.

"He'll be fine until I get my hands on him," Peter growled. He met Saturday's eyes and they both smiled. Peter's bark was far worse than his bite. She'd been on the receiving end of that bark often enough to know. But then Peter's smile fell. His brow furrowed, and he cocked his head at her. She answered the question he didn't ask.

"I was the last to fall asleep," she said. "Trix bade me farewell, after he poisoned us all." So maybe it was fairy magic instead of poison, who cared. It worked the same way. "I tried to talk some sense into him, but he'd made up his mind. I offered to go with him, but he refused my help. He left. I got mad. And then I broke the world." She pointed at the wide-open door leading to a wider-open landscape.

Slowly, Peter, Mama, and Papa stood and followed Monday

into what was left of the backyard before it fell away into endless waters. The sun burst through cracks in the clouds now, and the sea was calmer. But it was still the sea.

Saturday stood with them, her strength fully returned, and breathed in a deep lungful of salt air. She'd sat beside lakes and creeks and rivers, but this water was alive, mesmerizing and chaotic, gorgeous and unforgiving. It scared her. Who knew how many innocent lives she had taken in her heedlessness? She had no business making such a thing happen, and yet here it was. Papa put his arm around her.

"Nothing small for you, eh, m'girl?"

"No, sir," said Saturday. She prayed that the gods had spared as many lives as they could. Miracles, like Monday had said. Hundreds and hundreds of miracles.

"What's happened to the barn?" cried Mama. "All that lovely dry hay wasted! And no place left for the chickens to run, and nowhere to hang the laundry. Good thing I kept the goose in the pantry, despite everyone's grumbling. There will be no pies this winter if the apples are gone too."

Chickens? Pies? Saturday had possibly just murdered hundreds of people. There were waves lapping upon their back doorstep, and all Mama could think about was hay and laundry? And the racket that goose made—it's a wonder one of them hadn't crept downstairs in the wee hours and put it out of its misery. Saturday could hear it in there now, barking louder than the gulls.

"Next time I call the ocean, I'll ask it please not to encroach so far onto the property."

"See that you do," was Mama's reply.

"Who's normal now?" teased Peter.

"I'm still just me," Saturday snapped. "The magic was in Thursday's mirror." That's right — part of this devastation was Thursday's doing, and she would have them know of it.

"You have a mirror?" asked Monday. Saturday wondered if her sister was regretting the talk they'd had earlier.

"Had," said Saturday. "It wasn't a looking glass like yours. Trix and I tried to see in it. It didn't work. It didn't do anything."

"Except split the earth and fill it up with seawater," said Erik.

"Well, yes, that."

"Mirror," said Peter. "That fancy silver one from the trunk this spring?"

"The mirror you hated and hid the moment you received it and never looked at again?" Papa clarified.

Saturday rolled her eyes. "Yes."

"Wasn't it a set with a brush?" asked Peter.

"Best keep that brush in a safe place," Erik said to Papa.

Saturday opened her mouth to object to the insinuation that anything in her possession would be deemed unsafe, when the air filled with bright spots of sunlight and tinkling bells. Everyone stopped what they were about to say and involuntarily smiled as one at the sound. Even the gulls seemed to silence and wonder what new divine presence had manifested. Saturday could have sworn she smelled sugar on the briny breeze.

Monday was laughing.

It was odd that such a sound would present itself during

such a stressful occasion, and from such an unlikely source, yet it was refreshing as candied lemons. Monday's profile, backed by the sea and crashing waves with her iridescent skirts and gossamer hair swirling about her, would have made master artists weep if they'd known what a sight they were missing.

Saturday tried to look past that, tried to block out the sunshine and the happiness and the loveliness that dazzled so hard it made everyone forget, if just for half a moment, all their worries and pains. She tried to see Monday for who she was, and not just the pretty packaging. Trouble was, the beauty was both within and without; an integral part of her soul.

Saturday shaded her eyes from the brilliance. "What?" she asked, while the rest were still dumbstruck.

Monday lifted a slender arm to the eastern horizon, where the sea met the parting storm clouds in a thin line. As if realizing it had been noticed, the morning sun split through the gray cover, showering both Monday and the far horizon in light. A rainbow appeared, bold against the exiting darkness, framing a small, dark gray blur on the water. Perhaps there had been some miracles after all.

Peter squinted into the distance. "Is that a rock?"

"A tall tree," guessed Papa.

Monday smiled, and the sun shone all the brighter in competition. "It's Thursday."

4

Sulfur and Stone

THE PRIVY CAVE stank of brimstone. More than usual, since Peregrine's nose didn't typically register the acrid smell anymore. The stones of the walls and floor took on an orange hue and began to perspire. Peregrine hiked up his skirt and hopped from foot to foot out through the archway, barely making it around a corner before a burst of flame engulfed the narrow stone hallway.

This particular alcove probably wasn't the safest place to do one's business, but Peregrine couldn't beat the cleanup. The perpetual venting flares came with a decent enough warning and kept the place from smelling like anything worse than the usual sulfur and stone. He'd been singed a time or two, but it was worth it.

Peregrine swung his lantern and watched the shadows dance along the shimmering, uneven walls of the tunnel. He danced a jig with them, his skirt swirling around his legs as he stomped gleefully through Puddle Lake. Disturbing the water marred the reflection he didn't care to see.

"Hello there, boy," Peregrine said to Shaggy Dog in greeting. "Find any good treats today?"

Shaggy Dog said nothing, just like it always did. Peregrine patted the giant rock formation on its hind leg.

Leila had selected exactly the right target on which to perform her spell. The witch's daughter and Peregrine had shared the same build and the same dark features — it would have required far more magic to curse some tiny, fair young thing into taking Leila's place at the Top of the World so that she could escape her mother and the dragon who slept here.

But Leila (he realized now) was not capable of that level of magic, and so her curse had not completely transformed him, thank the gods. He'd retained his manhood, for all the good it did him here in the White Mountains, on a peak higher than time itself. Though his height remained the same, the line of his jaw had softened and his skin had paled, taking on a subtle olive shade. His muscles had thinned and corded, like a dancer's, not surprising with all the climbing and exploring he did on top of all the housework . . . or whatever one called chores when one's home was a great mountain of fire and ice.

Peregrine passed the mushroom forest and growled at the stone bear that met him there, peering down from the ceiling.

Big Bear marked the spot where the air began to grow cool again. Peregrine stopped to don the boots he'd been carrying. He took the shawl from his waist, pulled it over his bare arms, and continued on with his thoughts. At least his thoughts were still his own.

He'd collected every mirror he found and hidden them away in a cave beyond the dragon. He'd learned to ignore crystals and reflecting pools as he encountered them. Over time, he'd become quite adept at not seeing the face that wasn't his: the black eyes beneath arched eyebrows, or the silver-blue streak in the thick black hair that always fell to his elbows in the morning, no matter how many times he hacked it off with implements, enchanted and otherwise. He'd learned to wear skirts and speak in whispers. Peregrine had kept the witch at arm's length enough to fall beneath her notice. After a while, those habits had come as naturally as breathing.

He had considered exposing the ruse to the witch, in those first days. He'd contemplated revealing himself and facing the witch's wrath simply to end his imprisonment. But Peregrine never quite found himself ready to forfeit both his life and the dream of triumphantly returning to the world of men. Eventually, he'd grown to enjoy the puzzles that these caves provided him. He relished the idea that he would never age or die. He didn't even mind the witch so much, on the days when her demon blood wasn't running wild.

And then that nice young woodcutter had stolen the witch's eyes and made Peregrine's life so much easier.

The cave floor grew drier and more even beneath the soles of his shoes; his breath turned whiter than the walls. Inside the kitchen, Peregrine banked the smokeless fire and swapped out the steaming laundry pot with another he'd readied with that night's supper. Betwixt — currently a very ugly dog with a rattlesnake's tail — twitched in his sleep in response to the reduction in heat.

Peregrine smiled. Betwixt was the main reason he stayed.

Betwixt was a chimera who'd been captured by the witch long before Peregrine, so long ago that he remembered neither his name nor his original shape. While the witch held him captive he had no control over where and when and how he changed form, but he was always some creature betwixt one animal and another, so the moniker suited him. And as Betwixt had not cared overly much for Leila, Peregrine's presence suited him as well.

Peregrine nudged the dogsnake with his foot.

"If you intend on waking me up before I'm ready, you'd better intend to share some of that stew as well," Betwixt growled without opening his eyes. "And a bowl of water."

"Absolutely!" Peregrine said cheerily. "I was hoping you'd taste the stew for me. The spider meat is fresh, but it's possible the brownie bits have gone rancid. And some of the mushrooms might have had a touch of color on them . . . it was hard to see. But then, it always is in this place."

"Pantry Surprise again already?"

"Waste not, want not," Peregrine replied.

"I'll choose 'want not,' thank you," said Betwixt.

Peregrine laughed at the retort. When one was forced to stay in another's company in a cave beyond time, it was best to keep the atmosphere jovial. Peregrine and Betwixt explored together, hunted together, and avoided the witch together as best they could. In the time of Peregrine's imprisonment Betwixt had become his best friend and closest confidant. It was a rare bond Peregrine had shared with no one since his father.

Peregrine took up a dagger and set to chopping shards of icerock out of the wall. He collected them in a bowl fashioned from an old warrior's helmet and set them nearer to the fire to melt. After the fourth or fifth shard chipped away, the dagger snapped. The blade flew across the room and landed behind a clump of pillarstones.

"Troll blade," said Betwixt. "Shoddy workmanship."

The dagger might have also been a thousand years old. "I'll try to select a dwarf blade next time." Forced to move on to another task, Peregrine lifted the laundry pot and dumped the dirty water into a runnel that led back down to the heart of the mountain. One by one, he began wringing the clothes out for drying. "I had a vision of her again last night."

"You had a *dream*. Stop calling them 'visions' or I'll start calling you 'witch.'"

"Fine, I had a dream. Of Elodie."

And what a lovely dream it was. They'd lived in a rose-covered cottage at the edge of the forest. A low rock wall surrounded a garden and a small barn. The kitchen had two ovens and a pantry and a pump house for well water. The bedroom had been up a long flight of stairs that reminded Peregrine of one of the turrets at Starburn, but he had never seen this place before. He only knew that he was warm and safe and loved and that she was there, smiling at him over the dinner table. The light from the sun twinkled in her bright eyes and caught her hair and turned it gold.

"Or not," said Betwixt. "You can't be sure it's her. You haven't seen her since you were small children."

"You're such a killjoy." Peregrine slapped the witch's ratty dress against the side of the cauldron and wrung it out in frustration.

Betwixt sighed and gave in. He was too kind to demean any visions of loveliness, however fleeting, insubstantial, and wholly untrue. "Go on. Tell me about her."

Peregrine nodded. "I see her as a goddess wrapped in waves of blue-green sea, or a terrible angel in a white gown sullied with blood, rising like the moon above a battlefield. Sometimes she holds a sword in one hand, sometimes an ax. Day or night, rain or shine, there is always a wind in her long golden hair and a fire in her bright eyes." Peregrine sobered and moved on to the next item of laundry—it fell to pieces as he lifted it. He flung the rent fabric into the pile he used for torch rags. "I am a fool for getting myself cursed on the way to fetch her."

"You can't keep torturing yourself," said Betwixt. "If the circumstances had been different, who knows what might have happened. If Leila had encountered you together, you or Elodie might have come to harm."

"I might have fought back. Or declined her accursed wish." Oh, all the things he might have done then. He'd gone over each scenario in his mind, futilely weighing his chances of success and defeat. "But you don't think the woman I'm seeing is Elodie? I don't see how it can't be. I don't know any other women." Except the witch, her daughter, and some chamber and scullery maids he recalled as a child.

"Peregrine." That name was never uttered in the company of the witch. The chimera used it now to get his attention, and he had it. "You were an earl's son betrothed to a towheaded little girl with pigtails. The woman you're envisioning might be Elodie fully grown, but she might just as easily be one of those goddesses you're always praying to, or a figment born of desperation and Earthfire fumes. I just wish you would stop using her to regret your past. Fact or fiction, she wouldn't want that. I don't think the real Elodie would want that either."

"You're right." But saying the words did not dispel the guilt he would forever feel for disappearing before he'd even had the chance to get to know his betrothed. He wondered if Elodie ever thought about him, or if she still waited for him. He wondered if she hated the idea of an arranged partnership, or if it would have afforded her the same freedom it had him. He wondered if similar visions haunted her sleep. Sweet Elodie. He would return to her one day, when he had learned all there was to learn. When he was worthy of her. For now, he would settle for visiting her in his dreams.

"Stop it," said Betwixt.

"What?"

"You're beating yourself up again! I can tell by the look on your face. She's a dream. Let her fade into memory like dreams are supposed to."

Peregrine stuck his tongue out at the dogsnake. Betwixt could decide what that facial expression meant.

"If Elodie of Cassot still thinks of you at all, I'm sure she feels what the rest of us do: pity that you never had a chance to live your life once it finally belonged to you."

Peregrine's childhood had been consumed with caring for an ill father, so he'd never enjoyed a life outside his family estate. Elodie embodied everything that might have been. "She was the only thing I was ever responsible for, and I let her slip through my fingers."

"So go back to her. The mountain is waiting."

"Waiting to kill me," said Peregrine. "If it had been that easy, I would have left long ago."

Betwixt swatted at Peregrine with his tail. He wandered to an opaque section of the wall where calcite had dripped down long ago in rippled lines and scratched his back against it. "You didn't exactly have a choice. You got cursed, remember?"

"How could I forget?" Enough of this folly; it was time to lighten the mood. "But if I hadn't been cursed I never would have met you, my dearest friend."

"That *would* have been a pity," Betwixt agreed, and they chuckled in unison.

Neither was ready when the first tremor struck.

Startled and confused by the sudden sense of vertigo,

Peregrine lost his footing. Betwixt—fully awake now—snapped the sleeve of Peregrine's shirt between his massive jaws and dragged him away from the fire. Peregrine huddled with Betwixt in a small archway. The mountain shivered beneath him. Fingers of icerock that had pointed down from the ceiling now joined them on the floor. Some crushed the pillarstones that grew up from the ground, splintering into white shards and glittering dust. Crystalline protrusions rang out like church bells as they crashed. Mighty columns that were created with the mountain toppled and fell. The air grew thick with ice and chalk. Peregrine coughed and hoped that slow, molten Earth-fire was not soon to follow. Betwixt howled, his tail rattling madly.

"Dragon?" Peregrine yelled to Betwixt over the thunder of the cave. "Could it be?"

Happily, Betwixt's canine hearing had not been compromised. "If so, it's been lovely knowing you," said the chimera.

The thought of death had once given Peregrine a great sense of relief. Now he prayed to gods unknown to preserve his meager life, pretense and all.

After what felt like a lifetime, the vibrations dulled like a forgotten note on a harpsichord and the caves wrapped themselves once more in a shroud of cold, dark silence. Peregrine shook debris out of his hair. He was unhurt. In the dim light of the dust-covered fire he examined Betwixt from head to toe, giving his unscathed friend a hearty pat on the hindquarters in both reassurance and gratitude. He retrieved the overturned

lantern, all the while silently counting to himself. Shortly there-
after, the shrieking started.

"Thirteen seconds," he said to Betwixt. "She must have
been knocked unconscious."

Betwixt huffed, sneezed, and rattled his tail for good measure. He pointedly ignored the banshee wail, returning instead
to the fire and nosing rocky debris from his former spot there.
The screeching began to resolve itself out of the echoes.

"HE'S ALIVE!"

The witch's familiar burst out from behind a still-standing
column, a flurry of black wings. Cwyn's usual perch had been
upset by the quaking, so she flew once around the room and
landed on Betwixt's giant head. The chimera snapped at the mis-
chievous raven.

Now that Cwyn could see the room, so could the witch:
she used the bird's eyes as her own to move about the caves. The
witch had summoned the bird in the mad wake of her blindness
for just this purpose. Peregrine had worried about being found
out, but this secondhand sight was less than perfect. Even better, the witch had a new obsession to distract her from sensing
that her daughter no longer shared her demon blood.

"JACK WOODCUTTER!" The witch stood in the arch-
way, eye sockets gaping blank holes in her pale blue face, a con-
trast to her pink, gaping mouth.

"That scoundrel again? I will summon him directly and order him to clean this up." Peregrine had found that jesting and
teasing were the best way to converse with the witch. Betwixt
had found that the best way was not conversing at all.

The witch blamed everything on Jack Woodcutter, from burned hair to errant farts, so this conclusion did not surprise Peregrine. Jack was the only human he'd ever known to venture this far up into the White Mountains by choice. The witch had captured Jack and forced him to complete her list of impossible chores. Jack had repaid her by stealing her eyes. Peregrine had helped Jack escape her clutches and disappear back down the treacherous mountainside.

Oh, what fun that had been. It felt like a million years ago and only yesterday that Jack had left them. Peregrine had no way of knowing if the bravely stupid man had survived, but he hoped so. He wished Jack well in his adventures. He did miss the company, but not more than he treasured his immortality.

The witch did not glare at him with her hollowed sockets as she might have looked at him with eyes, but Peregrine could feel Cwyn's unyielding stare. "Snip-snap-snurre-basselure! No man alive could shake the bones of the earth so, except him. That rascal stole my eyes! I will have them back!"

Peregrine went about the business of resetting the room to rights, demonstrating to the witch just how seriously he considered her histrionics. "You haven't found Jack in all this time, Mother. What makes you think you'll locate him now?"

"Shivers and shimmies! Every earthquake has a center. Jack is at that center. I'd bet my eyes on it."

Peregrine was tempted to take that bet. "Even if he is, how do you propose to find him? Betwixt isn't exactly in any shape to travel."

The chimera in question feigned sleep on the hearth. The

snakehound's eyes were closed, but Peregrine marked his still, shallow breaths. Betwixt was the only one among them who could descend the mountain unaided, albeit perilously, and only when he was in a form that afforded him both wings and skin thick enough to withstand the unbearable cold. Peregrine had seen Betwixt assume a form like that only once. He wasn't yearning to see it again anytime soon.

"I will cast a spell," said the witch.

"Of course you will, Mother. How silly of me."

"Yes, you are! A silly girl, I always say." The witch was hit-or-miss when it came to spellcasting, but it was her favorite hobby. She kept at it every day, siphoning off the sleeping dragon's magic, trying to open a portal back to the demon world from whence she'd come. She rarely succeeded in doing much more than infusing light into stone or summoning strange magic objects from afar. Once, she'd succeeded in making the cave walls taste like cake. Peregrine missed that particular spell, stomachache or no.

The witch's spellcasting lair and bedchambers were a series of caves very close to the dragon's tomb—proximity to the dragon boosted a spell's power, for better or worse. Every spell she cast drained her physically—the stronger the attempted spell, the quieter she was afterward. She often retired directly to the adjacent room, when she didn't pass out in front of the cauldron. If she was deep enough into a spell, she could waver indefinitely between the lair and her bedchambers, disappearing for rather notable lengths of time. This could go very well or very badly for Peregrine and Betwixt. Possibly both.

"I'll need a map for the scrying," she said. "East and west. West and east, and always south."

The whole of the world was south of here; she could mean anywhere. "They're in the library," answered Peregrine. "I'll fetch one for you." He didn't want the witch anywhere near that particular cave.

"Thank you, my silly green darling." Idly, the witch scratched the dark blue stumps of her horns beneath her hair. "We'll go prepare." Cwyn launched herself off the rocks to fly back down the tunnel. The witch followed like a tethered ghost, all white hair and blue skin and gray rags against the shadowed archway.

The "library" housed the few precious scrolls Peregrine had collected from the witch's hoard . . . and from the skeletons of those who'd met with the dragon once upon a time and hadn't lived to tell the tale. There were some spells but more maps, all with vague descriptions of how to reach the dragon's treasure using tunnels long since buried under ice, crystals, Earthfire, and time.

Peregrine and Betwixt took their time journeying up to the small, out-of-the-way alcove. Betwixt's great hound's feet slipped on the steep path, which made for slow going. Peregrine had selected this particular niche for its dry warmth, its proximity to the dragon's lair, and its difficulty to reach. Betwixt often had a hard time getting there while sporting particularly large shapes, or aspects without wings. Peregrine was only forced to bow his head to avoid the low ceiling, and watch his knees on the knobby floor.

He slipped off his soft boots, lit the library's lantern from his torch, and then scrubbed the torch out against the rough, pitted ceiling. "There were a few maps of the continents that I recall . . ." Peregrine muttered. He set the lantern on the gnome-shaped icerock pedestal beside the piles of books and papers with a "Thanks, Old Man."

Betwixt sniffed from pile to pile, sneezing at some particularly old documents and rendering them into dust. "Oops."

"It's okay. That one was Trollish. I never could read it. I put all the maps over on this side, but I thought I had separated out the ones that weren't just of the mountain . . . yes, here." He gently unfolded a large, wide sheepskin sailing map of the three continents, with the ocean between them. Above the ocean, at the highest point of the map, a star marked the Top of the World. The shadows on the wall bent over to examine the work of art with him. Whoever had created this map had been quite the traveler. Before seeing this, Peregrine had had no sense of exactly how large the world was.

"You're not going to give her that one, are you?" There was a growl in the chimera's voice. "She'll probably just destroy it."

"I know." The map itself didn't matter; Peregrine had long since memorized it and every other scrap of vellum and skin he'd collected here. But holding the thing gave him some wistful measure of hope, reminding him that there was still so much of the world yet to see.

"Copy it on the wall, here," Betwixt rattled his tail at an odd blank space to the left of the niche's entrance. "For safekeeping."

As long as the dragon slept on, as it had for centuries, everything here at the Top of the World would be safely kept. And if the dragon ever woke . . . well . . . there would be nothing left worth keeping.

Peregrine took up a sizeable chunk of charred coal. On the right side of the alcove's opening were hash marks he had begun making when he'd first discovered this place, both drawn and scored with a knife, in an effort to mark the passage of time. Eventually he'd tired of the exercise and progressed to more productive things like bettering his artistic abilities, or teaching himself how to play the silver flute he'd found on a wispy old skeleton of unknown origin.

He sketched the lines of the map onto the uneven wall from memory; it was easier than trying to hold the skin open, balance himself, and scratch on the wall at the same time. The coast of Arilland sloped downward into the desert wastelands. Also in the south lay the island kingdom of Kassora and, an ocean beyond that, the Troll Kingdom.

Peregrine leaned back and held up the lantern to see how closely he'd come to recreating the map. Betwixt, who had spent the time sniffling and sneezing and rattling through more stacks of papers, stumbled over the bumpy ground to have a look.

"It's amazing how you do that," said Betwixt.

"What?" Peregrine slapped his hands together and tried to dust the worst of the coal onto his skirt. "Draw something from memory? I've had quite a bit of practice."

"No, I mean telling yourself you're drawing one thing, and then painting another picture entirely."

Peregrine lifted the lantern higher and scooted back from the wall. The shadows fell away to reveal his masterpiece. As close as he had been, he could only see the coasts of the continents outlining the sea. From this vantage point, he realized that he had drawn the woman from his dreams.

Peregrine's shoulders dropped. "Not again."

"I'd expect nothing less from a man obsessed."

"Or a lunatic." Peregrine joked to mask the fear that his mind would one day run rogue and leave him, just as his father's had. Thanks to Leila's curse there would be no living death for him, only death, swift and sure. Not that he needed to hide anything from Betwixt.

"You're in good company, my friend," the chimera said, and nosed the back of Peregrine's hand. "Let's go. The Queen of Lunatics is waiting."

Peregrine rolled the map and secured it inside his shirt, his hand brushing his father's ring on the chain around his neck as he did so. He looked back at the woman who haunted him, hair streaming lines of continents, eyes bright even when outlined in dark coal. She meant the world to him, and he had failed her. This isolation was the price he must pay.

Peregrine lit the torch again from the lantern. "I'm sorry, Elodie," he whispered to the drawing, and then blew out the lantern, banishing her once again to the darkness of his dreams.

Betwixt led them under the swollen ceiling and down the

slide to the witch's sanctum by scent more than torchlight; even Peregrine could discern the acrid smell of spells in the air. The cold met the heat in the chambers just outside her caves, creating drafts that sometimes threatened to blow him off his feet. All around him the stones perspired, dripping both clear and cloudy tears to the floor. He carried his shoes; it was easier for him to find purchase on the slippery ground. Betwixt was not so lucky.

His bare toes paused at the edge of the moat surrounding the witch's lair. Even after all this time he'd never gotten quite used to the natural illusion this stretch of still water created, mirroring the high ceiling above into a yawning chasm below, while only in truth a mere finger's-length deep. It was a constant reminder of the falsehood in which Peregrine lived: lies built on top of other lies living inside yet even more lies. Before his reflection could add to the treachery, he kicked a stray rock into the moat and broke the spell.

The walls of the witch's spellcasting lair were opaque and dull; they contained none of the flecks that caught the lantern light like fairydust. Crystals did not grow here, nor did any other living thing. Strange spells had long since stripped this cave of any color or life it had ever had. Nothing remained except madness and ancient bones covered by centuries of calcified rock. As he always did when he entered this chamber, Peregrine prayed to Lord Death that these fallen warriors did not know the insanctity of their resting place.

Betwixt sneezed several times in succession at the foul

odor. Peregrine fought back tears himself at the stench, so much worse than usual this time, like burned flesh and urine. He quickly located the source: the witch's infernal cauldron. Had she filled it with Earthfire?

"I brought the map," he called out, his body still mostly obscured by the steam from the cauldron. "I'll just put it here for you." He tossed the map onto the closest table and turned to leave as quickly as he'd arrived.

"Thank you, my dear." The words were even in tone, sober, seductive. When the witch channeled this much of the dragon's magic, her demon aspect was fully visible. Her skin darkened to lapis lazuli and her hair took on an ethereal indigo sheen. Her knobby fingers were tipped with rough claws, and her horns seemed to have grown. Her hollow eye sockets were black enough to mask the face of Lord Death himself.

This was the true face of the witch — the true face of all witches, though their demon aspects varied by element. As the fey were children of the gods, witches were the children of demons. This particular witch was a lorelei: a water demon.

"I do wish you would stay," said the lorelei. "This magic will be one of my finest works." Cwyn hopped anxiously from pillarstone to pillarstone, flapping her wings and stirring the air. The bracelet of stones at the witch's wrist burst to life with an inner fire.

This display of power frightened Peregrine; he took small comfort in the fact that it would lay the witch low for some time in the aftermath. "I worry about you, Mother. I fear this magic is too taxing for you."

"You're a sweet girl," said the lorelei, meaning nothing of the sort. "Hold the map for me, darling."

So much for getting out quickly. "Of course, Mother."

Intoxicated by the sheer pressure of magic filling the room, the compulsion to do the lorelei's bidding overwhelmed him. He shuffled to the table to retrieve the map where he'd tossed it. Betwixt remained glued to his skirt; Peregrine almost tripped over the chimera twice. In his hands the map buzzed with energy, as if reinfused with the life of the animal from whose skin it had been made. The steam made the hairs on his arms and neck stand on end.

The lorelei's voice echoed, deep and melodic:

"From Earthen fire let cauldron bubble,
Reveal to me Woodcutter trouble."

Sparks of lightning from the cauldron cracked against the cave walls. The cauldron's contents became a small sun, blinding with a bright yellow light. Rooted in place by the spell, Peregrine could not turn his face away.

The map began to bleed.

Somewhere north of Arilland a pinprick of blood welled up out of the skin and ran, dripping onto the ground and instantly vanishing into smoke like liquid flame. The map turned to ashes in Peregrine's fingertips and danced away on the gale-force drafts of wind now swirling about the room.

Relieved of his duty, Peregrine felt his limbs tense and come back under his own control. He slowly backed away from the lorelei and her cauldron. He froze when she turned in his direction, away from the cauldron, but the rapture on her empty face was not directed at him. She was focused on the bird.

The ball of the bright yellow light from the cauldron swallowed Cwyn, holding her just above the fire in the center of the cavern. The raven began to spin—or the colors around her did—either way, Peregrine's stomach rolled sickly on the bird's behalf. Betwixt's low growls vibrated through Peregrine's skirt and into his legs. The chimera's snake tail wrapped around Peregrine's wrist and guided him slowly backwards, away from the spell.

From the reflection in the moat, Peregrine watched the ball of light and feathers in the center of the room spin faster and faster. Then it began to grow larger and larger. Peregrine swayed. He blinked several times. Lights flashed. His head throbbed. He closed his eyes. Blood roared through his head. He slipped, lost his footing, stumbled into the water. He opened his eyes.

The roaring was not in his head. From far above, pieces of the cave ceiling began to fall all around the lorelei. Fingerstones trapped her in a crystalline cage before crumbling to the floor. The rumbling got louder and the pieces got larger. A tiny shaft of daylight hit her hair, and then another, reflecting blue on the walls around them. The lorelei threw back her head and screamed to the sky.

The witch was making a hole in the mountain.

Terror swept through Peregrine. The lorelei could bring the mountain down with her insanity. If she woke the dragon, the world would soon be finished with them all. The lorelei needed to harness the dragon's magic for her infernal spells. Surely she wouldn't be so stupid, but he knew she had the potential. Right now, he had no idea what Fate had in store for him.

Betwixt, however, had other plans. The snake tail yanked his arm, almost pulling it out of the socket. Peregrine landed quite unceremoniously on his backside in a lump of skirt and hair and chimera. He rolled under a very large, very old outcropping and prayed it would be enough to withstand the chaos.

Before them, in a raven's shriek and a shower of glittering blue calcite, the ceiling collapsed.

5

Earthbreaker

OMEHOW, MAMA had fresh bread in the oven and a bowl of fruit on the table by the time the gray-sailed ship weighed anchor. Papa and Peter were hard at work on the well, pumping out water into buckets and testing each. Papa was worried that the salt brought by the new ocean might taint the groundwater. Saturday had a vision of bodies shriveled up beside the lapping waves, crusted in crystals and parched to death. She wondered if she could solve this problem as easily as she'd caused it, but trying anything now would put Thursday and her crew in jeopardy.

Mama had ordered them all to diligence save Monday, who had held up a graceful finger and stopped Mama mid-sentence. So Monday was the only one who watched over the ship that carried their beloved, long-lost, pirate-wed sister until her feet touched the meadow now acting as a reluctant shore.

"She's here!" Monday ran down to meet the skiff. Saturday watched to see if her eldest sister's feet touched the ground.

Saturday and the rest of the working brood paused to look at Mama, who wiped floury hands on her apron and said, "Well, let's go, then," as if she'd been waiting impatiently for hours. The words broke the spell, and they dropped their pails and pots and made their way toward the shore. Having banished the dark clouds far to the west, the shining sun sparkled mercilessly on the magical sea.

Monday embraced Thursday with an eye for never letting go. Saturday could only make out two tanned arms wrapped about Monday's pale satin waist and a mop of burnished copper curls buried into Monday's shoulder.

When she was near enough, Thursday escaped Monday's heavenly clutches and almost tackled Saturday in her enthusiasm.

"You're stronger than I remember," said Saturday. "And skinnier. And shorter."

Thursday threw back her head, gave a raspy laugh that scared the gulls, and kissed her sister on the cheeks. "Well met, Earthbreaker," she said. "I am here to escort you on your travels! My humble boat is at your service, Mama."

Mama's joy at the reunion quickly hardened. "Then you know about Tesera."

"Yes," said Thursday. "I cannot imagine."

"But——" Saturday started, and then silenced at the look

Thursday gave her. Effectively, the Woodcutters had lost most of their daughters over time: Monday to marriage, Tuesday to Death, Thursday to her Pirate King, and Wednesday to Faerie. Sunday, in the palace, was still close enough to home, and Friday's apprenticeship wouldn't be forever . . . but it was enough to make Saturday keenly aware of what it would be like to never see one of her sisters again. For all that she wished it aloud sometimes, she never really meant it.

"You saw this in your spyglass?" Mama asked.

"I did." Thursday still looked pointedly at Saturday. "In a manner of speaking. Mine is a very different sort of glass from the one that summoned us here."

"What was it *supposed* to do?" Saturday asked cheekily.

"Does it matter? Sea glass isn't *supposed* to be shattered into a million pieces . . . but I should have expected nothing less from you. Where's your bag?"

"My bag? But . . . how do you know . . . ?" And then Saturday remembered the properties of Thursday's enchanted spyglass. It could not only see across leagues to other sides of the world, but it could also see certain events through time. Thursday must have known that Mama would want Saturday to accompany her.

Finally, a chance to leave the towerhouse, and on a pirate ship to boot! But what should have been excitement over a journey on the high seas was dampened by the thought that Saturday would spend the whole trip looking for Trix's dead body floating among the waves.

"Erik ought to go with you," said Monday. "He can accompany Mama and Saturday to their destination once they reach the northern shore." Erik bowed deeply to Monday, as if she had just bestowed upon him some very important royal honor.

Thursday tilted her head a moment in thought and then said cheerily, "The more the merrier! Always nice to have another hand on deck. Mama, Saturday should really get a move on before the ocean dries up again."

Saturday considered the new horizon. Was that even possible? Anything was possible today, it seemed.

Mama clicked her tongue. "You heard her, Miss Molasses. Fetch your things so we can be off."

Saturday grumbled sullenly and stomped back into the towerhouse, compelled to collect her things at Mama's enchanted behest. Clever Thursday, using Mama to shoo her along. Peter followed her up to her room, as Saturday knew he would. He was the only one besides Papa — and Thursday, apparently — who knew about her bag.

Though she had been quite young, Saturday clearly remembered the day Thursday ran off with the Pirate King. There had been little warning. Thursday had spent the morning as usual, full of chores and breakfast and stories. She'd disappeared sometime that afternoon. No one thought to look for her until dinner. Wednesday came down from her aerie and delivered the note Thursday had left upon her tidy bed, and that was that. The Woodcutters were left with nothing but a sheet of paper and an echo of bright laughter on the wind.

That day, little Saturday rescued an old feedbag from the

barn and started putting things in it, readying for her own journey. The feedbag became an old pillowcase, then a laundry sack, and finally a threadbare messenger bag that Friday had mended for her after a certain amount of bribing and begging. The summer of her sixteenth year, Saturday had been so sure that adventure would call her that she took the bag to work in the Wood every day.

She was ready for anything, but anything never came.

The summer had passed uneventfully, and she stowed the bag in her room once again. She'd found a hinged floorboard beneath her bed, cleaned out what looked like ash and dried leaves and bound sticks to make room. It was the perfect hiding place.

Now Saturday shimmied behind the stout headboard and Peter got a firm grasp on the footboard. Together they shoved the bed aside. Peter hopped onto Saturday's mattress and sat cross-legged while Saturday fetched the bag.

"You must be thrilled," said Peter.

Saturday was not especially thrilled about breaking the world, but that wasn't what he meant. She always knew what Peter meant. "Overjoyed," she said sarcastically.

"Unemployed," rhymed Peter.

Saturday wasn't in the mood for games. In one great yank, she extracted her bag from its hiding place. She plopped both it and herself on the bed beside Peter. Almost as an afterthought, she added the ebony-handled comb to its contents.

"I knew this day was bound to come." Peter made a face at the bag. "When will I see you again?"

"When there are stars in the daytime." Judging by Peter's

forlorn expression, he wasn't really in the mood for games either. "Oh, Peter, don't worry. I'll be home as soon as I find Trix." Even as she said them, the words sounded like a lie. Jack hadn't come home either, once upon a time.

Peter caught Saturday's upper arm in a grip that would have bruised any of her other sisters. "You haven't killed Trix. He's fine. The animals will help him. They always do."

But the animals couldn't have helped him if they had all died in the flood as well. "He's fine and I'll bring him back," she said determinedly.

"Just make sure he's safe." Peter's voice was soft now. "Only bring him back if he wants to come."

The idea was preposterous. "Why would he not want to come home?"

He indicated the bag between them. "Adventure is the vice of all Woodcutters."

It was true enough; even with its one castle-worthy tower, the tiny cottage was stifling. "Fine. I will make sure Trix *wants* to come home before I tie him to a horse."

Peter nodded, taking her sarcasm as oath. "And protect Mama," he added.

"Mama doesn't need protection. She could kill a bear by staring at it." *Or by telling it to die.*

"Will you please think about someone other than yourself for five seconds?"

"I'm thinking about Trix," said Saturday. She hadn't stopped thinking about Trix; the guilt and litany of unanswered questions were taking their toll on her.

Peter growled at the ceiling. "Gods, you drive me mad."

"That makes me glad," Saturday rhymed.

"You make me sad," said Peter.

"I'll find our lad."

"I'll stay with Dad."

"You're going to miss me so bad," said Saturday, even though she really meant it the other way around.

"Yes, Whirlwind, I am." He caught her up in a hug and then stared at her face, as if memorizing it. She did the same, etching in her mind her brother's sky-blue eyes, his wind-tossed sandy hair, the line of his eyebrow, the curve of his lips, the shadow of stubble on his dimpled chin, the freckle beneath his right eye. He hugged her again. "Don't forget about me while you're off adventuring."

"I'll bring you back a chest full of gold and a pretty girl to keep you company."

"See that you do."

She wanted to linger with her beloved brother, but the moment Saturday slid her arm through the strap of her bag, the compulsion to comply with Mama's order became irresistible.

"And one more thing."

"Seriously, Peter?" Saturday walked backwards down the steps so that she could see her brother deliver whatever preposterous addendum he had in store.

"Try not to stink too badly."

"I will sleep with pigs, just for you!" She leapt down the last half-flight and sped across the sitting room with Peter hot on her heels.

"I think I'm going to be sick," Mama said on the skiff to Thursday's boat. She had finished braiding Saturday's long hair and was now unable to distract herself with anything else.

Thursday patted her hand. "I'm sorry, Mama. This new sea is a rough one. Once we get to the ship you can lie down in my quarters. My cabin boy will fetch you anything you need. And if she gives you any lip, you have my permission to throw her overboard."

Mama smiled a little at the jest, but kept her lips tightly shut. Her skin turned faintly green. She breathed deeply, swallowed hard, and pinched the skin between her left thumb and forefinger. Why didn't she just tell herself to not be sick? Mama's stubbornness truly knew no bounds.

Erik worked hard at the oars, fighting the waves that tried unceasingly to punch and toss them back to shore. Mama pushed Saturday away to heave what remained of the accursed porridge over the side. The shove caused Saturday's sheathed sword to knock into the side of the skiff and almost topple her into the water, but Erik's hand shot out to steady her.

"Thank you," she said.

Erik only grunted before returning his attention to the waves, and Saturday officially gave up being polite. She was about to board a pirate ship, after all.

Once on the ship, Saturday was glad to have her sword at her side to keep her from succumbing to the sickness that already held Mama in its thrall. Thursday ushered Mama into her quarters at what Saturday assumed was the front of the boat. The aforementioned cabin boy was a skinny little thing in a stocking cap, but Thursday expected her to lug Mama's belongings anyway. Saturday had offered to help, but the cabin boy just narrowed her big blue eyes and gave a scowl worthy of Saturday's own.

Realizing her assistance was neither required nor wanted, she excused herself to explore the deck of the ship. The rest of the crew busied themselves around her, calling out orders she didn't understand. Saturday held fast to the railing and turned her face into the wind as the sails caught and moved them out to sea.

A large shadow passed over the sun; she shielded her eyes with a hand to see a few birds with very large wings diving into the ship's wake. Three were white; one was smaller and dark, but with a wingspan just as wide as that of his fairer cousins. The white birds seemed more skilled at snatching prey, though the dark one was just as adept at thieving from the others' beaks.

"Mollymawks," said a voice behind her. "The dark one is a frigate bird. Don't see many of those this far north. But then, one doesn't typically see the ocean this far east."

Saturday braced herself for the sisterly drama, but none came.

"The mollymawks bring luck, if they stick around. Their dung's good luck too. High Simon wears an umbrella for a hat."

Saturday squinted up into the bright sky at the crow's-nest. Simon was a common name on the sea for men hiding from the law. "How many Simons are in your crew?"

Thursday took a moment to count them all. "Seven," she said finally. "Plus Crow and Magpie, whom you've met."

Ah yes, the duo that had delivered Thursday's trunk full of treasures that spring. The daggers in their boots had fascinated Saturday almost as much as the men themselves. One of them had a funny accent. She couldn't remember which. She looked forward to seeing them again. "And your cabin boy," added Saturday.

"Ashes-on-the-Wind."

"She doesn't seem like much."

"If her brains were as smart as her mouth, she'd be Queen of the World," said Thursday. "Pay her no mind."

If the girl had half as much gumption as Thursday and Saturday, she was in the right place. A gust of wind whipped Saturday's hair over her shoulder, and she was glad Mama had taken the time to braid it. The birds screeched at each other overhead, dancing in and out on the currents of air as if they were braiding it themselves.

From beneath her brightly colored kerchief, Thursday pulled several strands of hair and handed them to Saturday. The bits of titian curled around her fingers. "Monday said I should give this to you. Not quite sure what for, though."

"My bracelet." Saturday slipped the small dagger from the opposite side of her swordbelt and pressed gently at the seam in the blue-green fabric. Two small stitches gave way, and she shoved Thursday's hair into the thin sleeve. When the rough edges were pressed back together the fabric seemed to melt back into itself, as if there had never been an interruption.

"That looks familiar. Friday's handiwork?"

Of course Thursday recognized the fabric; it had been she who'd sent it to the towerhouse in her infamous trunk. That same trunk had borne the brush-and-mirror set.

"She made me a dress for the first night of the royal balls, just like you requested," Saturday told her. "But then I . . . I wasn't able to go the second night, so Friday used bits of my dress to gussy up everyone else's gowns. She sewed up pieces of their hair into this remnant as a memento." Saturday had hated those balls and everything about them. The bracelet was a trophy, marking her triumph of will at defying Mama's wishes.

"That's sweet of her."

"That's Friday, silly and sentimental. After the evil king was dead and the dust cleared, Trix and Peter and Monday gave me bits of their hair to add to it. Yours was the only one of the siblings' I didn't have."

"Besides Jack and Tuesday."

Saturday gave her pirate sister a sideways glance. Had the sun bleached her brain along with her hair? "Right," she said. "Besides Jack and Tuesday." Not that she meant to go digging up graves.

Thursday had to shade her eyes to look up at Saturday. How had she ever won a fight being so short?

"You've certainly grown quite a bit bigger since I last saw you," said her tiny sister.

"Her mouth has grown proportionately. So has yours."

Erik's presence delighted Thursday — as did almost everything else, it seemed. The seaman's garb he wore now still covered as much of him as possible, but the material was lighter and blew like the sails in the wind. Saturday would have thought it strange to see Erik without livery and armor, but the relaxed look suited him.

"It's been too long, Erik," said Thursday.

"You were but a girl when Jack was cursed, and little more than that when you eloped with your Pirate King. I'm not sure I've forgiven you for not saying goodbye."

"You cared about me too much," said Thursday. "You would have talked me out of it."

"Damned right, I would have." There was a hint of that serious, disapproving look on Erik's face with which Saturday was all too familiar. She was pleased to not be the only recipient.

"So, considering a life on the sea yet? I could do with a Red Simon."

Erik chuckled, and the seriousness vanished. "I've missed you, lass, but I'm not sure I could. I'll give it some thought."

"You've got time," said Thursday. "The sea is patient. Unless it's called up by one of my sisters."

Saturday changed the subject. "Your skin seems to be faring better." On the skiff it had been close to blistering; a pale pink blush was all that tinted Erik now.

"Simon Cook gave me a pot of salve to use to ward off the sun. Said he stole it from a witch on a troll ship." He looked to Thursday for confirmation, but the Pirate Queen only shrugged. "He also told me you bested a kraken on the way here."

"A kraken? Really?" asked Saturday.

"Really," said Thursday, as if fighting giant sea monsters was something she did every day. "All sorts of things got churned up when your ocean decided to visit."

"Do you think we'll get to see anything like that?" Saturday asked. Knowing her luck, they never would.

"With permission, milady," hissed a soft voice above her.

High Simon alit on the deck from the rigging above. He landed gently on bare toes as yellow-green as the rest of his compact, muscular body. His eyes were slits above a long nose with a bit of a hook to it. His waist-length black hair was wrapped in a leather tail. He wasn't wearing a hat at the moment, but Saturday could see bumps in the hair along his crown where one had sat.

Saturday guessed that one of High Simon's parents had been a goblin, not that she'd ever seen one. She sensed that her usual brusque attitude might cause him to disappear back into the crow's-nest just as quickly as he'd arrived, so she tread lightly.

"Yes," Saturday said politely. "What is it?"

A strong green arm pointed steadily out to sea beyond them, toward the back of the ship, where the giant-winged mollymawks still dove for treats in the wake. "Look there, along the horizon. Can you see the strip of indigo?"

Saturday squinted hard into the bright sun, not sure if she was actually seeing something or forcing herself to believe it was there.

"Here," said Thursday. Saturday turned and realized that Thursday was offering her magical spyglass. She hesitated, but her pirate sister dropped the heavy glass in her hand anyway. The gold was warm in her palm. "Go on. Take a look."

Saturday lifted the glass to the spot where High Simon had pointed and gave her eyes a moment to adjust. Then she twisted the focus ring and the indigo line sprang into crisp view. She swayed a bit and steadied her elbow against a thick, coiled rope hanging from the nearest mast. "I see . . . are those spikes or spines? And are those two heads? What is that thing?"

"A lingworm," Thursday answered. "A legendary creature few have ever seen. It has three heads: one for truth, one for compassion, and one for wisdom. I'm guessing one of the heads was damaged in the storm. But not to worry," she said at the furrow in Saturday's brow, "it will grow back."

"Will it attack us?" asked Saturday.

"I feel it safe to say that no Woodcutter is in danger from that particular lingworm." There was something else Thursday wasn't telling her. Instead of intriguing Saturday, the mystery only rankled.

She slapped the spyglass back into Thursday's hand. "I'm not a fan of secrets."

"Some secrets aren't ours to tell, Saturday."

"Nor are they ours to keep!" She was beginning to feel as trapped on this ship as she'd been at the towerhouse.

Thursday collapsed the spyglass and fit it back into her belt, next to the sheath where she kept a thin rapier with a cupped basket hilt. "Shall we settle this properly, then?"

Saturday's hand fell to her own sword. "Oh yes, please."

The two sisters drew their weapons and the crew cheered and gathered round. Erik leaned back against the rail to watch his student apply his teachings.

Saturday's sword was longer and wider than Thursday's rapier, but its weight put Saturday at a disadvantage, as did her balance. The constant shifting of the deck was second nature to the Pirate Queen. They were not evenly matched, but what Saturday lacked in experience, she made up for with exuberance. And a magical sword.

"Here, Captain, use mine." One of the Simons offered Thursday his strangely curved scimitar. "You might break that piskie stick against her hand-and-a-half."

"No, use mine!" Crow offered up the mop with which he'd been swabbing the deck.

Saturday's sword could be used in either a one- or two-handed attack; the soldiers on the practice grounds called it a hand-and-a-half. At the moment she held the sword in both hands, squaring her shoulders, while the lower half of her body stubbornly concentrated on keeping as much of the soles of her boots as possible on the swaying deck. Saturday also knew, from practicing with Erik, that in order to have any sort of upper hand in this fight, she needed to make a preemptive strike. She lunged at Thursday, forcing her sister to jump back in surprise.

"Ten bones on the Giantess," called Erik.

"Twenty on the Captain," yelled one Simon.

"Fifty on the Harpy," shouted another Simon.

"Which one's that?" asked a third.

Thursday hopped up on the rail and walked down the length of it far enough to jump onto a collection of barrels that had been lashed to the deck. Saturday was forced to pick her feet up and follow her scampering bilge rat of a sister, shifting her weight and throwing her strikes off. Thursday attacked from each new position and Saturday parried. Thursday was all nimbleness and upper body strength. Saturday tried getting in past Thursday's defenses and forcing her to lose her grip, but the larger blade only slid across the metal basket hilt of the rapier and left Saturday open for Thursday's attack.

Thursday winked, pulled Saturday's braid, and skipped up to higher ground.

Sweat got in Saturday's eyes, as well as the sun, and she began to see why men around the world both hated and admired her sister at the same time. Thursday wasn't a pretty figurehead on a ship — she was a captain. Saturday knew what it was like for a woman to be measured as a man. Thursday couldn't just win *some* fights; she had to win every one until she'd earned the respect of her crew. Even then, she'd always have to fight just as long and hard as the best of them.

Judging by the cavalier insults they tossed about, these men respected Thursday quite a lot. Thursday was toying with her, and Saturday knew it. It was good of the men to play along, but she did wish she could land even one decent strike against her sister.

Saturday took her mind out of the fight a moment and instead of assessing Thursday's attack, she assessed the field of play. The practice grounds were flat and typically free of obstacles; this was an area in which Saturday definitely needed improvement. From her current vantage point there were only two places for Thursday to go: back down to the deck, or a flying leap across to the roof of the captain's quarters. Saturday decided which one was more likely and lunged.

Thursday stopped on the roof to examine her torn sleeve and the thin scratch now visible down the outside of her arm.

"First blood, little sister. Well done."

The men paused their taunting, waiting for Thursday's next move. Saturday squared herself on the deck and readjusted her two-handed grip on the sword.

"The gloves come off now," Thursday said, and launched herself into the air.

Saturday wasn't quite sure where her sister was going with this — overboard? — until she noticed High Simon lying up in the rigging. He reached down and caught Thursday's arm up to her elbow in what must have been a practiced trick. Thursday flew through the air like a bright, wingless mollymawk and landed on a stack of crates with the sun directly behind her.

Saturday was blinded. "Cheater!" she yelled.

"Pirate," Thursday corrected.

Saturday squinted, but the sun was overpowering. Without anything to shield them, her eyes began to water. She weighed the risks of letting one hand off the blade while Thursday . . . danced a jig? Saturday couldn't quite make it out. Whatever it was, the men began catcalling and throwing things at their captain.

Mercifully, large black wings blotted out the sun. The frigate bird.

Thank you, fellow outcast.

The shadow grew as the wings closed in upon the ship. It wasn't the frigate bird. This beast was much darker and much bigger. It headed straight for them, and Saturday was directly in its path. The crew unsheathed their weapons, switching from humor to business in the space of a breath.

"Heads up!" Thursday cried. The Pirate Queen's blade scratched down the length of the enormous black bird, excising more feathers than blood, but doing some little damage all the same. Saturday leapt and swung her own blade at the bird, but it reared above the deck. Before Saturday could regain her balance, it caught her up in its giant talons.

"MINE!" it seemed to call from its giant beak. "MINE!"

"Give her back, beastie!" yelled one Simon.

"There's already one crow on this ship," yelled Crow, or Magpie.

"And that's one too many!" added the other.

"Chicken dinner!" yelled the cook.

The giant raven let out a harsh caw that brought several of the crew to their knees.

One of the men still standing drew an arrow from his quiver.

Erik grabbed for Saturday as she slipped away. He managed only a solid grip on the tail of her long braid. Saturday cried out in pain. The winged monster launched itself higher into the air, easily taking both Saturday and Erik with it.

Saturday watched the ship shrink as they ascended. With her advanced healing ability she might survive a fall from any height, but Erik certainly wouldn't. Before they gained any more altitude, Saturday freed her sword arm, and her sword with it.

"Let go," she said to Erik.

"No!" he cried.

"That's what I thought you'd say." With that, Saturday cut off her braid.

Saturday's heart sank as Erik fell back to the ship. The archer pulled back on his bowstring, but Thursday stayed his hand. Saturday looked down at the ocean below, her sister's ship getting farther away with every wing beat.

Erik threw himself against the railing and let loose a battle cry toward the sky; the Simons dragged him back. Thursday — tiny now, like a dolly of the sister Saturday knew — sheathed her sword and placed a closed fist on her left breast in salute. The rest of Thursday's crew saluted her as well. From inside the talons of the great bird, Saturday saluted them back.

She never saw her mother.

6

The Deepest Wounds

A CRASH ECHOED from the witch's destroyed lair, cries both human and inhuman, and then silence. Wherever the witch's raven had disappeared to, she'd obviously returned. Peregrine set aside the daggers he'd been sharpening at the whetstone. He slipped on his second-best boots and another fur wrap, having lost the first during the spell-induced collapse. He snatched the nearest torch from a notch in the wall and took off running.

Betwixt scuttled out of his hiding place in the shadows and tried to keep up. The witch's spell had triggered the chimera to change again; he was now a large scorpion with chicken legs and tusks where pincers would otherwise be. Running wasn't one of Betwixt's strengths in this new form. Nor was this one of the species that lent itself to communication, though his carapace did change color with his mood. After his transformation, Betwixt had been a shiny, serene shade of purple. Now he was red as apples and dragon's blood.

As the archways opened into the ruins of the spellcasting caves, Peregrine pulled the fur up over his head to protect him from the freezing wind. Cwyn's return had been awkward and messy. She'd slid in and tumbled over, trailing blood and feathers along the ice as she came. The massive bird was still the size of an ancient roc.

The witch was slumped against the wall beside her familiar's body, spellspent and blessedly unconscious. The deep blue tint of the skin around her eye sockets, behind her ears, and down her neck had faded.

Cwyn's feathers stank of salt and sweat and copper. Peregrine worked to extract her giant head out from under her body as gently as possible before she crushed herself under her own weight. Despite the grief and aggravation the witch's familiar brought to his life, Peregrine worried about her. Every time he was tempted to hate Cwyn he reminded himself that the raven was just another prisoner in these caves, another slave to the witch's desires.

Betwixt carefully nudged himself under Cwyn's body, wedging his tusks deeper and deeper between the dark feathers and the icy floor until he was almost completely obscured. Peregrine backed up against the bird's gently heaving side, using all the strength in his legs to roll her over and assess her wounds.

They only managed to budge her a fraction . . . but budge her they finally did.

"There's an angry scratch here under her neck." Peregrine always spoke, even if Betwixt could not reply. He hoped the wound had been caused more by storm than sword. "I can't tell how far down it extends, but it doesn't look deep, or poisoned."

Betwixt nudged Peregrine gently in the calf with a tusk. His carapace had already lightened to a sunset shade. Did that signify relief? Concern? Peregrine patted the chimera on the tail, careful of its deadly stinging tip. "She'll be fine, my friend."

Betwixt, unsatisfied, nudged again.

From the opposite side of Cwyn's hulking girth came a soft groan, lower and less keening than the moaning of the bitter wind that howled through the hole in the ceiling.

Oh *no*. She didn't. She couldn't have.

Peregrine mumbled another prayer to any god that might be listening and ran around Cwyn's giant tail. There was Jack Woodcutter, grasped tightly in Cwyn's great talons, a long, trouser-clad leg and a shock of frost-covered golden hair. Peregrine's prayer turned to a curse. The lorelei had captured her prey after all.

"Help me," Peregrine implored Betwixt. He hugged one of Cwyn's talons while Betwixt hooked a tusk around another, and they pulled in opposite directions. Peregrine shouted a halt when he heard the telltale sound of steel against shell. He extracted Jack's sword and laid it aside before it did either Betwixt or himself any damage.

Finally, the two of them pried the bird's foot open enough for Peregrine to get a decent grip on Jack and pull him free. Jack was as tall as Peregrine remembered but a great deal thinner. The long flight through the frozen atmosphere had taken its toll. His clothes were torn and coated with blood and rime, save for the brilliant slash of blue-green fabric at his wrist. He needed to get Jack warm immediately. Peregrine rolled his friend onto his back and swore. This was not Jack Woodcutter.

The witch's familiar had captured a woman.

Still, the resemblance was remarkable. She must be a sister. Jack had kept Peregrine amused on many a chilly evening with tales of his sisters' colorful exploits.

Whoever she was, Peregrine's arms were now filled with a woman. Even broken, battered, and half dead, she was the most beautiful thing he'd seen in a very, very long time. So he kissed her.

The cold, chapped lips warmed beneath his. "Sword," she whispered.

"It was only a kiss," mumbled Peregrine, but his heart leapt with happiness. A new friend! He should be worrying about her plight or her health or her family, but the desire for human companionship overwhelmed him.

Betwixt pushed the sword along the ground until it was within Peregrine's reach. Peregrine dutifully offered the sword with a chipper "milady," but her once-again-lifeless body did not take it. Awkwardly, he shifted her in his arms and sheathed the blade in the scabbard at her belt. Regardless of whether or not it was wise to leave her armed, keeping the sword there would be safer for everyone while he moved her out of the snowy cave mouth.

"I need you," he said to Betwixt. Strong as he might have been from all his active spelunking, this girl was too large and unwieldy for him to carry like the romantic hero he'd once pretended to be. He hoped—and was pleasantly surprised—that she fit along Betwixt's back. Her neck curved up his tail, and her legs trailed out over his tusks. His six stubby chicken feet seemed to bear the weight without strain.

Peregrine led Betwixt to the cave he used as a bedchamber and rushed to throw coals on the fire pit in the center of the room. He pulled his sleeping pallet as close to the fire as he felt was safe before ungracefully rolling the girl off the chimera's back. Even in the dim light he could tell that the blue tinge had miraculously vanished from her skin. She began shivering. That was a good sign.

He decided to remove her frozen shirt and trousers and replace them with fresh ones from his own wardrobe. He had a much harder time coming up with the latter than the former—skirts were less restraining and more adaptive to the extreme temperatures. He unearthed some hose and a pair of short pants and decided against them both—the short pants had been made for a much smaller man and while they might have fit in the waist, they would have looked ridiculous on Jack's sister. He finally found something suitable enough that hadn't rotted to shreds and returned to where she lay, still shivering on the mattress.

He took a deep breath, steeled his nerves, and proceeded

to undress and redress her. It took far longer than it should have, as he kept his eyes half closed most of the time for her modesty. As if she'd care, unconscious as she was. Though Jack might have had something to say about the manhandling of his sister, and that something kept going through Peregrine's mind as he pulled her deathly cold legs and arms through the unwieldy fabric.

Betwixt, thankfully unable to laugh in his current state, merely hung his orange head and shook his giant tusks.

When Peregrine finished, he covered her gently with several fur blankets. It would have to do for now. As much as he hated to leave the girl, he still needed to tend to the witch and Cwyn before the two of them froze in the cave mouth. If the witch died, then her hold on the dragon would be lifted. He didn't need some freshly woken beast of legend burning him out of house and home, or more cave falling down around his ears, thank you. He was comfortable enough with the way things were, leagues above the world of the eternally dying, down where clocks ticked seconds away and counted breaths that, once exhaled, could never again be taken.

He jogged back to the windy cave mouth. Cwyn had blessedly shrunk to a manageable size. The witch looked so small and fragile now: a bag of bones in a tattered gray dress with a white mop for a head. Her eyelids remained closed over the one aspect that ravaged her features. Betwixt prodded her foot, and it flopped over. Peregrine pressed his fingers into the wrinkled flesh of her neck and felt for a heartbeat. It was there, faint but steady.

"Still alive." Peregrine glanced up at the looming, frosted fingerstones above them. All the witch's spells would be lifted upon her death. As a water witch, the lorelei's talent had aided in the formation of these icerock caverns. Without her beating blue heart, the mountain would collapse on top of them.

Assuming they hadn't been roasted by the dragon already, of course.

Betwixt patiently resumed his role as stretcher and bore the witch down the opposite side of the rubble to her bedchambers, the lantern dangling precariously from the deadly, hooked stinger of his tail.

Peregrine followed the chimera, his arms full of the still-rather-large and unwieldy Cwyn. He administered a healing salve to Cwyn's angry scrape before tucking the witch beneath her patchwork fur blankets. The witch and Betwixt were the closest thing he'd had to family beyond his parents. How strange it was to care for someone and hate her all at the same time.

Betwixt prodded Peregrine in the leg again, reminding him of the girl — as if it were possible for him to forget. He needed to be present when she awoke. Even after all this time, he still remembered what it had been like to come into this cave of majesty and madness; the least he could do would be to guide her through her first steps. Poor lost soul. She would be so frightened! He would be as gentle as he could, easing her into these new circumstances. He would be her friend. After all, they had someone in common: her brother.

Peregrine banked the fire in the kitchen caverns, covering the stewpot so that it might still be warm when the witch and her familiar awoke later. He set more clear ice to melt in another pot. His mother the countess had always had tea to calm her nerves. Peregrine had taken up the affectation in memory of her, what little memory there was left.

By the time he returned to the Woodcutter girl, he was relieved to see that her cheeks had regained a rosy flush and her breathing was deep and regular. Her face was unblemished; what he thought had been a bruise along her jawline must have been just a shadow. There were no gashes or lumps, only pink scratches on her arms and across her ribs. The blood on her clothes must have been Cwyn's. In his panic, he must have imagined the worst. If he didn't know better, he'd have guessed she'd merely fallen asleep after a long day's work instead of being dragged half dead against her will to the peak of the tallest mountain in the world.

But he did know better, just as he knew that the deepest wounds were not always visible from the outside of the body. Peregrine lay down next to Jack's sister and held her tightly, willing his body's heat into her. Having been without human company for so long, the embrace was as much for his own healing as it was for hers. He breathed in her tangled mass of hair; she smelled of frost and bird musk, but beneath that he imagined he caught the scents of salt and sunshine. She sighed in her sleep.

It was a lovely sound.

7

Welcome to the Madness

HE AIR tasted like the kitchen in winter, all frost and cinders. Her coverlet was rough in patches. She was excessively warm. Saturday opened her eyes and tried to focus on the stone blocks in the ceiling of her tower room. Had Papa let her sleep past dawn again?

And then the shrieking began.

Saturday sat up and put her hand on the hilt of her sword. The very warm lump on the pallet beside her cursed, and from the blankets jumped either a very handsome girl or a very pretty boy in a skirt. Not a nightgown, a *skirt*. What sort of person wore a skirt to bed? And what was he . . . she doing in Saturday's room?

But she wasn't supposed to be in her room either. She should have been with Mama on Thursday's ship. Room . . . sea . . . ship . . . Saturday blinked as memories swam before her.

"She's awake early."

"She" seemed to designate someone other than Saturday. The strange boy cursed again. He . . . she . . . took Saturday by the shoulders and shook her, forcing her to concentrate on . . . his, definitely his . . . maybe . . . face. Either his skin was slightly green or Saturday was sicker than she felt. "Doesn't matter. It's my fault. Look, I'm sorry I don't have time to explain. Just *don't say anything.* If you don't say anything, you will stay safe. Can you promise me that?"

Saturday was too confused to do anything but nod. She'd promised Peter that she'd find Trix and come home. She had promised to protect Mama and then vanished without a word to her. She didn't seem to be very good at promises lately.

"Good girl." The strange boy kissed her forehead. "Welcome to the madness." He leapt from her bedside to the far side of the circle of stones in the middle of the room.

Circle of stones. White, glittering rocks. Definitely not her room.

The strange boy dumped half a bin of coal into the stone circle — only the very rich could afford to waste coal like that — and haphazardly stirred it with a poker. The room warmed and brightened bit by bit, though there was no smoke from the fire. The pit smelled of brimstone. Perhaps she'd gone to Hell and the raven who'd captured her was an angel delivering her to Lord Death.

The boy straightened his shirt and skirt. He wound his long black hair back into a knot and fixed it at the base of his skull. Friday had that same talent; Saturday had watched her sister do it enough times before starting the mending at the kitchen table. Her hand drifted to her own hair, grasping at nothing but air until it came to her chin. A vision flashed in her mind of Erik . . . the slice of a sword . . . a battle cry. At the same time, the light from the fresh coals began to fully illuminate the space around them.

Above her, undulating, milky-white stone spilled down from the heavens. The ceiling lifted like a wild cathedral over archways and crevasses and up again into empty shadows. Giant protrusions stretched down from above or up from below, reaching in to fill the space with curious waxen fingers. This was no palace but a cave, one as old as the gods, or older.

"Where *are* we?"

The strange boy shushed her. She remembered his advice about staying safe and closed her mouth.

Before the vapor of her breath could dissipate, an enormous, long-tusked crimson beetle-thing came scuttling around the corner on . . . chicken legs? Right on his wickedly pointed tail flew a large bird with deeply violet wings. Behind the bird stalked a small, wraithlike woman with giant empty holes where her eyes should be. Her skin was slightly blue, though she didn't appear cold.

Madness, the boy had said. Oh, how right he had been.

Saturday was instantly on her feet with her sword in both hands.

"Forgive me, Mother, I did not expect you up and around for some time. That spell took a lot out of you." The boy gave the crimson insect a look that Saturday might have given Peter, if he hadn't woken her in time for breakfast.

Wait . . . had he called her *Mother?* But the boy wasn't blue. And spells? She was no fairy, so that meant this wraith was a sorceress or a witch. Judging by her hue and the small horns on her forehead, Saturday guessed the latter. What had become of her eyes?

The witch ignored the boy and pointed a bony finger at Saturday. "How dare you mess with my familiar! Who ever heard of a purple raven?" Those terribly empty eye sockets gaped accusingly in Saturday's direction, but slightly to the left, as if there were someone standing behind her. The effect was unnerving. Saturday resisted the urge to turn and look. "I'll take that sword, dearie."

Over my dead body. Saturday stretched the fingers of both hands, wrapped them tightly around the hilt again, and settled into a defensive position on the pallet. She sized the witch up. The insane old woman was no physical match for her. If she attacked before the witch could loose a spell, the fight would be over and done with quickly. Then Saturday could give her full attention to getting out of this bizarre cavern and back to the swordfight from which she'd been so rudely kidnapped.

"There's no escape from here this time, my terrible troublemaker. Hand it over."

This time? Saturday had never been to this place before. She definitely would have remembered.

"Just take it, Mother. Use your magic," said the boy.

Saturday scowled. So much for thinking the boy was on her side. Saturday calculated the distances in the room, deciding how close the witch would need to come to her before she could spring her attack.

"Snip-snap-snurre-basselure — I can't grab hold of it! There's something protecting her."

There was?

"*You* take the sword," the witch told the boy. "You're about his size."

His? Saturday did turn then to see if someone really was standing behind her, but there was no one else in the room. She turned back to the witch . . . and was treated to a face full of violet feathers. Saturday spat and swung but the bird was too close; the weight of the sword shifted her off balance. She kicked the furs aside and the raven-that-should-not-have-been-purple came at her again. Saturday gritted her teeth and growled, as a battle cry would have left her with another mouthful of feathers.

Stop fighting. Give her the sword.

Saturday stopped fighting, but only because THERE WAS A VOICE IN HER HEAD. A voice coming from inside one's own skull was not something a fighter trained for. Then again, it was exactly the sort of stunt she would have expected Velius to pull.

You're going to think yourself into an early grave, girl.

"Who——?" The boy moved closer and she remembered to keep her mouth shut.

He stretched out a hand. "Woodcutter, please."

He knew her name? Her suspicions grew. This was no random abduction. Did they plan to ransom her back to Sunday and Rumbold? Not without shedding a few drops of blood first. Saturday wouldn't make this kidnapping easy on anyone.

NOW, CHILD.

The words echoed so loudly between her ears that she winced and loosened her grip on the sword.

GET OUT OF MY HEAD, Saturday thought back, but it was too late. The boy plucked the sword from her grasp and the air began to sing. As if burned, he quickly dropped the weapon onto the pallet.

"It's hot!" he cried.

Saturday cocked her head at the bold-faced lie. She recognized that strange singing——it was the same sound her nameday gift had made in her hands the night it had changed from an ax to a sword. The boy knew her sword was enchanted and, for whatever reason, he did not want the empty-eyed wraith touching it.

"Charmed," said the witch. "Ooh, how wonderful! Back up, sweetling, and let Mummy take care of it." She crossed the room as efficiently as anyone with sight, then knelt and gingerly swaddled the sword inside the fur blankets without touching any part of the hilt or blade.

Saturday lunged for the witch with her dagger. The witch held up a blue-palmed hand and Saturday froze in mid-strike. She strained with all her might, but not so much as a finger moved. She tried to cry out, but the sound died in her throat.

The witch clasped the sword to her skinny chest and strutted out of the cave with all the confidence of a woman who had two very good eyes. "Come, Cwyn," she said to the bird. "Betwixt, please sit on our guest until we return," she said in the direction of the bugaboo. "I'll deal with you later, Jack Wood-cutter," she said to the space beside Saturday's head, and then cackled madly on her way out of the cave.

Jack? The witch thought she was her dead brother? Had these people lost their minds, or had *she?*

Saturday shook her head to clear the cobwebs, happy to find that she was able to move again now that the wraith and her bird had left the area. The next body part she freed was her index finger, which she pointed at the boy.

"You," she commanded with a voice not unlike her mother's, "will tell me exactly where I am and what is going on. And *you*" — she pointed at the bugaboo — "if you so much as attempt to sit on me, I will throw you out the nearest window." If there weren't any windows in these caves, Saturday would make one. "And then I will sit on *you.*"

The bugaboo shook its tusks, and his carapace turned a light shade of ocean blue.

"Did you just . . . ? Gods, I am not colorful enough for this crowd."

"His name is Betwixt," said the boy.

"Betwixt. I'd say I'm pleased to meet you, but this is all a bit too strange for me. And if you know my family, that's saying a lot." Betwixt's shell shimmered and changed again. "What's green mean?" Saturday asked the boy.

"Not sure, but I think he's in love with you."

"Huh. So no crushing me with your massive bulk." Betwixt waved his tusks back and forth in dissent. "Excellent. Your turn." Saturday raised her eyebrows at the boy.

"What do you want to know first: my story, or your brother's?"

"Do you know where Trix is?"

"Who's Trix?" asked the boy.

"Not the brother you were referring to, apparently," said Saturday.

"Jack," he said loudly and slowly. "Do you want me to tell you about *Jack?*"

"Sum up whatever you can fit in before the witch returns, or I punch you." Saturday raised her fists. "I may just punch you anyway, for good measure. I'm not big on patience."

The boy took a deep breath and then spoke as fast as he could. "The witch is a lorelei—a water demon. She's not very talented when it comes to spells, so she siphons magic off a sleeping dragon in an effort to open a doorway back to the demon home world. Her daughter, Leila, ran away after cursing some fool with similar features to take her place." He curtseyed. "The witch sees through the eyes of Cwyn, her raven familiar, because her eyes were stolen by one evil, conniving Jack Wood-cutter in an effort to thwart her spellcasting." The boy crossed his arms over his chest. "The end."

Saturday hailed from a family of storytellers, but this tale bordered on preposterous. "*Where* am I?"

"The Top of the World."

"And you are . . . ?"

The boy curtseyed again, and then bowed. "Peregrine of Starburn. Cursed on the way to fetch his betrothed."

Saturday couldn't imagine anyone wanting to marry this fop. "But the witch thinks that you are her daughter."

"Leila. Yes."

"And she thinks that I am my brother?"

"I saw the family resemblance right away. So which day of the week does that make you?"

Oh, how she wanted to punch the self-serving grin right off his face. "Saturday."

"Splendid!"

Saturday's clenched fists itched. She was trapped on top of the highest mountain in the world, without her sword. The situation had all the earmarks of a Jack-worthy adventure, but she didn't see anything particularly splendid about any of it. "Where is she taking my sword?"

"To her bedchambers, most likely."

"I'll just go and find it, then," said Saturday.

"It won't be that easy," said the boy. "She stays there most of the time. When she's not sleeping she's casting spells. Or preparing for spells. Or generally making a mess of everything."

Saturday harrumphed. Next to swinging a sharp weapon and scowling, it was one of the things she did best.

"Did Jack tell you about this place?" the boy — Peregrine — asked.

Saturday wavered between anger and jealousy. "You've seen my brother more recently than I have." She chose not to be more specific.

When she was but a toddler, Jack Junior had been cursed by an evil fairy and turned into a dog at the palace in Arilland, then subsequently presumed dead. Earlier in the year, when Sunday had rescued Prince Rumbold from his own curse, it was revealed to the family that Jack had not died, but in fact had gone off to live a full and adventurous life until he'd been eaten by a wolf. Or not. Sunday believed Jack was still alive. Saturday didn't know what was true anymore. As a result, she abhorred secrets about as much as this conversation.

"I should go. The witch will be back soon to assign your impossible tasks. There might be as many as three. You will have to complete them unless you can tell her where you've hidden her eyes."

"But I don't know, because I'm not Jack."

Peregrine snapped his fingers. "Got it in one. And if you know what's good for you, you won't tell her you're not who she thinks you are." He shook out his skirt, picked up a lantern, and began walking away. "Up here, no one can hear you scream."

"Wait . . . so what am I supposed to call you? Leila, right?"

"If you have to, refer to me as 'the maid,' but it's really best if you don't say anything at all." He turned back to add, "I'll try to help you when I can. Just ask." The bugaboo followed him out through the archway.

He'd left before telling her anything else, like where to find a drink of water, or breakfast, or where to relieve and wash herself. It would have been nice to have her messenger bag with everything she'd prepared for a journey like this. If she ever got it back it would never leave her side, even on a place as theoretically secure as her sister's ship.

Well, she'd just have to go exploring in the caves before the witch found her. She would find a way out of this place or die trying—if Jack had found a way out, she could too. Gods knew what sort of trouble Trix would be in by now. If he were still alive. She had to believe he was. But the sheer size of that ocean . . .

Saturday's heart ached in her chest. Perhaps this prison was the gods' way of punishing her for breaking the world.

She stepped off the pallet where she'd been standing onto the uneven stone floor and a chill raced up through her bones. She hadn't remembered removing her boots . . . or her sword-belt . . . or changing her clothes. The shirt and trousers she wore now were old, but not ill-fitting. She found her boots resting beside the stone pit. There did not seem to be another lantern handy, so she removed one of the small torches from the wall and used the fire to light it.

Saturday had a measure of experience with dark mazes.

She'd been lost in the Wood many times—more frequently as a little girl than now. It happened to every woodcutter from time to time, even Papa. No one but the piskies knew their way around the Wood.

This cavern was nothing like the Wood at all.

Within minutes, Saturday's head ached from her eyes' constant refocusing. The icerock walls with their odd patterns confused her, robbing her of her depth perception. The shadows played tricks on her, sometimes revealing a dead end, other times leading Saturday to chasms down which she might fall forever.

Every time the light moved, the cave changed. Around one corner was a forest of trees, hundreds of them, completely encased in snow and dripping with icicles, frozen into a timeless winter. They even smelled of damp cold. Stone faces stared at her from the shadows. Stone icicles rimmed the caverns like bared teeth protecting unknown treasures.

Making rock piles to mark her path in this space would have been futile; there were so many pillared protrusions, tall and knobby and many looking like broken rock piles themselves, that she didn't bother. She took out her dagger and scratched the walls in a few places, two straight cuts, angled inward to look like her mother's discerning brow, but from even a few paces away they disappeared into the sheets of white and ice and crystal.

Saturday banged her head for the umpteenth time. No matter what the stories said, caves were meant for dwarves, not giants. Having her sword would have at least helped with the massive headache she'd developed—foul witch. She rested beside a steep drop-off and something dripped onto her. Water cascaded down from the ceiling; she turned her head up to catch the water in her parched mouth. The air had gotten warmer, but rain? Inside? What a curious thing!

She stretched out her arm over the chasm in an effort to keep her balance and was surprised to see *two* torches casting shadows.

"Why, you're not a chasm at all, are you?" Her voice did not echo like she thought it might in a maze this size.

Saturday dipped a boot in the mirage and discovered that naught but a shallow pool of water had cast the massive reflection. Laughing, she leaned over the rock on which she sat and prepared to drink.

A stranger's face looked back at her.

All her life, it had never occurred to Saturday to cut her hair. Girls had long hair and boys had short hair, and that was just the way of the world. She tied it up when she was in the Wood or tucked it under a cap before sword practice and never thought twice about it. Her golden locks were gone now, close cropped at the nape of her neck, while the longer tendrils by her face dipped their ends in the pool. She couldn't be sure exactly how much she looked like Jack, but it wasn't the first time she'd been mistaken for a boy.

Saturday stuck her face in the pool and drank deeply. The water tasted of grit and soot. When she'd had her fill, she raised the torch again and moved on through the stone forest.

Oh, what stories Sunday would have told about these

decorated monoliths, sparkling in the lantern light, frowning down upon her with their protruding, frostbitten brows. Friday would have imagined the icicles as rows of needles standing at attention among yards and yards of lace. Thursday would have seen the history of these caves through her spyglass, back to when this mountain was nothing but a rolling hill in the landscape. Wednesday most likely would have recited poetry to the dancing shadows, stumbling across a spell or two by design or by accident before growing thick wings and flying herself to safety. Saturday wished she had such wings. The lantern showed them everywhere now, twin peaks of shadow feathers mocking her with their insubstantiality.

One of the shadows flew straight up and slapped her in the face with warm feathers. Saturday recognized that smell. The witch's familiar had found her.

"Silly troublemaker. Were you trying to escape again? I've blocked this way, as you can see."

Saturday saw no such thing, nor could she see the witch. She held the torch back, squinting into the darkness until she made out the soft light of a stone bracelet infused with magic. In the hand of the skinny arm that wore the circle of light was a long-handled rake with rusted tines.

Saturday subtly pushed the blue-green fabric of her own humble bracelet under her sleeve. Out of raven-sight, out of mind. The witch had taken her sword; she wouldn't part with this last memento so easily.

"I have your first task." The witch giggled and cackled with pride.

"I'm ready," said Saturday.

"Ha!" shrieked the witch. "You think you're going to sweep the stones or empty the water pots or tame the basilisk? The tasks I set were all too easy the first time."

"You have new pets?" Saturday guessed.

"No more pets. Tired of them. Killed them and ate them. Slow-roasted them over the fire while they died screaming. They were best that way." The witch licked her lips, and the raven fluttered restlessly.

"You're worrying the bird," said Saturday.

"Cwyn is not my pet. She is my familiar. She serves as my eyes, until you find them. And now you will clean her nest."

Saturday took the rake the witch thrust at her. Clean the nest of a single bird? How was that harder than taming a basilisk? But Saturday remembered the strange boy Peregrine's advice and kept her mouth shut lest the witch come up with something more difficult. "Lead on," she said. "It seems I don't know my way around these caves as well as I once did."

"That's because the ways of these caves are not your ways. They are my ways, and I change them as I will." The witch threw her arms open toward the false lake and the wall of rocks beyond it. "Here we are!"

The witch ducked through an archway into a small alcove filled with stone pillars and outcroppings. Beneath them, on the patch of somewhat-level floor, was a small amount of dried moss. Saturday wrinkled her nose at the smell, reminiscent of the chickens at home. Why did birds stink worse than horses and cows?

"So, if I clean this up, you'll give me my sword back?" asked Saturday.

"If you clean this up, you get to keep your life," answered the witch. "Think, while you work, about where you put my eyes. You will find them, and find them soon, or I will take yours instead. Snip-snap-snurre-basselure!"

8

Epiphany

ETWIXT! PRAISE the gods. I had quite despaired."

Peregrine halted his as-yet-infernal lute playing to greet the chimera slinking into the cave with quiet grace. It had been a good long while since Peregrine had last laid eyes on his friend. The chicken-footed scorpion body had morphed into a sleek black gryphon of the smallish variety, much like a young panther with charcoal-gray wings.

"If you despaired, it's only because you tired of your own one-sided prattle." The chimera's head was thankfully more leonine than bird, leaving his mostly mammalian mouth free to converse, though the words that came out were a bit high-pitched and nasal.

"You know me so well. Shall I play you a tune to celebrate your triumphant return?"

"Have you learned to play anything even closely resembling a song on that?"

Peregrine gave his companion a wide and silly grin and curled his toes against the pillar on which he perched. "Not at all. But I could get the flute . . ."

"Don't trouble yourself." Betwixt wandered around the room a bit before circling and settling himself in a cold spot away from the lantern. The chimera craved warmth when he was in a solid state. Right before a change, or right after, he craved the cold. His wings folded neatly over his haunches and his tail waved back and forth lazily. "So, how goes it with our young prodigy?"

Peregrine resisted snapping a lute string, as he wasn't likely to find a ready replacement. One learned to take good care of one's belongings when there was a limited supply. "She's still digging herself deeper into that bird's nest. I don't think she's ever going to ask me for help. Jack Woodcutter neglected to mention that his sisters were stubborn brats."

Betwixt scratched his jaw with a hind leg. "There are six other days of the Woodcutter week. They can't *all* be so badly-tempered."

"I pray not, for Jack's sake." Peregrine's hopes for conversation and companionship had so far been dashed by this girl. She worked harder than her brother ever had, and tirelessly. Peregrine had woken and slept three times since the witch had set her to her task. He'd checked in on her, but she hadn't spotted him, so he didn't interrupt. Deeper and deeper she buried herself in the filth of the witch's familiar. She had yet to figure out the trick to the enchanted rake, and Peregrine refused to involve himself where he was not wanted. He had eventually tired of waiting for her to ask for help and had gone about his daily business as usual.

Only, there was nothing usual about his daily business anymore. He'd been lonely as a child with an ill father, but that loneliness had been eclipsed by his years of solitude at the Top of the World. And yet, having someone else close at hand who pointedly ignored him made him feel worse than he ever had before.

This hadn't been the case when Jack had scaled the mountain. There had been the swapping of laughter and stories. When Jack had asked Peregrine to escape with him, Peregrine felt comfortable enough beneath Leila's disguise — especially now that the witch had been blinded — to be secure in his decision to stay and sabotage the witch's experiments. The world would go on as it should, none the wiser, for as long as he could manage it. "When Jack was here, he spoke of his family as if he'd only just left them."

"Did he? It was so long ago, I barely remember."

"It wasn't *that* long ago." Betwixt did tend toward hyperbole. "But the day Saturday arrived—"

"*That* day I remember."

"Saturday mentioned not having seen Jack since his voyage to the White Mountains. Do you think something's happened to him?"

"Oh dear. I hope not."

"As do I," said Peregrine. "The Goddess of Luck seemed to be ever at his side; I only pray she still is."

"Luck can be bad as well as good," Betwixt pointed out.

"I wish I had better luck with Saturday," said Peregrine. "I want to help her. What's so terrible about that?"

"You're just bothered that she doesn't give two figs for you," said Betwixt.

"Of course I am. Do you think the skirt is putting her off? I fear it makes her see me as weak."

"I think the witch has put her off more than you or me," Betwixt suggested. "To be honest, I don't believe she's seen you at all, weak or not, since she's been here."

The idea took away some of Peregrine's bluster. He didn't want to think of what would happen when "Jack Woodcutter" finished all the witch's tasks and still couldn't find the eyes. "She's obsessed with that room. She'll work herself into the arms of Lord Death at this rate. What kind of person burdens herself so much when help would be given freely and willingly?"

"A very strong person. And a very stupid one."

Peregrine laughed. "Spoken like a true cat."

"Why don't you just ask Saturday herself about her intentions?"

"She'd have to stop burying herself in bird dung long enough to talk," he said.

"Then the Goddess of Luck is with you this day." Betwixt tilted his head to the sloping archway through which Saturday was determinedly making her way to them. There was a rake in her hands and fire in her eyes.

Everything about her was so familiar to him, as if he'd known her for a lifetime. Pity she didn't feel the same. They could have been such good friends.

"Hmm." Peregrine leaned back and casually picked up the lute again. He wanted his image of lassitude to irk her. He should have been ashamed at this pointless goading. He wasn't.

"Jack Woodcutter! As I live and breathe." He yawned, and then instantly regretted it: Saturday reeked like a sewer. "Just between us girls," Peregrine whispered, "that cologne doesn't suit you."

"Good morning, *Lie*-la." Saturday purposefully mispronounced the name. Oh, he did like her gumption. Shame about the brattitude. "Or day, or afternoon, or evening, not that anyone can tell."

"Every greeting is welcome in a land beyond time," Peregrine said poetically, plucking idly on the lute as if he might compose a song with the words.

"Then I should have hugged you and mugged you with slime," Saturday rhymed glibly.

Peregrine was surprised at her show of cleverness and continued the verse. "Look at Woodcutter! Not bad with a rhyme."

Instead of answering in kind Saturday turned her face to the floor, as if someone had just scolded her for having fun. "It was a game I played with my brother. Peter, not the one you know."

Not the one he knew, and not the one she sought. So many siblings! Peregrine could hardly imagine a family so large. "My compliment still stands. If I had your gift, I would write a hundred songs to your malodorous beauty."

"First, you'd have to learn how to play," she said. At the snuffled sound of cat laughter, Saturday raised her lantern and spotted the gryphon. "Hello there."

"Well met, Miss Woodcutter."

While she had her lantern held high, Saturday turned slowly and examined the sparkling pillars in this cave, like castle turrets made of fairydust. The fingerstones here looked like tall, dripping candles waiting to be lit. It was one of Peregrine's favorite spots.

"All these caves look mean," said Saturday. "Full of teeth, like they intend to eat me alive."

Peregrine blinked at the scene, trying to see it with new eyes. He'd felt the same way when he'd arrived, but in the period that followed the caves had changed. Mellowed. As he had. "The longer you stay, the kinder they appear."

"Is it true that time doesn't properly pass in this place?"

"Oh yes," answered Peregrine. "There is no day or night here, only sleeping and waking. The sun and moon pass overhead, but Lord Time and his brothers have no hold on this mountain. We could live up here a thousand years and never age or die."

"How do you know?"

Peregrine shrugged. "I'm not dead yet."

He dodged the swat she intended for him. "You try my patience."

"Take care with that. If he decides he likes your patience, he'll take all of it," Betwixt chimed in.

Saturday pointed at the gryphon with the rake. "Did you used to be the beetle-thing?" Peregrine had to give her credit; he hadn't caught on to Betwixt's nature so quickly. Her cleverness aggravated him, but he quashed the feeling. Now that she'd finally come to him, he did not want to ruin it.

"I was. Forgive me for not introducing myself earlier. My name is Betwixt." The gryphon bowed his head.

"Is that really your name? Or is 'Betwixt' a part you're playing as well?" She looked askance at Peregrine. He simply shrugged his shoulders helplessly.

"It might have been something else so long ago, I've forgotten it. Betwixt is the only name I have to give you."

"I'm sorry," said Saturday.

"It's not *that* bad a name," said the gryphon.

"I mean that you've forgotten your old name," she corrected. "That happened to a brother-in-law of mine when he was enchanted. Are you enchanted? Is there anything I can do to help? I'm a maiden," she said bluntly.

"So am I!" said Peregrine.

"You are an im——" Saturday stopped before she finished the insult. Her restraint surprised him. He really wished she'd stop impressing him. It made her lack of interest that much harder to bear.

"Cat got your tongue?" Peregrine asked her.

Betwixt yowled in nasally feline laughter.

Saturday stuck out said tongue to prove that she was still in full possession of it. "I need help," she said.

Finally! Peregrine resisted the urge to hug the lute giddily. "You need a bath" was all he said in reply.

"Are you going to help me or not?" said Saturday. Her knuckles around the rake handle were white.

"Are you asking or not?"

Saturday put her head down, sighed, and started again. "The witch gave me this"—she thrust the disgusting rake in Peregrine's direction—"and told me to clean her wretched bird's nest."

Peregrine backed away from the rake. He didn't want it to accidentally touch him. "And . . . ?" he prompted.

"The cursed thing doesn't work! The more soiled peat I rake, the more there is, multiplying instead of diminishing. It's some sort of foul magic."

Peregrine wrinkled his nose. "Something in this cave is certainly foul."

"I gave up on the rake and tried shoving out the moss with my bare hands for a while."

"Oh no," said Betwixt.

"Oh my," said Peregrine. He wasn't sure even he had the stomach—or the nose—for that level of degradation.

"But nothing happened! I worked from the time I woke until the time I fell asleep and the room looked the same as it had when I started."

"So you tried the rake again," said Peregrine.

"Yes," said Saturday. "Disaster. Can you help me?"

Peregrine sat and stared at the girl for a while, letting her stew. He suspected she knew what he was doing, but she remained quiet. "Yes, I can help you," he said finally.

"Name your price," said Saturday.

"I didn't say there was one yet."

"I have siblings," said Saturday. "I know how this works. Go on, state your conditions."

Peregrine was torn between the desire to kiss Saturday and the desire to strangle her. It was an intoxicating feeling that amused him no end, but her stench made the decision for him.

"I will you give you a number of sacks," said Peregrine. "When you clean the bird's nest, collect the soiled moss in these sacks."

"Done," said Saturday. "Is there a supply of clean moss to replace the old?"

"I'll make sure you have it," said Peregrine.

Saturday nodded, but she did not thank him. And because she did not thank him, Peregrine continued his list of demands. "I will also have a bath ready for you. When you are done cleaning the nest, you will take it."

"All right," she said easily, for this was more of a benefit than a hardship. He'd hoped she'd take it as such. But she still conveyed no expression of gratitude.

"You will come with me wherever I decide to take you, and you will keep a civil tongue in your head."

"Fine," spat Saturday. "Is that all?"

"One last thing," said Peregrine. "You have to fight me for it."

"For what?"

"For all of it: the sacks, the bath, and the answer to your enigma."

The smile she gave him was wicked and wonderful. "My pleasure."

~eelee~

He might have returned the lute first and taken a longer, more circuitous route to the armory, but the girl's smell was more than he could bear. Betwixt led the way, half slinking and half flying, ever keeping upwind. When Peregrine passed through the archway to their destination he lifted his lantern and turned to see her expression, hoping that he might catch a glimpse of happiness, however small.

He was not disappointed.

Peregrine saw a moment of unabashed joy on Saturday's face before she noticed him watching and stifled it. "Where did all this come from?" She set down the rake and brought her own lantern in for a closer look.

"If there is one thing a dragon's lair does not lack, it is the weapons of defeated foes." One by one, Peregrine lit the torches around the room. He had chosen this section of the caves for its natural shelves, on which he'd separated the weapons into categories. "Axes, maces, lances, bows, arrows. The swords are in a pile over there. There are so many, I'm never quite sure how to sort them."

"And clean, polish, and sharpen them?" Peregrine nodded in answer to her question. "This must have taken *ages*."

"It's an ongoing project. I enjoy a hard day's work."

"Me too," she said. Peregrine heroically refrained from comparing his "hard days" with her exhausting path of never-ending masochism.

"The results of my work on the weapons are easier to see. Armor is less salvageable as a whole, but there's still plenty to be had, and it's excessively useful. Even a dented helmet makes a passable mixing bowl."

"A mixing bowl." Saturday seemed to find the notion blasphemous. She let her hand hover over a shelf of oddities, but did not touch them. "I don't even know what some of these things are."

"Nor do I," Peregrine admitted. He picked up one item that had very long spikes connected by a chain. "This one could be a very dangerous whip."

"Or a collar," Saturday suggested. "Maybe something attached to a helmet?"

"More likely. Though the skeleton I took it from had it like this." Peregrine wrapped the chain around his fist, so that the spikes pointed out from his knuckles.

"Wicked," said Saturday cheerfully.

Peregrine tossed the chain back onto the shelf. "And completely pointless when fighting a dragon. If you're close enough to punch it, it's close enough to roast you and eat you."

Saturday walked to the next shelf, which was full of daggers and sharp throwing implements. "May I?"

"Of course. They come in handy when one needs to chop ice from the walls." Peregrine had replaced his own broken dagger earlier.

He'd destroyed many a dagger while hacking at the walls of his prison, but there was still a plethora to choose from. Silver, iron, bent, curved, and serrated, they stretched out before Saturday like a smorgasbord of pain. After lifting and balancing a few of the knives, Saturday added only one more to her swordbelt with its empty scabbard.

"Did you bury the skeletons?"

"Of course! Thankfully one of the knights who died here brought a magic shovel that could cut through icerock like freshly churned butter."

Saturday rolled her eyes at him but did not stomp away. Perhaps there was hope for a friendship between them yet. "Bones have useful properties," he said seriously. "The warriors here are long dead, as are the ones who mourned them. The only living being to come up this far in recent years was Jack."

"Right," said Saturday. "You mentioned that."

Peregrine took her hand. "You really haven't seen your brother, have you?"

Saturday pulled her hand away, scalding him again with those eyes of fire. The feeling that he'd known her forever struck him again.

Peregrine wondered why he kept trying to please her and

realized it was because of Jack, but Jack had enjoyed himself during his stay. Peregrine couldn't stop from asking, "Do you enjoy *anything?*"

Saturday exhaled. "Can I just fight you now? Please? I'd rather die than continue this conversation."

"Oh, this is going to be *fun.*" Betwixt leapt to a shelf beyond sword's reach and settled himself comfortably.

Peregrine curtseyed. "As milady wishes. But you can't have so little faith in your abilities. I'm sure you've had teachers more recently than I."

"My sword was my nameday gift. As you know, it's enchanted. I'm not so good without it, despite my teachers' attempts."

Peregrine indicated the pile of swords. "So choose another one."

Saturday put her hands on her hips. "None of them is my sword."

"But many of them are enchanted," said Peregrine. "Most of them, I'll wager. One doesn't hear many tales of men going up against beasts like our dragon with only their wits and cold steel."

"Unless those tales are about Jack Woodcutter," she said under her breath.

Peregrine had heard few tales of such men as a boy in Starburn; bedtime stories in the north typically ventured into the realms of gods and monsters. But having met Jack, he could imagine the kinds of stories that confident swagger left in its wake. As many hearts broken as curses, he'd wager.

"Well, then, let's see if you live up to your reputation, Mister Woodcutter." Peregrine pulled a sword from the pile at random and unsheathed it. The hilt's basket was ornate and set with dull jewel chips. The blade was thin and glowed a red that tinted the crystal walls around them a sinister pink.

"What does that sword do?" asked Saturday.

"No idea," said Peregrine. "Hurry up and pick one so we can find out. Who knows? You might decide you like something here better than the one you had."

"Doubtful." Saturday took a little longer over her selection. The sword she chose was far less decorative, with only crude runes etched haphazardly into its pommel, grip, and cross guard. It looked ancient, and heavy, and didn't have much of an edge. She'd have more luck using it as a club. Perhaps that was her plan.

Peregrine took up the stance his father and swordsmaster had taught him: arm held up and blade pointed down. Conversely, Saturday held the hilt at her center of mass with blade pointed skyward. He tried to remember which of the regions of Arilland Jack had said her family was from. *"En garde."* He hoped she knew what he meant.

He did not expect her to say, "This grip is warm."

"You're welcome to choose another sword," he offered. "We have all day, night, afternoon, and evening, or until the witch finds us."

"No, this sword is fine. It's just . . ." As she spoke, the sparkling runes from the hilt duplicated themselves on the skin of her hands, her wrists, and then her arms. She drew in a sharp breath, but she did not let go of the blade.

Peregrine worried for her safety. "What's happening? Saturday, talk to me. Are you all right?"

She looked up from her silver rune-covered arms and her bright eyes flashed above that impish smile. The dirty locks of her hair framed her face. "I'm perfect," she said, and struck out at the red blade.

Peregrine dropped his sword.

He did not drop it on purpose; he'd fully intended for the two of them to fight evenly and fairly. But what Peregrine had just seen beyond that ancient blade, atop smelly limbs and a neck now covered with glowing runes, was neither the face of Jack Woodcutter nor that of his far less likeable sister.

The face that had grinned at him with those bright eyes was the face of the woman from his visions.

Betwixt had been right: Elodie of Cassot was not the woman of his dreams after all. The image he'd been seeing for most of his life had been that of Saturday Woodcutter.

The familiarity he'd been sensing crashed like a wave in his heart. No words sprang to mind to describe the feelings this epiphany swept through him, but the ones that came closest were not meant for mixed company.

"Peregrine?"

Peregrine snapped out of his trance. "I'm sorry," he said to the chimera, and he picked up the sword again. "You're completely covered in those runes now," he said to Saturday.

"Are you sure you're all right?" He was amazed *he* was all right enough to string coherent sentences together.

"Perfectly lovely," Saturday said pettily. "Are we doing this or not?"

He wanted to stop the argument, sit her down, and ask her a barrage of questions. But more, he wanted to watch her, to see the face burned on his soul bearing down on him in real life. Peregrine resumed attack position. "Best two out of three?" he asked cheerfully.

"Prepare to die," said Saturday.

9

Decision

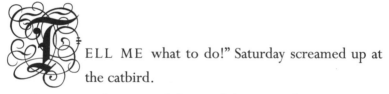ELL ME what to do!" Saturday screamed up at the catbird.

Betwixt took wing and dropped down to where Peregrine now lay dying at her feet. "I don't know," he answered.

"I didn't mean it," she said, "when I told him to die. I didn't really mean it."

"I know that. So did he. It's all right."

"This"—Saturday pointed at Peregrine's prone form—"is *not* all right." She was a killer. She'd killed Trix and heavens knew how many innocent people, and now she'd killed Peregrine, when she was just starting to like him.

Saturday's mind spun. She begged the gods to hear her:

she hadn't really meant it. Mama's oft-spoken warning repeated itself in the back of her mind: *Words have power.*

The message had always been meant for her little sister, or for Mama herself. It had never applied to the ax-wielding giantess who traded quips in the Wood with her father and brother all day but couldn't tell a proper story to save her life. Yet here she stood, over a boy she'd threatened to kill, watching him die.

"Think, Saturday, think!" She tossed the heavy blade aside and felt the runes fade from her body. He'd been right; the feeling was reminiscent of her own sword, not that it could ever take its place. The symbols had turned her skin into armor, impervious to any blow. By all rights, Peregrine should have won first blood with his ruby blade, but thanks to her magical protection, he had not.

They had fought long and hard, longer than she should have and not half as hard as she'd wished to. They were well matched: he was as rusty with his weapon as she was untrained. After much teasing and taunting and running and jumping, she'd turned the tables and scratched him first instead. Peregrine fell to his knees almost immediately, but not in mock defeat as she'd first supposed.

Saturday's blade hadn't just been decorated with enchanted runes. It had also been poisoned.

The moment Peregrine's hand left the hilt of his sword, the blade's red glow faded and the walls around them regained their shimmering powdered-sugar whiteness. Similarly did the blood leave Peregrine's face, rendering him deathly pale. It had been only a scratch on his wrist, but he was already beginning to shake.

Saturday's hand instinctively moved to the bag that was not at her side. "If I were in the Wood, I would have crushed jewel-weed," she told Betwixt. "Is there anything like that here?"

"Maybe in the witch's caves," he said. "But they are far from here and difficult to reach. And it wouldn't be a plant."

"Right." Proper plants couldn't grow in caves. Saturday didn't know the first thing about magic spells, but she knew a little bit about poison. There was one option left.

Saturday removed the ornate dagger Peregrine had sheathed in his belt and used it to cut deeper into the angry wound. Moving his confounded skirt out of the way, Saturday lowered her lips to Peregrine's wrist.

The gryphon put a paw on her shoulder. His dark fur was soft and his feathers tickled as they brushed her dirty skin. "You might be poisoned too."

"I'll be fine," said Saturday. She hoped the catbird took her at her word. She didn't have time to explain her recent inde-structibility, though it would have been nice to have her sword to help her on that front. She sucked the blood from Peregrine's wound and spat it onto the icy stone floor. She could taste the poison's taint amidst the copper on her tongue. Peregrine's eyes rolled back up into his head.

Saturday sucked and spat again. "Go find that witch of yours. Tell her that her daughter is dying." She didn't want to involve the witch, but she saw no other choice. Jack Woodcut-ter would take the blame for this, though it was Saturday who deserved the punishment. She resolved to tell the witch every-thing if this boy died.

Betwixt did not argue. He leapt toward the archway through which Saturday had entered, only to be stopped by a mass of cerulean wings. The raven was blue now? Fantastic. She'd probably be blamed for that, too. Well, if that loathsome bird was here that meant the witch wasn't far behind. Saturday hoped the lorelei wasn't too addled over the state of her "daughter" to cast some sort of antidote spell.

Saturday wiped her mouth and laid an ear flat against Peregrine's chest. She feigned calmness in an effort to discern a breath and heartbeat that were not her own. His shivering increased. His skin was clammy. Saturday's lips tingled. She should have asked him which of his gods he'd like for her to pray to. Perhaps the catbird knew.

"Step aside, daughter."

The words were not the witch's, and the daughter referred to was not Peregrine. Saturday recognized the voice as the one that had echoed loudly inside her head upon her arrival, deep and rough as a chimney sweep's.

Betwixt hissed. Where the raven had once been now stood a sturdy, blue-robed woman of average height with a face like Mama's: grim, no-nonsense, and full of lines. Her messy hair was as rich a blue as the raven's feathers had been and her build was thick, as if she were no stranger to hard work. The woman rushed to Peregrine's side.

An enchanted bird turning human did not surprise Saturday. One of her sisters had done the same thing just that spring, and that goose had been as white as a wedding gown. "Did you bring the witch with you?" Saturday asked the woman.

"This will go far more smoothly without her," she replied. "We have to act quickly. Is there a container of any sort handy?"

Saturday hastily scanned the armory and returned with a smallish helmet, a metal gauntlet, and a finger-claw. There might have been something more suitable in the room, but she didn't want to waste Peregrine's breath trying to find it.

The woman smiled at the choices Saturday laid before her. "Well done," she said, and leaned over them. Saturday had no idea what the woman was looking for. Hadn't she said they were in a hurry? Curious, Betwixt leaned in too. The woman gently reached out a hand as if to pat his dark ears reassuringly, but she grabbed a whisker from his muzzle and pulled it out instead.

The catbird screeched, hissed, and flapped his wings. He unsheathed the wicked claws on his right front paw and snapped at the woman with his beak. She held his head down. "Tears," she said to the chimera. "Don't waste them."

Betwixt stopped struggling. The woman placed the gauntlet under the cat's beak and coaxed the tears from his eyes with the finger-claw. She did not touch the tears herself.

"You deserve to be pecked," Betwixt said from beneath her arm.

"I could have told you a sad tale and waited, but your friend is in quite a bit of danger," said the woman. And then, to Saturday, "Hold his arm still."

Saturday placed her hand in Peregrine's, turning his arm so that the festering cut on his wrist pointed heavenward. There was little blood, but the skin was red and angry. Around the cut, the veins ran black and blue and green.

The woman tilted the gauntlet and let the tears fall — one, two, three — directly onto the wound. Almost immediately the blood dried and the redness began to fade. The flesh turned pale again but for a thin blue line of scar marking the original cut. His shivering stopped, but not in a bad way. Saturday placed her other hand on his chest and felt his breathing, slow and deep and even.

"Was there a need for all that?" asked Betwixt. "He cannot die in this place."

"Just because a man cannot die does not mean he cannot be crippled," said the woman, "and there are many ways to cripple a man." She dipped her finger in the tears again and traced Saturday's lips before gently placing the gauntlet aside. "Gryphon's tears have healing properties. Do not waste the rest."

"Thank you," said Saturday. Her lips still felt swollen, but the pain had stopped.

"Who are you?" asked Betwixt.

The woman sat back on her haunches, crossed her legs, and rested her folded hands on her belly. "I have many names," she said. "In these mountains I am usually known as Vasilisa. Here, the lorelei calls me Cwyn. That will serve."

Saturday gave a half-laugh. "No one else in this cave is what they seem. Why should you be any different?" She felt a gentle squeeze and realized that she was still holding Peregrine's hand. She let it go immediately and leaned away from him. Thankfully, he didn't seem to notice.

His eyes were open now, staring at the blue woman. "Is that . . . ?"

"Yes," Betwixt finished before he could bother asking, just as Peter would have done if Saturday had posed the question.

"Smart bird. Never did that before." Peregrine sounded euphoric. Either a gryphon's tears also reduced the amount of oxygen to one's brain, or the cure had somehow rendered him drunk.

"I did not have the power before," said Cwyn. "It takes much for me to resist the geis."

"Before what?" asked Saturday.

"Before you," said Cwyn. "Don't worry. It will not last long."

What an odd thing to say. What cause would Saturday have to worry? "Are you a goddess?" she asked.

"You flatter me, daughter. You are closer to the gods than I."

"You're a demon," said Betwixt.

"Another witch," said Peregrine. "Bah."

"I've been called worse things." Cwyn brushed her hair back to reveal two small horns protruding from high on her forehead.

"Tooo many bluuue witches," slurred Peregrine.

"I am not a *lorelei*." The witch said the word as if it were a curse. "I am a pyrrhi, a fire witch. I'm only blue because the lorelei's imposter daughter cured my wounds with a salve made from rancid cave mushrooms."

Peregrine giggled guiltily. "Oops."

"A healing for a healing," Cwyn said to Peregrine. "My debt has been repaid."

"Bad mushrooms dye your skin?" asked Saturday.

"The ones up here do," Betwixt answered. "As they wither, they change colors."

"Like leaves in the Wood," said Saturday.

"Like leaves that run the spectrum of the rainbow," said Betwixt. And then to Cwyn, "How can you stand to be her familiar?"

"How do you stand it?" Cwyn shot back. "Her need drew me here, amplified by the dragon's power. She summoned me from the Earthfire at the heart of this mountain."

"S'not very good at spells," mumbled Peregrine.

"Indeed. Acquiring a familiar to restore her vision was what she intended. Acquiring me wasn't." She looked pointedly at Betwixt. "Nor do I plan to enlighten her about my true identity. While I act as her eyes, she sees only what I want her to see."

"Understood," said the chimera.

"I don't think you do," said Cwyn. "The lorelei must be stopped. She is attempting to open a doorway back to the demon world from which our ancestors came. If she succeeds, it will rip this world apart."

"Never happen," said Peregrine. "She's rubbish. No worries."

"Jack took her eyes to slow down her progress," said Betwixt. "Peregrine and I have been doing what little we can to sabotage her, but mostly, she sabotages herself."

"Your efforts have not gone unnoticed by me, though they remain unseen by our mistress," said Cwyn. "Until now, her spells have been fueled by what little magic she can siphon off the dragon. That's changed, thanks to our new visitor."

"Me?" asked Saturday. "But I don't have any magic. You must have me confused with another sibling. It's a common occurrence lately."

"You were not born with magic, nor can you create it," said Cwyn, "but you are a vessel. You can channel magic, contain it, and control it. Through you, others may do the same." She clasped Saturday's hand in her own. It was small and strong, like Mama's. "At the moment, you are the most powerful being on this mountain. You must use that power to defeat the lorelei."

Cwyn was talking too fast, saying impossible things quicker than Saturday's mind could process them. "I'm not fey," she told the fire witch. "All my brothers and sisters are. Not me."

"It isn't fairy magic she's talking about," said Betwixt. "This is godstuff."

Erik had said that exact same phrase back at the tower-house. *Godstuff*. Saturday remembered the taste of Trix's stew on her tongue and resisted the urge to vomit. She stared at her hands, large and unwieldy and never good for more than hefting an ax or a sword. Now she was supposed to believe that those hands could throw lightning bolts? Impossible. And yet, she'd already called an ocean and endangered—or ended—countless lives. She could not deny what she had witnessed with her own eyes.

Poor Trix. He should never have been burdened with a sister like her.

"No more killing," said Saturday. "These hands have done enough damage on behalf of the gods. I won't be used as an instrument to kill the witch who holds you prisoner."

"If you don't kill the lorelei, she will destroy the world," said Cwyn.

"And if she does kill the lorelei, the dragon will wake and this mountain will fall," argued Betwixt.

"Save a few, or save the world." Cwyn kissed Saturday's hands and released them. "The choice is yours." The outline of her human form was already beginning to fade, her blue skin and hair quickly turning to blue down and feathers.

That was no choice for a mere woodcutter; it was a choice for a hero.

"What do I do?" Saturday asked no one. What would Jack do?

Have faith, the pyrrhi said inside Saturday's mind. With the last of her energy, the witch's familiar lifted her raven wings and flew from the cave.

"Did she answer you?" asked Peregrine. "What did she say?"

"Nothing helpful," said Saturday. "Are you all right?"

"I—" Peregrine's eyes widened and his face softened dreamily. "You're beautiful."

Fantastic. As if she didn't have enough on her plate, now she had to deal with insults from a boy drunk on magical cat-snot. "You're delusional."

In a flash, Peregrine's dreamy expression was gone. "Yup. Just as I thought." He stood up, brushed his hair back, and straightened his belt and skirt as if he'd done nothing more than trip and have a bad fall.

Saturday felt as if she'd been tricked into something. "What just happened?"

Peregrine put his hands on his knees. He leaned down to speak to her, still on the floor, as if she were a child. "How can someone so clever always be so lost? Let me help. We fought with magical swords. You almost killed me. I was saved by someone who I didn't realize owed me a debt, only to be told I'm going to die soon anyway . . . unless I'm miraculously rescued by an idiot who thinks beauty is a weakness." Peregrine crossed his arms over his chest. "Forgive me if I'm a little upset."

What in the world did beauty have to do with anything? And why was he putting those words in her mouth? Saturday may not have been beautiful, but she certainly wasn't weak.

"I'll find a way," said Saturday. "I'll find a way for us all to escape. I'll get us all safely down from this mountain and then no one has to die. Just let me think." She was very good at problem solving as long as she had the peace of mind to work things out.

"She doesn't get it, does she?" Peregrine asked Betwixt.

"Don't make this harder on her than it already is," said the chimera.

"Why not?" yelled Peregrine. "It's not only her life in the balance here!"

Is this what she and Peter did all the time? So much talking without actually saying anything helpful! Saturday's patience reached the breaking point and she lashed out at Peregrine. He recoiled enough for her arm to miss sweeping his legs.

"You already almost killed me once today, *Jack*. Isn't that enough?"

Saturday jumped to her feet and reached for the red magic sword between them. "Apparently not."

Peregrine rushed to the pile for another sword; this one's blade burst into flames as he raised it against her. "Let's finish this, then."

"Children, please," said Betwixt, but Saturday ignored him. There were no cords of wood here for her to chop in frustration; this was the next best thing. Besides, if anything happened, there were still some gryphon's tears left.

Saturday lunged at Peregrine. "Why do you have to be such a jerk?"

He lifted his flaming sword and the two blades met. "Why are you so selfish?"

She sliced a wide arc across his middle, but he had already backed away. "I have to choose between killing myself or killing everyone else. How is that selfish?"

He grunted as he blocked her next strike. "Because you haven't asked what I wanted."

"You want to rescue us all? Fine. *You* figure it out."

Peregrine caught his sword against hers and slid it up the length of her blade until their noses were almost touching. His breath was warm. "Maybe I don't want to be rescued. Maybe Betwixt and I are just fine where we are. Did you ever think of that?"

Saturday stomped on his foot and spun away as he winced in pain. She turned back to strike at him, but he was gone again, having jumped to the rows of pillarstones along the far wall.

As much as it irked her, she knew how he was feeling right now. The gods hadn't given her much time to consider her options as she tumbled from one mess into another. Saturday eased up on her attack, allowing Peregrine his time to think. "Why would you want to stay here?"

Peregrine stepped gracefully from one pillar to another without faltering. "When I first arrived here, I attempted to escape multiple times. Each one ended in failure. I pretended to be the witch's daughter because I valued my life. Betwixt seemed to think it was a good idea for me to keep breathing."

"I'll thank you to keep me out of this," said the catbird. He had returned to his perch on the shelf high above them.

"Eventually, I stopped trying to leave. I have a friend here. I can do anything I want, for as long as I please. I have, literally, all the time in the world. That's more than I ever experienced as a boy, and so much more than my father ever had. Which you would know if you cared to ask." Having reached the last pillar-stone, Peregrine jumped down and came at her with the flaming sword again.

Only bring him back if he wants to come. Trix had run away from his family, from her, and she had been too stubborn to let him go. Now here she was, doing the same thing again with Peregrine.

Peregrine kept coming at her, but without her nameday sword she lacked the energy to continue. She refused to fight anymore. She threw the red sword across the room, tossed her head back, and screamed her frustration at the ceiling. She did not realize that Betwixt had returned from his shelf until she felt the warmth of his fur and feathers by her side.

"Saturday?" the chimera asked tentatively.

Saturday lowered a hand to the soft spot between his wings.

In that moment, she missed her Wood as much as she missed her brothers. She'd spent most of her life looking toward the horizon, waiting for the moment to escape the mind-numbing simplicity of her daily routine. She never imagined she'd meet her fate alone at the top of a mountain frozen in time. "I destroy everything I touch," she said. "What sort of destiny is that?"

"Come, now. You're being too hard on yourself."

"I broke the world," she told the chimera. "I have no intention of doing it again."

Peregrine lowered his sword. The flame on the blade sputtered and died. "The earthquake? That was you?"

"Yes." She did not mention the mirror she had thrown, or the ebony-handled brush that had come with the set. Mystical or not, it remained in her bag on Thursday's ship. Probably for the best.

"My little brother ran away and I was angry," said Saturday. Who knew what price Trix had paid for that anger.

"Remind me never to make you angry," said Peregrine.

"Too late," said Saturday. She might have laughed if her limbs hadn't felt as heavy as her heart. Responsibility burdened her already-tired soul. Her defenses were so far down that she put up no resistance when Peregrine took her in his arms and kissed her.

He was warm and clean and his kiss was soft on her sensitive lips. He held her tightly and she held him back. She reveled in his embrace like a gift she did not deserve. She clung to the feeling as he stepped away, knowing that the moment she let it go, the guilt and filth and exhaustion would subsume her.

If Peregrine started reciting love poems, she would punch him. But when he finally opened his mouth to speak, what he said was "Turn the rake around and shovel with the handle."

It took her a moment for his words to register. Saturday relaxed her clenched fist.

"You can sleep here tonight." He crossed the room to where he had fallen and slid the runesword into his belt before picking up the gauntlet, still damp with gryphon's tears.

Sleep here? In the wretched cold, with no fire or pallet or blankets? There were but a few torches on the walls . . . and then Saturday remembered the flaming sword. She'd make do. She thought she heard something scurry away in the shadows, but she paid it no heed.

"We'll find you tomorrow. Good night, Saturday."

And with that, they were gone.

10

Destined for Destruction

WHAT WAS that?" asked Betwixt.

"A very good question covering a myriad of subjects," Peregrine said in a scholarly tone. He'd waited until they were some distance away from the armory before wiping his face with the end of his sleeve. It would have been a rude thing to do in front of Saturday. He sniffed his shirt; her smell still lingered on him. It wasn't pleasant. The kiss, however, was another matter. Peregrine wiped his mouth again and grinned into the cloth. "Where would you like to begin?"

"Let's start with the kiss."

The kiss. The thought made Peregrine's knees tingle, and every fiber in his body that wasn't furious smiled. "Okay. So . . . you were right."

"While that's usually true," said Betwixt, "that's not the answer I was looking for."

"Does Saturday look familiar to you?"

"Of course," said the chimera. "She looks like Jack."

"That's what I thought too. At first." They came to a split in the tunnel. Peregrine decided there was more work to do in the kitchen, so he selected the one on the left. "And then I realized I'd seen a face like hers more recently than that. So have you."

The chimera whiffled through his beak. "I have?"

"It was her eyes that did it. Her eyes and that mad grin as we prepared to fight."

"When you dropped your sword."

"She looked at me with those bright eyes filled with fury, and I knew." He'd known her then for who she was, just as he'd known his heart and soul were lost forever. He should have recognized her when the gods delivered her to his doorstep.

"You knew that I was right?"

"I knew that Elodie of Cassot was not the woman in my visions."

Betwixt yowled. "Oh, gods. Your infernal sketchings. That was Saturday?" The catbird yowled again in affirmation. "That was Saturday!"

Peregrine balanced the tear-stained gauntlet and the torch while he lifted his skirt to maneuver around the small pillars and rock shelves in the floor. " 'Infernal.' So apt a description." Here and there the runesword scraped against the calcite, leaving a trail of glittering snow in his wake.

"What are you going to do?"

"I'm going to change my shirt and wash my face. I will not be kissing that girl again until she's had a proper bath. Then I plan on burning a few of my possessions before the witch can get her claws on them. Want to help?"

Betwixt swatted at Peregrine's skirt with a paw. "That's not what I meant."

"You mean what am I going to do about being in love with Stubborn-Britches Woodcutter when I'm betrothed to another woman?"

The gryphon's chuckle was more of a fluttery purr. "It is a dilemma."

Peregrine raised a finger. "You're not seeing the bigger picture, my friend. As a traitorous birdie-witch just told us, we're all about to die. That pipe dream I had of returning to the world? Never going to happen. For once, I hope that after all this time dear Elodie was smart enough to carry on without me."

"I hope so too," said Betwixt. "For her sake, and yours."

Peregrine was too wound up for serious conversation. Having reached the kitchen, he walked straight up to the shelves that contained most of his pantry items. He carefully poured the last few gryphon's tears into an empty vial, and then slipped the vial into his pocket. The next vial he picked up and threw into the fireplace. The glass broke and spiced mold spilled everywhere. The smokeless coals began to emit strange violet fumes.

"So, since our happy, comfortable lives will be cut short in the very near future, I feel that we should live every second as if it were our last." A hammered helmet full of dried mushrooms exploded against the back wall. Several pieces of coal shot out of the chimney alcove and sizzled as they burned shallow holes in the icerock floor. "Don't you agree?"

"I'm not so sure," muttered the chimera.

Every piece of armor held something in this pantry, and Peregrine was of a mind to destroy it all. A pauldron of brownie teeth followed the mushrooms.

"I am free to love Saturday Woodcutter all I want. I can hug her and kiss her and fight her and reveal my deep and abiding love for her as we're freezing to death on the mountainside or sucked through a demon hole. Which would you prefer?" He dumped out a poleyn of dried seeds he'd been saving. There was nothing to save them for now.

"You're still upset," said the chimera.

"Right again!" cried Peregrine. "Why have I never realized just how astute you are? We should celebrate. A shame there's no alcohol. We could have a toast."

"You never liked it anyway," said the chimera.

"Not the point! But since there's no alcohol, I say we continue burning things." Having reached the back of the shelf, he extracted Leila's handmade book of recipes and spells. The pages were a mixture of parchment and animal skins and other substances that Peregrine was happy not to know. Several loose sheets fluttered to the ground as he carried it to the fireplace. He snatched them back up again — every shred of this book must be destroyed. Leila herself had instructed as much in the frontispiece, and now Peregrine knew why: the lorelei needed more avenues for her power like the world below needed a waking dragon. He'd risk forgetting these tidbits of wicked wisdom in the short time they had left in this prison.

"Peregrine, I've never seen you like this," said Betwixt. "Should I be worried?"

Peregrine did not answer, watching the fireplace as the flames licked the pages. The edges blackened and curled in on each other. The smoke that rose from the book was chartreuse and white, and the overpowering smell of cinnamon filled the room.

"Snip-snap-snurre-basselure. Is this a housecleaning or a tantrum?" The witch entered the kitchen through the entrance farthest from the fireplace.

Cwyn remained safely back against the wall. Smart move. Peregrine wanted to throw the pyrrhi in the fire as well. Betwixt shook his feline head in disapproval at the murderous look in his friend's eyes, and Peregrine backed down. As a fire witch, Cwyn more than likely would have basked in the burning.

The bird's blind mistress wandered closer, sniffing her way to the fireplace. "Dinner, perhaps? A new recipe? Or could it be . . . a spell?" This last choice made her the happiest. "I do detect the distinct presence of your handiwork! It's been so long, I thought perhaps I imagined it. My darling daughter, walking in her mother's footsteps! I am so proud of you."

It wasn't impossible for humans to perform some small magic spells, but Peregrine could evoke nothing like the elemental manipulation the lorelei played at, nor did he know how to fake that distinctive burned cinnamon smell. She had forced him to attempt working magic a few times, but the amount of energy required had drained him to the point of exhaustion within moments. He'd begged the witch to forgive the loss of aptitude she'd once seen in her daughter and allow Leila to excel at her own pace.

Now he would have to pretend he'd learned something.

"You honor me, Mother," said Peregrine, dreading the imminent maternal contact.

The witch awkwardly hugged Peregrine, pressing her frail body against his lean, muscular one. "Tsk, tsk. So skinny," she scolded. "We'll have to work harder at fattening you up, my sweetie." Peregrine attempted to block her from the fire, but she pushed him aside as she followed her nose. "What's this?"

At the flick of a bony wrist, Cwyn crossed the room and landed on the witch's shoulder. Peregrine wrinkled his nose at the bird in disgust. The raven squawked back at him.

"Play nice, dearies," said the lorelei. She waved her hand; the top layer of icerock melted into the fireplace and extinguished the coal in a puff of rancid steam.

"What have we here? Lovely things. Mushrooms . . . brownie teeth . . . ooh, and the pungence of a nicely fermented mold." No stew Peregrine had ever made had garnered a grin as wide as the one that now split the lorelei's ghastly face. "And seeds. Hmm. Oh yes."

He'd hoped that the charred seeds would be indistinguishable from the coal dust. Of more dire importance, though, was

Leila's spell book. Some things even the raven couldn't unsee. The witch pinched the book between two blue fingers and held it up. The crisp black pages dripped purple blood.

"Cauldrons are used for more than just laundry, child. Remember that. It's easier to alter ingredients in a pot than in the"—she sniffed the pages—"fire. Not Earthfire or coal but proper, elemental fire. Plus seeds from life yet to be, and pages from life that once was. I've been doing it all wrong."

"Mother?" Peregrine hoped the witch didn't mean what he thought she did.

The witch jumped to her feet and did a little dance. Sweeping Peregrine up into her bony blue arms she yelled in his face, "I've been doing it all wrong!" She kissed both his cheeks. Her breath stank of rotten brownie meat, brimstone, and chalk. Given the combination of odors already in the kitchen, Peregrine preferred kissing Saturday.

"My beautiful daughter has discovered the key! She's a genius, you know," the witch said to Betwixt. "Shells don't wash up too far from the tide. Thank you, my girl!"

"The key for what, Mother?" Peregrine pitched his voice slightly higher, filling his question with youthful innocence. He was afraid he already knew the answer.

"For the spell," the witch supplied. "The only spell that matters—to open the doorway home! And you, dearest daughter, will be with me as I cross the threshold to the demon realm. We will return to the birthplace of the basselure and claim our rightful thrones as queens of our element."

"I don't want to intrude," said Peregrine. "It's your spell,

Mother. This is complex magic. I'm afraid my presence will cause a disturbance." Peregrine's absence also meant that whatever Saturday planned, she would have to carry it out by herself.

"Nonsense, my brilliant babe! As the seed and the page, so are we the beginning and end of one life. I wouldn't do this without you. I will have you see your mother's triumph!"

Peregrine tried another tactic. "But I don't have any more of these ingredients," he pointed out. "In my . . . passion, I used them all up in this fire."

The witch waved a bony hand over the drenched fire. "Snip-snap. I'll just have Jack fetch them before I drain his blood for the cauldron. I think I'll keep his eyes to replace my own. As long as there's blood and bone, I don't imagine the spell will miss them."

"Poor Jack," said Peregrine.

"You won't mind, will you, dearest? You probably think he's a handsome specimen, but I assure you there are plenty more men on the sea."

"It sounds like you already have your mind made up, Mother. Who am I to dissuade you?" They were doomed. He'd come straight here and accidentally given the lorelei exactly what she needed. Peregrine had run out of ideas for thwarting her.

Betwixt, hiding on high again, was no help at all.

After a few random swats in the air, the witch found Peregrine's cheek and patted it. "There, there. You can thank me properly later by helping me with the spell! Oh, isn't this exciting! I must prepare. Come, Cwyn!" The witch continued her wild, swirling dance of joy, trailing her fingers along the wall to guide her way out of the kitchen area.

Cwyn did not follow right away. She stayed perched on a pillarstone by the fire, staring Peregrine down.

He stared back, thinking over his next words and actions carefully. Cwyn could not pass on his exact sentiments to the witch, but she could convey his actions through her eyes at any given moment.

Rage boiled beneath the calm he forced into his body. "This is your doing. I would never have destroyed this pantry and burned that book if you hadn't come to Saturday spouting your messages of doom."

Betwixt landed behind the bird, claws unsheathed. "You knew the missing pieces to the spell all along."

The raven cackled almost as well as the lorelei.

"You're forcing Saturday to kill the witch for you. And you've used me to do it." Peregrine wanted to wring the bird's neck and roast her for dinner.

Cwyn's voice reverberated in his skull. *Saturday could leave the lorelei to work her spell. She could let the doorway open and watch as the world burns. The choice is still hers to make.*

Mind-to-mind dialogue was always painful for Peregrine, either because he had no aptitude for it, or because his brain was not used to such intrusions. He raised a hand to his pounding temples — his fingers were purple and black with soot. "She will never choose herself over the world. You know that," he said. "You've known that all along."

The bird spread her wings and took to the air. Her maniacal

laughing caw echoed down the tunnels as if a murder of ravens had joined in her celebration.

Peregrine collapsed to the hard floor in the mess that had once been a fire. The only light left in the room was the one small torch he'd brought from the armory. "It seems Miss Woodcutter is not the only one destined for destruction," he said to his companion.

Despite the cold and damp floor, Betwixt curled up beside him and placed his beaked head in Peregrine's lap. "We can help her stop the witch. We can help her escape from the mountain before the dragon wakes. It might work."

"And a flea might stop a giant." Peregrine stroked the soft, downy fur behind Betwixt's ears in an effort to calm the emotions warring in his breast. He couldn't remember the last time he'd felt this strongly about anything. Now that Saturday had entered his life, he seemed to be feeling everything all at once.

"When the witch dies, every spell she's used to form these caves will falter. If we do somehow manage to dodge the falling rocks and rivers of Earthfire all the way to the cave entrance, how do we descend from the tallest mountain in the world without being frozen to death by the wind and snow?"

"When the witch's spells break, I will have control over my form again," argued Betwixt. "I can take you both down quickly enough."

"It might take time before you have control again. It might take energy you won't have because the witch has siphoned every bit of it away. Do you trust your nature enough to bet our lives on it? And then, after all of that, we'll be chased by a very angry dragon. You know full well that surviving the dragon is impossible."

"I'm being optimistic," said Betwixt.

"I'm being *realistic,*" said Peregrine.

"Well, don't let Saturday catch wind of your realism, or she'll never go through with killing the witch."

"We forfeit our lives in every scenario."

"This is no life," said Betwixt.

"Funny," said Peregrine. "Then what exactly is it we've been doing up to now?"

"We do not live here. We merely exist. And we would have gone on doing so while the dragon slept, but it is not a life. Lives have suns and seasons. Lives have happiness and sadness and birth and death." He lifted his wings to make great shadows on the walls. "Time rises up here to die. Down there is where it is lived, felt, and remembered."

"And regretted." Peregrine could not help but think of Elodie and the sweet dream of a simple life he was never meant to lead. He ran a thumb across the blue scar on his wrist and allowed himself the brief fantasy of a quest-filled future beside the giant, sword-wielding brat who'd stolen his heart the moment he'd met her.

"As you choose. That is freedom: the ability to choose. One day, I will once again be able to choose my own form. That is how I will know I am free."

"Death is also freedom," said Peregrine. "It seems to be the only choice left for Saturday. And for us."

"And here I thought cats were supposed to be the annoyingly

wise ones," said Betwixt. Peregrine ruffled his fur, and Betwixt snapped playfully at his fingers. "I plan to help Saturday kill the witch, but I also plan to help her escape these blasted caves. Are you with me? If we're going to die here on this mountain, I say we do it in a blaze of glory."

Peregrine cracked a smile. "From the gullet of a dragon."

11

A Nonsense Never Hoped For

SATURDAY WOKE up shivering in the dark-ness. She reached for her blanket, but Trix had stolen it again. Scamp.

As sleep left and reality crept in to set up shop, Saturday remembered where she was and how she'd gotten there. What she'd done to Trix. How she'd abandoned her mother. She sent up a prayer to the gods for her brother's well-being and Mama's safekeeping, then turned her face to the icerock floor of the ar-mory and refused to give in to the urge to cry. She needed to get up and start saving the world. It's what Jack would have done. It's what Trix would have wanted her to do.

Too bad their last exchange had been a fight. Lately it seemed like most of Saturday's conversations were arguments.

The moment she raised her head, she wished she'd had that bath. Her dirty skin crawled over her aching muscles and her head itched. It wasn't a state she was a stranger to, but she never slept this way. Mama always made her, Papa, and Peter wash before dinner. Time-consuming as the custom had been, Saturday had grown to enjoy ending the day clean and fresh. She looked forward to ridding herself of this filth when she was done mucking out the bird's cave. She tried not to consider the quality, quantity, or temperature of the water to come, or what dubious means Peregrine had of providing it, but he had promised her a bath, and she'd hold him to it.

He had also kissed her.

Saturday pressed her lips together. There was no more sting left from the poison, only the memory of the pressure of Peregrine's mouth upon hers and the ghost of his warm arms around her. She had dreamt of being kissed, once when she was a little girl and once when she'd been kidnapped from Thursday's pirate ship. She wondered now if that second time had been a dream at all.

To Saturday, falling in love was a nonsense never hoped for. Love and marriage and family would mean the end of her adventuring. She had only just begun to live her life outside the towerhouse. So far, that life had been full of swords and witches and life-or-death decisions. Kissing had no place there.

And yet, Saturday couldn't bring to mind a tale about Jack in which he'd banished evil or bested a beast without winning the heart of some girl in the end. Saturday sighed. Did romance *have* to be part of the adventure? It just seemed so unnecessary and distracting.

Worst of all, she had *liked* the kiss. She wanted to do it again, and that annoyed the hell out of her.

Fighting with someone was so much easier than caring about him, and caring would make Saturday's final decision that much harder. It wasn't just herself she'd be sacrificing by killing the witch and waking the dragon; the deaths of Peregrine and Betwixt would be on her hands as well.

She stood up and collected the rake. If she could not conquer her emotions, she could at least conquer this day. A hard day's work might not solve everything, but it would help her sort out her thoughts.

Saturday got lost on the way to the privy cave. This mountain was a piskies' parlor, mazes upon mazes of dark tunnels and chambers in which even a kobold could get lost. She arrived just in time to do her business and avoid being burned by the cleansing fire. Clever, whoever had discovered this particular alcove. Cruel, that Peregrine had not mentioned the marsh-gas odor that heralded the cleansing fire. But then, she hadn't gone out of her way to be kind, either. She decided to make an effort to be nicer.

And then she wondered why.

Stupid kiss.

Too bad she couldn't leave her clothes behind to be incinerated as well. The privy cave smelled better than she did. She stayed close to the fire, missing the feel of warm sun on stiff muscles. She found a lantern and used the embers left in the wake of the privy fire to light it, coaxing them to her with the handle of the rake. She tossed the rest of the useless pebbles into Puddle Lake. She'd started keeping a handful of pebbles in her pockets to toss whenever she suspected such a mirage.

Her stomach growled angrily. Dubious of the multicolored mushrooms guarded by the bearlike rock formation, she tried to locate a place in the walls where she could chip away at the icerock. What clear ice she finally did manage to carve out melted disappointingly on her tongue. Her stomach was not fooled and loudly voiced its opinion about her trickery.

The caves wound down and around, up and through, with sometimes sloping, sometimes jagged floors and ceilings low and high. Somewhere in between Saturday realized she was even more lost than when she'd started. Tired of knocking her sore noggin on cleverly concealed protuberances and fingerstones, she sat back against the wall with the rake beside her. Someone would find her eventually. She secretly hoped that someone would be Peregrine, even though she still hadn't decided what to say to him.

His kindness reminded her a little of Peter, always offering to help, always letting her get under his skin. Peter was compassionate without being soft, so what was it about Peregrine that bothered her so much? She should try harder to consider him as she did her brother.

Except for the kissing part.

There was a shuffling noise in the shadows, the same

scurry of little feet she'd heard in the armory the night before. Curious as to the source, Saturday did not move the lantern. She remained very still. Creatures in the Wood were often brave enough to sniff her out so long as she did not pose a threat to them. Not that any creature of the Wood could have stood her current scent, but cave dwellers might be a bit more forgiving.

Tentatively, a small, ginger-furred tailless rat-thing entered the golden ring cast by the lantern. It led itself more by its whiskered nose than its cloudy eyes. Its ears were wide and pointed, like a cat's, and the left one was missing a chunk. The light reflected off several sharp teeth. The rat-thing opened its mouth and snapped at the air.

Trix would have been able to tell her if the animal meant her harm, but Trix was not here to guide her. Not sure that she wanted it nearer, she shifted slightly. The animal backed away with a hiss and quickly retreated to the shadows.

Saturday heard a fluttering of wings from the opposite end of the cavern, but it was not Betwixt. The witch's familiar rounded a corner and landed on a fingerstone beside her. The lantern light revealed green in the bird's changing feathers today; the tips were the color of rich rye grass.

"Hello, Cwyn." The greeting was raspy in Saturday's dry throat, and she realized that these were the first words she'd spoken since waking. Yet another odd feeling. Members of the busy Woodcutter house were often expected to converse before fully leaving Lady Dream's realm. "I don't suppose you're here to lead me to a fine breakfast?"

"Caw!" said the bird.

"That's what I thought."

Saturday moved her weary bones off the floor and dutifully followed the raven down the tunnel to the bird's nest. The lorelei waited for her there, a ghostly vision of tattered rags dancing in the shadows up and down the corridor. Saturday tucked one of her daggers inside the waistband at the small of her back, in case the witch decided to remove the other one, in her belt.

"Shall I sing you a tune?" Saturday asked the witch, fully intending to do no such thing. Saturday had the melodious voice of a lizard. She only ever burst into song when Peter got on her nerves.

"The rocks sing their own tune," said the witch. "When I had my eyes I did not know how to listen."

"Perhaps losing your eyes was a blessing," said Saturday.

"Perhaps I will cut you into pieces and eat you for dinner." The witch licked her lips. The raven settled on her mistress's shoulder. Her talons made deep furrows, but if this was painful the witch showed no sign of it. She looked pale beside her richly colorful pet, the yawning sockets of her eyes like puddles of shadow unable to catch the light.

"I have more tasks for you," said the witch. "I need you to bring me seeds and mushrooms and spiced moss. And if you do not clean this mess today, my bird and I will dine on your bones."

Saturday was suddenly glad she'd gone to Peregrine for help despite . . . everything else. "I suspect I will make a lovely supper," she said boldly, "if a bit tough and chewy."

"I will cook your meat until it is tender," said the witch. "You will melt on my tongue."

"But if you cook me, how can I find your eyes?" asked Saturday.

The lorelei grasped Saturday's arm in an iron grip. Her seemingly frail and withered appendages were as much muscle and bone as raven's claws. "If you do not find my eyes," said the witch, "I will simply take yours."

Not if I kill you first, thought Saturday. She considered the dagger in her waistband. She could do it now, dispatch the witch and be done with all of this. But she wanted to find her sword first and, if possible, a way off the mountain. She knew there would be very little chance of survival against the dragon, but she had to try.

Saturday turned her face away, but the witch's hand found it anyway, lovingly tracing the contours with her wrinkled blue claws. "Your skin is smooth," the witch said dubiously. Her cheeks flushed a deeper blue. She smelled of frostbite, cold and sharp.

Saturday tried to hold her jaw as arrogantly as she could. *Jack,* she repeated the lie to herself. *I am Jack.* She let her voice fill her whole chest and deepen in tone. "I should get to work."

"Work!" The witch threw back her head and cackled at length, all soberness melting into hysteria. "Live to fail another day, Jack Woodcutter! Come, Cwyn. Your mistress tires and there is much to do." But the raven had already taken wing, quietly riding the chilly drafts down the cavernous hall, her glowing wings illuminating the path with soft green light. "Foul fowl," the witch grumbled.

Taking one last lungful of icy air from the hallway, Saturday entered the disgusting bird's nest. Immediately her nose wrinkled and her eyes watered. Before her towered pile after pile of once dried, now soiled, moss, easily four times the amount there had been when she'd started. Saturday brushed her uneven forelocks behind her ears, sickened by the griminess of herself, and set to work. She lifted the rake like a club and thought about Peregrine's armory, procured from an era's worth of fallen warriors.

"What idiot came to best a dragon with a rake?" Amused at the images the thought evoked, she took a shallow breath. "Here goes nothing."

She grasped the rake just below the business end and poked the handle into the moss pile. As if skewered by an invisible pitchfork, a heaping helping of soiled moss rose into the air. Ridiculous and implausible it may have been, but Saturday could not deny what she saw. It was nothing that lifted the straw, nothing that held it, and nothing that tossed it away from a pile that this time shrank instead of grew.

"I'll be damned," she whispered.

The soldiers in the practice yard used this expression all the time, but it wasn't one Mama encouraged. The Woodcutters' lives were strange enough without tempting Fate with a request for punishment. Considering her circumstances, Saturday wasn't terribly worried. It would be considerable work for the gods to make her life more complicated than this.

Before going any farther, Saturday dropped the invisible forkful of moss and exited the cave again. She poked around in the crystalline darkness for Peregrine's promised sacks and found them behind a large pillarstone, about thirty yards from the cave opening, far enough away that a meandering witch wouldn't have tripped over them. Three were full of fresh, clean moss. The rest were empty. Saturday filled her arms with the sacks—it took her several trips—and then dutifully began filling them one by one.

While she worked, Saturday thought about every member of her family. She made up rhymes about them all, and what they might be doing. But she couldn't stop her mind from constantly drifting back to the swordfight with Peregrine . . . and that kiss. On and on she worked and thought and blushed and worked some more. She considered what Peregrine had said before about the length of a "day" in these caves. Saturday could go on for hours in the Wood without getting tired. She didn't even stop to eat unless Papa or Peter reminded her. If left to her own devices, exactly how long might a full day's work be?

The chill air kept Saturday from sweating profusely, but she was forced to stop and carve untainted ice chunks from the wall as she grew more and more weary. Saturday filled fewer and fewer sacks between breaks until, finally, her body gave up.

She woke to water splashing in her face and a chunk of ice wrapped in linen at the base of her neck.

"Wake up, Woodcutter. You're too big for me to carry, and you're no good to me dead."

Wasn't she? Without her, the witch would have her blasted

stew, may it give her heartburn and spoil her stomach and ruin her spells. Peregrine and Betwixt could continue on with their freedom to live, if not their true freedom. Freedom. Sword. Water. Trix.

"Trix," she croaked. "I'm so sorry."

"I'm the one who's sorry. If I'd known you were going to wake up and work yourself to the bone straight off, I would have left you some food. Why didn't you come find us first?" Droplets of water on her face again. "No, no, come back to me. Here, drink this."

Saturday could not manage to open her eyes, but she knew a cup of cool water in her hands when she felt it. She drained it.

"More," she croaked, but her stomach was louder.

"This first." The cup was ripped from her reluctant hands and replaced with bread. Gods of heaven and earth, a small roll of bread. Saturday could imagine it was still warm from her mother's oven. In her kitchen. At home. On a winter's day. Or maybe Friday had baked this one, because it was chalky and flat and had a funny spice to it. Her chair at the table was freezing.

"Peter, shut the door."

There was a crack and a sting in her cheek as Peregrine slapped her.

Saturday's eyes flew open. In the next heartbeat, she had her dagger pointed at his throat.

He caught her hands in his easily, too easily, and lowered his head to look deep into her eyes. "There she is."

"Welcome back," said Betwixt.

"Where—" But Saturday didn't need to ask. The answers

came and disappointed her as quickly as they had upon waking. "Right. Sorry."

"I hit her and *she* apologizes!" Peregrine said far too loudly. "I was going to congratulate her on not having lost her mind, but now I'm not so sure."

The food settled in her nauseous belly and sanity slithered back under her skin. Saturday watched Peregrine's mouth as he spoke, imagining what it would be like to kiss him once more and telling herself to stop. *Warm,* she thought. It had been warm in his arms. She'd like to be warm again.

"Her brain's still addled," said Betwixt.

Saturday was inclined to agree.

Peregrine handed her another rough bread roll and the cup, which he'd replenished from the helmet at his feet. She drained the cup again and inhaled the roll while he refilled the cup once more. Peregrine emptied the bags of fresh moss and scattered it across the clean room while she chewed and drank and slowly came back to life.

"I'm okay now," she said finally, glad that he had goaded her into conversation before she was conscious enough to worry about what to say. Actions spoke louder than words and he was helping her, despite the fact that she was about to be the cause of his death. "The witch gave me new tasks. She wants me to find her mushrooms and seeds and some sort of spiced moss."

"No brownie teeth?" asked Peregrine.

"She must already have some," said Betwixt.

"What's a brownie? Wait, no . . . If it has teeth, I think I saw one earlier. What's spiced moss? And where am I supposed to find seeds in a cave?"

"Don't worry. I'll help you with all of it," said Peregrine. "But first things first. Are you okay enough to help me lug these bags across the mountain?"

Saturday groaned.

"I have a wagon," he said.

"Really?"

Peregrine shrugged. "It's a small thing, more of a litter or a wheelbarrow, I suppose, but it's useful enough. And it functions! Sort of."

"Sort of?"

"When it doesn't, he fixes it," said Betwixt.

"Works for me," said Saturday.

"And I've brought you a change of clothes for that bath I promised."

"*Gods,* yes." Those were the very words she'd wanted to hear. She expected some small retort from Peregrine at her blatant enthusiasm, but when none came, she turned to find him staring at her like an idiot. Seizing the opportunity, she moved to return his earlier favor by slapping him out of his dazed state. He caught her hand before it connected.

"Don't start," he said, shaking off his brief catatonia. "That look on your face just reminded me of . . ." He shook his head again and dropped her wrist. "I'll explain later. Let's go."

Saturday jumped up. "Yes, sir!" She wavered a bit as the blood rushed to her head. That was dumb—she should have remembered to rise more slowly. Mama called it the curse of the tall folk.

Peregrine shot her a look. "Remember who you're addressing, Woodcutter."

"Yes, *ma'am?* Whatever." Saturday tapped her temple. "Addled brain, remember?"

"Fools," said an exasperated Betwixt.

"Cats," mocked Peregrine.

The cat in question stuck out his large pink tongue.

Now that her belly was temporarily sated, Saturday's muscles complained as she hefted the bags onto Peregrine's strange cart. It had been stupid of her to faint and lie still on such cold ground for so long—the frost from the unforgiving icerock had seeped into her sinew and frozen her limbs stiff once more. As much as she longed to be clean, she loathed the thought of bathing from a metal helmet-basin the same temperature as the walls, but she'd suffer through it if it meant not having to smell herself for another night. Peregrine might even take pity on her and let her sleep by a fire again. If she didn't open her gob and screw it up first.

Peregrine's "wagon" had been cobbled together from what looked like the broken wooden handles of axes, spears, and maces. She'd noticed a dwarf's hammer or two in the armory before their sparring match, but she wondered what Peregrine had used for nails. The wheels of the wagon were shields, hammered down and reinforced with leather straps. It wasn't the smoothest device she'd ever pulled, but it was indeed functional.

Once the cart had been filled, Saturday grabbed the handles and began jogging down the corridor. "Where are we off to?"

"Let me carry that for a while," said Peregrine. "You've already done enough for today."

Why was he being nice to her? She'd been nothing but rude to him, and that was before the pyrrhi had come bearing tidings of doom. When Peter was nice to Saturday like this, it was always because he wanted something.

"I need to stay warm," she told him. "I'll hand it back over to you when I tire. I promise."

Peregrine agreed, silly boy. Peter never would have accepted such a deal. He knew that Saturday never tired.

True to her word she ferried the moss all the way to their destination. Peregrine called out twice to get her to stop and change direction, and twice to pick the mushrooms and moss for her second task.

"Do you think it's wise to collect these ingredients for a spell we're trying to stop?" she asked him.

"With the amount of magic at her disposal, thanks to your presence, I suspect the ingredients don't matter much," he said. "And fulfilling her task will keep you alive long enough to fulfill your destiny."

"Destiny" was a kind word for the chaos Saturday was meant to unleash here. She only hoped she found her sword first. It would be a shame to die without it.

Saturday did not recognize any part of these caves. She had no idea where they were. It hurt her head less to concentrate on stretching and keeping her footing instead of the twists and turns around and through as their path gently sloped heaven-ward.

She was grateful that most of the way had been level and wide enough for the cart—only once did they have to unload and reload the wagon, after moving it to an opening several feet off the ground. The air was considerably warmer here. Her muscles relaxed even as her boots slipped on the perspiring rocks beneath her.

Once Saturday was able to relieve herself of her burden, she looked around and lost her breath at the sight.

They had climbed all the way to paradise.

12

Beyond Saving

O F ALL the nooks and crannies Peregrine had discovered in the caves, the garden felt the most like home. Under different circumstances he would have kept this room from Saturday, but their time on the mountain had been cut short. In a fortnight, the garden might no longer exist.

The walls here were solid quartz crystal instead of cloudy calcite and icerock. Ironically, these towering, flowering crystals looked more like ice to him than the rest of the rime-ridden caverns. The ceiling came to a point, creating a clear pyramid, with walls thin enough to let the sunlight through when there was any and the starshine in when there wasn't. Currently, there wasn't.

Not that one could track days reliably under this skylight

by any means. In Starburn the sun came for summer days and fled for the winter ones, but the Top of the World lay even farther north. If one truly meant to monitor the passing of time, this room would only be good for marking seasons instead of days. Peregrine knew this because, eventually, he had given up on those as well.

He rubbed out the simple ward he'd drawn on the floor to keep the brownies away — something he'd learned from Leila's book — and led Saturday over the threshold with the wagon. Betwixt carried the lantern he clenched in his beak to a pillar on the far side of the room.

"The garden was here when I arrived," Peregrine said to Saturday's stunned silence. He removed a dagger and flint from inside his skirt pocket and set about lighting the torches he'd wedged in between various crystals on the wall. "It was much smaller then, but the rudiments had been started. We've built up the soil from the detritus of the other plants that can't survive this environment and Cwyn's used peat. That silly magicked rake turned out to be useful after all."

Saturday paid him little mind. She focused instead on the greenness around her, the life that this garden brought to the dead mountain as it stretched up to the crystal peak. Peregrine remembered feeling that same reverence once, so very long ago, and he hadn't been born and bred in a forest as she had. It meant the world to him that he could share this with her.

"This garden was Leila's alone; I've never heard the witch mention it, and we've never brought it to her attention. I suspect it was one of the reasons Leila devised her plan to escape. Being here does make one miss—"

"Everything," finished Saturday. Her voice filled with more emotion than he'd thought her willing to share. "The Wood. My family. So much work to do." The wistfulness in her voice trailed away with the thought. She reached out to caress a leaf of the closest plant. "Seeds. Where did you get the seeds?"

"The same place I got the swords and lanterns: from the dead." She did not shudder at his words as he might have, but she was a warrior, not he.

"Provisions," she deduced.

"Most of what they carried was rotted to nothing, but some desiccated seeds remained dormant. Whatever dust I found, I scattered here."

"Any dust is fair game for compost," Betwixt added. He flew to a crystal outcropping above the garden and stretched out like a sphinx. "Since most of the dust here is of a magical origin, seeds that might never have sprouted were convinced to do otherwise."

"We had a garden at home," said Saturday, "and the Wood has its own bounties, but I don't recognize many of these plants."

"Nor did I," Peregrine admitted. "Some are still a mystery. Many times I didn't recognize the skeletons from which I took them. Some of the fruits of my labors—"

"*Our* labors," corrected Betwixt.

" . . . *our* labors—my apologies—have been tested by good old trial and error. Most are palatable. Others are just beautiful. There was a particular inedible orange specimen with incredibly tough skin that stank of sour milk when it blossomed."

"Trollish," said Betwixt. "Had to have been."

"That's the only plant I've ever weeded on purpose. There's a goblinfruit here that's unappetizing to look at but delectable on the inside . . . like goblins themselves, I suppose. I was lucky to cultivate a patch of wheat and corn for grains and tea for . . . well, tea. Then there are the more familiar vegetables: the potatoes and gingerroot took quite well, as did the onions and the—"

"—beans," Saturday finished for him, tilting her head back to admire the winding stalks that grew farthest up the wall, twining in and out and around crystals all the way to the peaked roof. This time she did shudder, but Peregrine hadn't the faintest idea why.

"But this is my *pièce de résistance*." Peregrine moved aside the large leaf that hid his tomato plants from view. Saturday's eyes widened. She quickly snatched one of the fattest ripe red fruits and sank her teeth into it. Her eyes closed in bliss and she made that face again, the same one she'd made when he'd offered her the bread and the bath.

She had yet to thank him in so many words, but at the moment he'd forgotten what a pest she could be. She couldn't argue with him if her mouth was full. Peregrine vowed to keep her clean and fed so long as she kept making that face.

Saturday groaned in delight and bit into the tomato once more. Peregrine smiled so hard, his cheeks hurt.

"Behave yourself," Betwixt said to him.

Peregrine raised both hands innocently. "She's the one making noises, not me." He took a full step away from Saturday for good measure, though, in case he accidentally ended up kissing her again.

Saturday took another bite and scowled at them both for interrupting her delightful communion with the divine fruit. She made to wipe the juice from her face with her sleeve and then stopped, no doubt reminded of exactly how disgusting she was from head to toe. "It's warm in here," she said with her mouth full, as if she'd only just realized that the change in temperature wasn't solely from the effort she'd exerted in lugging the cart far longer than she should have.

"The heat, damp, and sun make this spot ideal for growing things," said Peregrine. He motioned for her to follow his outstretched arm. He did not trust himself to touch her—let her think his need for space was because of the smell.

Their destination lay beyond a thick, low wall of crystal and stone that looked solid but for the steam that rose up from behind it, betraying the true breadth of the cavern. Saturday led the way around the wide outcropping, startling a colony of ice bats. The torchlight caught their clear wings, showering the floor beneath them with sparkles of light. Peregrine tried to stop her as she reached out to the crystalline wings, but he was not close enough to grab her filthy arm in time. Saturday flinched and pulled away fingertips scored with lines of blood.

"Sorry. Should have mentioned those. Crystalwings. They're as beautiful as they are sharp, and completely useless as a food source. Don't put that in your mouth." His fingers slid in the slime that covered her elbow and he quelled his gag reflex. He wasn't sure how she'd been able to stand herself this long. "Just wash it off."

The boulder they stood on overlooked a vast chasm, but one could guess from the steam that it was a real lake and not a mirage. Still, Saturday tossed a small handful of the pebbles from her pocket and watched the ripples mar the ceiling's reflection in happiness.

"Clever girl," said Peregrine. It had taken him much longer to come up with the same trick.

The water was clear as far down as the meager torchlight permeated. Now that the ripples had dispelled the deceitful reflection, the crystals under the water could be seen. Those at the perimeter were beautiful and sharply pointed. But unlike in most lakes, there was no wildlife, and no discernible bottom.

Peregrine attempted to coax Saturday forward with his voice in an effort to refrain from touching her again. "It's deep. Impossibly so. The water is heated from the heart of the mountain. This high up it's tolerable. Pleasant. Blissful, even."

"For humans," Betwixt interjected.

"A mile or so down and you'd be boiled alive."

"The witch would have her stew," said Saturday.

Threatening to put Jack in her cauldron was one of the witch's favorite pastimes. "Woodcutter bouillabaisse," said Peregrine. "Quite the delicacy. Now, if you walk back this way, there's sort of a path down to—" But she had already removed her clothes.

The soiled rags lay in a puddle at her feet. Above them

stood a statue of uninterrupted golden skin, save for that thin blue-green bracelet at her wrist. She was built like a man, her incredible upper body tapering down to a small waist, thin hips, and strong legs that went on for miles, but there were subtle curves there, if one knew to look for them. Her unfortunately matted hair — short in the back and long in the front — did not mar the perfection that was her body. Peregrine was fit and lithe himself, but he was nothing compared to this monument of womanhood now framed by equally giant and exquisite crystals. She raised her arms straight out to the sides, revealing little in the way of breasts, and in one fluid motion dove neatly from the boulder into the clear crystal water beneath them.

She took his breath away. His visions of this woman instantly morphed from enjoyable and innocent to absolutely torturous. He needed to concentrate on something else, quickly, before he completely embarrassed himself.

"Impressive," said Betwixt.

It all happened so fast that by the time it occurred to Peregrine to look away, she was already gone. He averted his gaze anyway, and busied himself by picking up her filthy clothing with as few fingers as possible and tossing it down to the water's edge. He took his time retrieving the sack from the cart that contained the fresh change of clothes he'd brought for her, as well as a hairbrush for her lank locks and a horse brush with which to clean her clothes. If they were beyond saving he'd chuck them in the privy cave. As his talents at fabric restoration had grown, he'd found few things in these caves beyond saving.

He carried all these items back to the water's edge, keeping his head down to watch his footing, and then tended to the washing. He glanced up only to make sure she had surfaced again, even though her intake of breath echoed in the crystal chamber and gave her away.

"If you swim gently along the edges of the pool, you'll find a yellowish sediment on some of the ledges. Rub it into your skin and hair—it's nothing like soap and smells a bit like rotten eggs, but you'll find it does a fair job of tackling the grime." Peregrine addressed the stains on her shirt instead of the dirty blond head bobbing in the water not ten feet from him. He did not raise his voice; the echo carried his words adequately.

"Aren't you coming in?" She asked the question in her normal voice, too strong for this chamber, but the tone was lighter than it had been. Peregrine could tell she felt better, and he was glad. "The water is lovely," she said, more softly this time. Almost sweetly. "And that skirt looks warm."

Right now, his skin felt hotter than the sun. No, Peregrine had absolutely no intention of going into that water. No, indeed. Not tonight. And never in her presence. "I'm fine, thank you," he replied. "You enjoy it. I brought a brush for your hair, if you want it." Without taking his eyes off the clothes, he nudged the wood-handled brush closer to the water's edge.

"What's the matter with you?" asked Saturday.

Peregrine dunked her soiled clothes in the water again, sprinkled them with sediment, and attacked them with the horse brush. Dirty clothes. Must get them clean. Very dirty. Whenever she was finished, they would unload the moss and

pick ingredients for a stew. Didn't need to unload the sacks tonight — that chore could wait for another day. Peregrine dunked the clothes again. Very dirty clothes.

"Hello?" said Saturday.

"What? Nothing," said Peregrine. "I'm fine."

Betwixt choked back a laugh, or a hairball. Either way, Peregrine continued ignoring his traitorous friend. He could blame his flushed cheeks on the fumes wafting off Saturday's dirty clothes. The clothes she didn't happen to be wearing.

"Come, now. You act like you've never seen a girl without her clothes on before."

"I haven't, actually." Peregrine said the words under his breath, but they reverberated throughout the crystal chamber regardless. He braced himself for the raucous laughter he felt sure would follow from his companions, but none came.

"Seriously?" Saturday asked.

Peregrine soaked the clothes again and wrung them out. "Serious as a night without stars." From what he could tell, what looked like dirt on the shirt and trousers was only stains now.

"Don't you have any siblings?" He could tell by the sound of her voice and the slap of small waves that she had drifted closer to where he was sitting. She would choose the moment when he was at his most uncomfortable to ask him about his life.

Betwixt continued to subtly hack up hairballs. Peregrine wished fleas upon him. "My father suffered from a forgetting sickness," he explained. "My mother felt it unwise to have more children. I was promised to a girl named Elodie of Cassot when she was a small child, but I never saw her again after that."

"Forgetting sickness? I've never seen such a thing," said Saturday.

"And I hope you never do. It is a living death, where a man's mind dies, yet his body lives on."

"That's horrible."

"You have no idea. We began to notice it, my mother and I, in the summer of my seventh year. He forgot small things at first, like phrases and appointments. Over the next few years he began to forget his past, and then his present. He forgot about Starburn—he could no longer leave his bedchamber because every room was strange to him. Finally, he forgot how to speak altogether. Mother dedicated her life to him, long after every memory he had of her was gone. I tried to be a son for as long as I had a father who remembered me."

"How long did he last?" asked Saturday. "His body, I mean."

"Too long," answered Peregrine. "Long enough for me to hope he would die and put us all at peace. A terrible, selfish thing for a son to wish on his father."

"But a sensible one. I assume his body finally complied?"

Peregrine laid the clothes out to dry. "It did. My mother followed him soon after." He leaned back against the jagged crystal rocks and looked at her. She idly rubbed sediment in her hair while he talked. The fabric bracelet at her wrist looked dry as a bone.

He forced himself to remain calm while he handed her the brush for her hair; he was amazed his pounding heartbeat didn't echo in the chamber louder than his voice. "I took my horse and escaped directly after the funeral, so eager was I to finally get away from that prison and on with a life of my own. I left Starburn in the hands of Hadris, my father's — my — steward."

"And you trusted this Hadris?"

"Enough to leave him in charge of the only world I ever knew," said Peregrine. "Leila met me on the road from Starburn. She pretended to be a fairy granting me a wish." He took up his long black and blue locks and shrugged with both hands full of hair. "I hate this stuff, but I can't cut it. The curse won't let me."

"What did you wish?" asked Saturday.

"To live a long and fruitful life until I lost my mind —"

"— or any other major organ," added Betwixt.

"Thought I was quite the clever young man for that bit," said Peregrine. "In hindsight, I probably deserved what Leila did to me. It was rash to leave like that, and not at all honorable. My father would have been ashamed."

"What?" Saturday gritted her teeth and growled at the ceiling. "Oh, you are a complete fool. I have half a mind to throw this brush at you." What she did instead was worse: she lifted herself out of the pool.

Peregrine closed his eyes, thought about solemn things, and listened for the telltale sounds of her dressing.

"If I were your father, I would have wondered why you didn't run away sooner. Do you honestly think he would have been happy knowing that he'd trapped his wife and son for so long? Would you wish the same upon your son? Or upon anyone for that matter?"

"No," said Peregrine.

"You went straight from Starburn to this mountain, from

one prison to another. No one deserves to be cursed, Peregrine, least of all you. You can open your eyes now."

He was blushing again, but this time he wasn't sure if it was from her presence or her words. He'd said as much to himself over the years, but like anything said too often, it had lost the weight of its reason over time.

"And yet I was cursed with you," he said. "I don't regret that one bit." Now that she was clean, the urge to touch her again was overwhelming. He wanted to bury his face in her hair and make sure all the stench was gone.

"My family would likely disagree with you." Dressed, though still damp, she'd finished with her hair, also still damp, and now stared at the small wooden brush in her large hands. "My sister gave me a brush like this once," she said softly. "May I keep it?"

Because the request had been so genuinely polite, it caught him off-guard. "Yes," he said, with probably more enthusiasm than he meant to reveal. She tucked the wooden handle inside her belt with its empty scabbard. She *did* look at him then and yanked his silver-blue lock of hair, just like a schoolboy.

"Maiden fair, oh, maiden fair,
What clever mischief do you dare?"

Her singing voice was not lovely, but it wasn't meant to be. Peregrine responded to her schoolyard teasing by mimicking one of the scowls she loved so much and he was rewarded with an actual smile. He dared to hope a laugh might follow it, but the blinding light erased all thoughts from his mind.

The crystals in the cavern were glowing.

Saturday and Peregrine both raised an arm to shield their eyes from the glare. Peregrine heard more than saw Betwixt fly down and land with soft cat feet on the crystal boulder above them. "Look," he said.

They lowered their arms. Peregrine no longer needed to squint at the crystals surrounding them. The harsh light was gone, as was any trace of torchlight or water's reflection. What shone now from every flat surface they could see was the face of a skinny young girl.

This girl also tried to hide her beauty beneath formless boy's clothes, but unlike Saturday the girl in the crystals would never be able to hide her porcelain skin, the curve of her full red lips, or her hair, thick and black as the night. Her large eyes were as blue as the twilight sky and just as full of mystery. Her dark brows, like thin raven's wings, furrowed in concentration or determination. She seemed to be climbing a rope into the heavens, surrounded by the billowing gray sails of a ship.

As quickly as it had appeared, the scene in the crystals vanished. The shattered speckles of torchlight returned to their places scattered about the cavern as if they'd never left.

Nothing broke the silence for a while but ripples in the clear water.

"Did you recognize that girl?" he asked Saturday.

"I think that was my sister's cabin boy," she answered. "I only ever caught a glimpse of her, so I can't be sure. But it looked like Thursday's ship."

Thursday the Pirate Queen—Peregrine remembered Jack's stories well. There was sure to be a certain amount of mischief on that ship, and this girl was doubtless the only maiden aboard. Peregrine tried to wrap his mind around the inadvertent spell Saturday had cast.

"You were too humble with regard to the extent of your god powers," he said.

"I did that?" she asked softly.

"Yes," said Betwixt. "You did."

So everything Cwyn had told them in the armory was correct, though Peregrine hadn't thought he'd be witnessing an example so soon. "You can work a magic mirror."

"I guess?" Saturday replied with little emotion. "I mean, I don't know. My eldest sister can. Does. Whatever. I don't have any magic."

For someone so strong, she was excessively hard on herself. Beauty and godstuff may not have been the fey powers she wanted, but they were powers she possessed, and it was foolish of her to eschew them.

"Cwyn said you could control magic," Peregrine reminded her, "not that you created it."

"There is no need to create magic here," said Betwixt. "Magic permeates the walls around us. You appear to siphon it far more easily than the lorelei can manage."

Saturday remained defiant. "But I don't know anything about magic."

"You don't have to know about it to wield it," said Peregrine.

"Still, it's a good idea to know about it so you don't get anyone killed," said Betwixt.

She threw up her hands. "How can you say that, while you look to me to lead you to your death?"

"I still have hope," said Betwixt. "I believe in heroes."

"What about you?" Saturday asked Peregrine. "You don't believe we'll survive the dragon, do you?"

She would value his honesty more than pretty words. "I don't. But our lives don't end here. There is still a spell to stop and a witch to kill and a dragon to wake, and I plan on doing all that next to the woman I love."

He did not expect smiles and shouts of jubilation at his statement, which was good, for he did not receive them. Saturday's brow furrowed. "You love me?"

Once more, he thought it best to be honest. There wasn't time left to play games. "The gods have sent me dreams my whole life of a wild young woman with golden hair and bright eyes. I have always been in love with her. I had thought she was Elodie. Turns out, she was you." He made no move to touch her.

"But what about Elodie? What about your betrothal?"

The last thing Peregrine wanted was for Saturday to think he was not an honorable man. "Elodie is a girl I never knew from a fate I was never meant to have," he said. "True to Leila's curse, I have experienced a long and fruitful life on this mountain. We may die up here in the next few moments, but I want to live those moments with purpose, filling them with as much as I possibly can. Don't you?"

"Yes," she answered, and he was pleased to see that her eyes were bright again. He hoped the last things he saw before his death were those eyes.

"We should make a plan," said Betwixt. "The witch may be comfortable enough walking into this spell blind, but I'm not."

"Agreed," said Peregrine. "She'll be preparing her cauldron even now. We'll usher Saturday to the farthest end of the mountain with her bag of ingredients to lure the witch away from her lair. Then, Betwixt, you and I can—"

Saturday raised a finger. "I just have one question."

"Yes?"

"You said I could work a magic mirror. Do *you* see a mirror anywhere?"

"Ah," said Peregrine. She had a good point, which meant there was even more to her abilities than he had originally believed.

"And what does 'ah' mean where you come from?"

"If I may," said Betwixt. "My dear, I believe you are a Transformer."

"A . . . what?"

"Perhaps 'mutant' is a better word," said Peregrine.

Saturday grimaced. "No. That sounds worse."

"Changer? Transmograficationist?" Peregrine drew the long nonsense word out, making up each syllable as he went along.

"That sounds ridiculous," said Saturday.

"That sounds familiar," said Betwixt.

"Whatever you want to call it," said Saturday, "I know I can't change *myself* at all. If I could, I'd be taller." She smiled at her joke. It was so nice to see her smile.

"Shapechanging is different," said the shapechanger. "Cwyn described you as a vessel. Think of yourself as a tool through which magic uses itself to alter itself."

"You are an enchanted weapon, all on your own." Peregrine indicated the runesword still at his hip.

Saturday thought about it a moment. "That doesn't make any sense."

"It will," said Betwixt.

"So . . . magic is *using* me?"

"This time it did, yes, like a petulant child wanting to be noticed. But only because you are ignorant."

"This conversation is making me feel so much better," said Saturday.

"Cats," Peregrine explained.

"You are not a chalice or an athame, an inert object with no say in how you are used. You have the power—if you'll excuse the expression—to choose what is done with the magic around you." Betwixt lifted his wings to indicate the cave. "Like transforming crystals and other reflective surfaces into magic mirrors."

"Or axes into swords." Peregrine hadn't meant to say the words aloud, but they echoed in the chamber nonetheless.

Saturday turned to him. "How in the world do you know about *that?*"

Peregrine tapped his temple. "Visions."

"The more you tell me about them, the more unsettled I feel," said Saturday.

"Imagine the subject of them landing on the doorstep of your prison," said Peregrine. "You are, quite literally, my dream come true."

"Now you're being preposterous."

"And you're being obtuse," he said. "But I think I can help. There's somewhere I need to take you." He stood and offered a hand. Predictably, she ignored him.

"Another place like this?"

"Not as beautiful, but hopefully as illuminating." He took up the sack of mushrooms and moss, adding to it a pomegranate, a goblinfruit, and two more ripe tomatoes. "For the journey," he said, tossing the sack over his shoulder. And because he had food, she followed him.

13

Mirror, Mirror

SATURDAY ONLY knew they'd reached their destination when Peregrine lowered the torch to light a brazier he'd come upon. She stayed by the brazier as the coals captured the flame. In her bare feet, wet hair, and damp clothing, it hadn't taken her body long to freeze back into an icicle. Her eyes followed Peregrine as he walked the perimeter of the room, lighting wall torches as he had done in the crystal cave. These sconces were more elaborate and perfectly anchored into the icerock, like the ones on the walls in Rumbold's palace. The brazier, too, was a work of art, not a crude stone fire pit like the one she'd woken up beside.

The light fought the darkness and quickly won. As each torch was lit, so was its reflection.

Saturday was standing in a cave of mirrors.

There were mirrors propped against every pillar and out-cropping. Some had even frozen into the walls. Large and small, plain and ornate, broken and intact, they reflected the firelight, the occupants of the room, and each other. Some of the thicker frames boasted carved woodland animals and gargoyles and de-mons and cherubs and lively trees and flowers. Every graven thing with eyes to stare did so, and their expectant gazes never left Saturday. Betwixt spread his wings in front of one particu-larly impressive mirror that Saturday guessed was about as wide as her house. Behind him, a thousand Betwixts stretched simi-larly into infinity.

"Is this one of the witch's caves?" Saturday whispered. "Will she find us here? She will be looking for me soon."

"It will take her some time to prepare for her spell," said Peregrine. "And like the garden, the witch does not know this cave exists. I'm not sure where Leila obtained these mirrors, or how long it took her. Some were scattered throughout the caverns, but I collected them here."

"Why?" Judging by the number of mirrors, such a project would have taken him longer than honing the edges of all the swords in the armory.

"While some features of this body are still my own, I have never enjoyed seeing someone else in my reflection."

And yet, he had brought her here, willing to face a face he despised to aid her in her quest of knowledge. "What did you look like before?"

"I can't remember." Peregrine waved the question away. "It doesn't matter."

Saturday considered how difficult it must be to forget your own face, especially after your father had forgotten his whole life.

"I knew these had to be more than just mirrors. I believe they were Leila's windows to a world in which she could not be and, ultimately, what drove her to escape."

"So these mirrors are magic but you can't make them work?" Saturday asked.

"Afraid not," said Peregrine. "I've rhymed and rhymed until I thought my brain would leak out my ears."

"Mine did," said Betwixt. "They were grueling exercises."

"What about you?" Saturday asked the chimera. "Did you try as well?"

"Such divination is beyond even my abilities," said Betwixt, "hampered as they are by the witch's geis."

Their comments only reinforced the fact that Saturday *had* performed magic back in the crystal cavern, all on her own. A thrill warmed her from head to toe. This is what she had wanted for her life, the ability to manipulate magic, important magic, magic that she could take on her adventures and use to make the world a better place. She wanted to be a legend, like the brother she'd been mistaken for, and legends needed more weapons in their arsenal than a sword and a decent work ethic. She only wished her family were here to witness her triumph before she died saving them all.

Saturday stood before one of the larger mirrors, its thick wood and gemstone frame tall enough to reflect her whole body. This was it. She couldn't wait. She knew exactly what she wanted—needed—to see. "Is a rhyme all I need to make this work?"

"I'm not sure which mirrors will respond to you," said Betwixt, "if any."

"It might be best for you to address the whole room," offered Peregrine. "Just in case."

Saturday took a step back from the large mirror, still facing it, but making sure her field of vision contained as many mirrors as possible. "I can do this," she said, as much to herself as to the others. She swallowed a yawn, not wanting her companions to realize how exhausted she still was, but she could not disguise her shiver. Peregrine's image stepped into the mirror behind her and gently placed a threadbare blanket around her shoulders.

The thin bit of fabric reminded her of the blankets on her bed at home. Typically Saturday was entirely self-sufficient; only Papa and Peter had ever braved her stubbornness to take care of her like this. But Peregrine had fed her and clothed her, seen her clean, and helped her in her tasks. And here in this room he had presented her with the chance to perform magic, real magic, like her sisters and brothers. She wanted to revel in her blissful lack of normalcy for a while.

Saturday let her eyes linger on the lines of his dusky olive face, the softness of his countenance reflecting his sympathetic nature. He was soft where she was hard. Saturday was sure that no matter what face Peregrine wore, she'd always be able to see that tenderness within him, a quality that she lacked.

Strange though its origins might be, Peregrine's affection for her was a beautiful thing, and she hoped she was worthy of it. Here, at the end of her adventure, she might as well let herself be loved. Like the heroes of legend. Like her brother Jack.

She just wasn't sure she knew how to love back.

"Thank you," Saturday said, and meant it.

"Tell me what you see," Peregrine said to her inside the mirror.

She hadn't rhymed a word to start the spell yet; the only things framed in the looking glass were the two of them. Together. They were of a height, though Saturday's body had experienced rougher work and better meals. He was dark where she was fair. She had stamina; he had grace. He was a flower and she was a tree.

"I see a boy in a girl's body and a girl in a boy's."

Peregrine smiled at her, making his face even gentler. "Which is which?"

Saturday laughed at that. It was a comment Peter would have made.

"You're beautiful," said Peregrine.

That, however, was *not* something Peter would have said. Saturday screwed her face up into a scowl at the compliment in an attempt to mar whatever feature happened to be catching his overly romantic eye.

"And you're an idiot," he added.

"The two do tend to go hand in hand," Saturday pointed out.

"No, they *don't*. Being beautiful doesn't make you an idiot, Saturday. Being stupid does." She felt the pressure lift as Peregrine pulled the brush he'd given her from her belt. "As a clean Woodcutter once said: You are a complete fool, and I have half a mind to throw this brush at you."

She wrenched the brush from his grasp and replaced it in her belt. "Stop being ridiculous."

"You really have no idea, do you?"

Why did they have to talk about this? People's outward appearance was Saturday's least favorite subject. "Yes. I know. I can be pretty enough. I've been forced to dress up for a ball before, but only because my mother made me."

"That's not what I mean." He turned her face back toward the mirror. "You cannot call yourself a proper warrior if you refuse to use all the weapons in your arsenal."

"Pshaw," sputtered Saturday. "Beauty is not a weapon."

Peregrine squinted at her. "Come now, Woodcutter. I thought you cleverer than that."

Beauty as power. Was he serious? But she considered Monday's ability to capture a room with a glance and release it with a wave. Saturday could not deny there was power in that. "Fine. You're right," she agreed. "But I'm not —"

"Saturday, I love you. You will always be beautiful to me."

Betwixt made mewling kitten noises.

It was difficult for Saturday to stay serious. "I'm the only woman you've seen in a very long time."

"You're the only *human* I've seen in a very long time," Peregrine corrected.

Betwixt's voice echoed from the far side of the cave. "The gods work in mysterious ways."

"Those ways aren't so mysterious if you're paying attention," Peregrine shot back.

"Paying attention is not one of my virtues," said Saturday. Despite that, she was very aware of how close Peregrine still stood; she could feel the heat of him through her damp clothes.

"Everything happens for a reason," said Betwixt.

"That's what Mama always says," Saturday muttered.

"Then it must be true," said Peregrine.

"You have no idea." She could almost see the outline of Mama's face swimming in the silver glass scolding her back to the task at hand. Peter's, too, as if he'd come to inspire the rhymes needed to ignite her spell. Saturday's fingers itched to perform this magic, on purpose, and on her own.

But if any of these mirrors were going to work, there was one face she needed to see above all others. For better or worse, she would know here and now the fate to which she had doomed her little brother.

Mirror, Mirror, Monday's rhyme had begun, and so Saturday's would as well. She stared into the one still framing her and Peregrine, but she raised her voice to address the whole room.

"Mirror, Mirror, stones and sticks,
Show my little brother's tricks."

Saturday hoped that the looking glasses—if any of them chose to wake from hibernation—forgave her vague request in light of the clever play she'd made on Trix's name in the couplet. And then she realized she was personifying an inanimate object.

"When I speak a spell like that, who's really listening?" Saturday asked her companions while they waited. "Certainly not the mirrors themselves."

"They say gods are the conduits," said Betwixt. "That is the reason for the rhyme: so the gods know you wish to perform a spell, with their blessing."

Saturday was skeptical. To the best of her knowledge, she and Peter had never drawn accidental attention with their Wood-born nonsense. And yet, she could easily picture the gods laughing at their witticisms. "The gods do have a sense of humor."

As if in response to her statement, five mirrors and a shard by the brazier burst into brilliance.

Peregrine cried out and threw his arm over his face. "Gah! You'd think I would have been prepared for that!"

The brightness had pierced Saturday's own skull as well. As she waited for the glare to die down, she offered another one of those silent prayers to the ether and whatever god she now knew was listening. No matter what the looking glass showed her, she wanted Trix to be alive. Preferably alive and safe.

The five mirrors showed the same vision at the same time, and then a few more joined in. The room began to warm from the magic. The familiar scene before them was the one from Monday's looking glass, though now Saturday knew what she witnessed. Saturday watched as the earth split below her and water sprayed to the heavens. Mudslides swamped forests. Flocks of birds fled the treetops. Relentless rains flooded houses and farms. Men, women, children, and animals alike were swept away by the angry tides.

Saturday's shivering now had nothing to do with the cold. "This is what I've done," she said. "This is the chaos I created. I don't understand how you could love a destroyer of worlds."

She could not turn away from the images, but she felt Peregrine's hand slip inside hers.

"The earth brought storms and floods long before you came. It created mountains and valleys and oceans many years ago, without your help."

"The only constant in this life is change," added Betwixt.

"But all those poor people . . ." said Saturday.

"I see suffering, but I don't see death," Peregrine pointed out. "You don't know for sure that you've killed anyone."

"I have no right to cause so much pain."

Peregrine squeezed her hand. "Look at them, Saturday. These are the people of your world. These are the people you will save when you stop the witch."

"When *we* stop her," said Betwixt. She felt the catbird's reassuring presence at her side.

"And we will," added Peregrine.

"Yes," said Saturday. "We will."

The visions blurred and the cave swam with colors—almost half the mirrors in the room were awake now. The colors resolved to settle on Trix. Saturday gasped.

Her brother's lifeless body was caught up on the back of a sea serpent. It was violet-scaled and segmented, but its movements were graceful and fluid. Large spines rose up from its head like stiff plumage. As it swam, the serpent tilted its head back so that the spines created a basket in which Trix's body was easily contained for transport.

Saturday worried about Trix's body remaining underwater for so long . . . but, too, she wondered at how the monster could swim with his head kept back at such an odd angle. Slowly, more of the scene was revealed. The monster had two more heads. One looked as lifeless as Trix.

Three heads. Saturday knew this beast. She had seen it herself from the deck of her sister's ship: the mythical lingworm. What had Thursday said to her? *No Woodcutter is in danger from that particular lingworm.* Her sly pirate sister had seen more than just a creature through that blasted spyglass, but she'd said nothing! She wanted to slap her sister for keeping secrets. Well, at least whatever Saturday was witnessing was not a threat to her brother. That must mean he was still alive. But Saturday hadn't been on the pirate ship for days now . . .

The mirrors grew bright again. This time when they dimmed, the mirror's eye looked up from the base of a tree.

"He's alive!" A dozen Trixes perched on a dozen branches in the looking glasses before her, every one of them alive and well. Saturday screamed in delight and grasped at the consoling arms Peregrine wrapped around her. "That's Trix! That's my little brother! He's alive!" She wanted to weep with the joy of knowing she had not killed him . . . or possibly anyone. Beside her, she heard Betwixt's wings flutter in happiness.

Trix had a golden apple in his hands. The vision flashed and he stood before a pretty young girl, but Saturday could not make out her features, outshone as they were by the brilliant gold of the apple's skin. Trix split the apple—a feat Saturday wasn't quite sure how he accomplished with his simple knife—but the two pieces he cut were not equal.

It was a trick. Saturday remembered this from one of Papa's stories. Did Trix know the story too? He was clever enough, to be sure, but he didn't look as though he had any supplies with him except that knife. He was mud-spattered and must have been starving. But he could not give in to his basic needs. Generosity must win out.

"Give her the larger half!" Saturday yelled at the looking glass. It was a silly gesture, but she couldn't seem to stop herself. Her voice felt cold and flat; the mirrors pulled the words out of her, but they died in the air. Trix couldn't hear her. There was no way he could. And yet, he turned his head and looked back over his shoulder at something before holding out a hand . . .

Before Saturday could see the outcome, the scene changed

again. This time Trix was at the top of another, even taller, tree. Saturday wasn't worried; Trix had always been at home in the treetops. It was where he'd been found by Papa that fateful winter's day when he'd become part of their family.

She was warier of the eagle that sat beside him. The bird looked almost as big as their house. Despite the raptor's wicked beak and talons, which made Saturday shudder in memory of her capture, Trix's face was unafraid. He and the eagle both looked out over the massive horizon. As they did, so too did the mirrors' eyes reveal what they saw. Plains and scattered forests spread out before them, leading to hills and valleys with harsh white peaks beyond. The largest of the mountains, dwarfing its brethren in size many times over, rose into the clouds and beyond. The Top of the World.

Saturday blinked. She didn't know if these looking glasses revealed the past, present, or future, but in this vision her brother was looking right at her.

She cried with all her might: "I'm here! I'm trapped! I'm here!" Over and over again she yelled into the thick, cold air, as if she might force the words through the mirrors and beyond.

She lunged toward the largest looking glass—at least, that's what she meant to do—but at the first footstep she collapsed. With Peregrine's arms still around her, she sent them both toppling to the ground. Her energy, forced once more to go on long after it was spent, gave out. The mirrors, every one now responding to Saturday's outpouring of power, went dark.

For a second time, Saturday's soul surrendered to blackness.

~elle~

Saturday woke where she had fallen: in Peregrine's arms. She did not see hide nor wing of Betwixt. The brazier had burned down and her muscles were screaming. Despite the amount of heat radiating from Peregrine's body, she was beginning to think that she would never truly be warm again, but then she remembered the heated lake. And the crystals. And the mirrors. And Trix. Saturday sat up and gasped.

Her body scolded her for her lack of proper stretching and the continued lack of her healing sword. She bent one limb at a time, slowly, attempting to placate her muscles before they seized up completely and her entire body became one large cramp. She knew better than to give in to her boundless enthusiasm, and yet she never seemed to be able to stop once she was in the thick of things.

She had done magic! It had cost her, worn her to the bone, but she didn't care. She considered doing it again immediately, checking in on Mama, or Papa and Peter in the Wood. Would she have the strength to perform that spell? Could she manage it before the witch found them?

Peregrine moved beside her, but Saturday refused to turn and look. She still wasn't sure what to do with this man whose gilded cage she was about to destroy. The closer they became, the more difficult her decision would be when her destiny arrived. She needed to approach her fate with a clear head. Love. Obsession. Saturday had only ever felt those things about her work. People were just too messy and unpredictable.

"Are you all right?" she heard Peregrine ask.

She was wonderful, terrible, elated, and confused. She pulled the thin blanket tighter around her shoulders, for all the good it did, and edged closer to the dying coals. Briefly, she considered setting her clothes on fire for warmth. "Fine," she said. "Cold." She brushed the floor beneath the brazier with her hands until she encountered the sack with her boots and quickly put them on. "Where's Betwixt?"

Peregrine put a hand to his head and Saturday realized how much her own ached. "That volume of magic would have effected a change. He'll have slunk off to change shape somewhere colder."

She didn't want to imagine anywhere colder than here. "It was too much power. I couldn't hold it."

"I'm sorry," he replied. "You should have focused on one mirror alone. I just didn't know if any of them would work, let alone all of them."

"But all of them *did,*" said Saturday. "I spent it all, everything I had inside myself, until my body shut down because there was nothing left to give. Perhaps I should try again. On only one mirror this time."

"No."

"Come on. Just let me try."

"No, Saturday. It's too much. I know how much you like working yourself into exhaustion, but I'd rather you not tax yourself to death."

She hated his logic. "Then we should probably get up. I can't imagine that went unnoticed."

Other than rolling onto his back, Peregrine gave no sign that he had any intention of moving. "I've done . . . okay, not worse, but spells just as ostentatious with far more devastating results, and neither the lorelei, nor the dragon for that matter, has ever batted an eyelash."

"Yes, but the witch wasn't looking for a reason to kill you." Saturday's ears pounded as she stood. "She's going to seek me out soon enough and expect my task to be finished. You need to find my sword and a way off this mountain." She picked up the sack with the witch's ingredients, and then checked the brush in her empty swordbelt and the dagger at her back. "I'll light a lantern. You get us out of here."

He seemed a bit taken aback at her gruffness, but she didn't care. He rose, twisted himself back and forth, adjusted the runesword in his belt, and then bent to touch his toes. He was down there so long, Saturday wondered if he'd fallen asleep again, ass over applecart.

"Here." She thrust the lantern into his hands. "Now *move.*"

They hurried, but the dark and winding path took far too long. Peregrine held a steady pace in front of her, but Saturday's impatience had the better of her concentration, and she smacked her head every ten seconds.

"You keep that up, you're going to be unconscious again."

"You keep slowing down when you talk, you really will be a girl." A set of yellow-gold eyes reflected their torchlight farther down the tunnel. Had the chimera shifted form so quickly? "Betwixt?" Saturday asked into the darkness. "Is that you?"

Nothing answered her.

"Get your dagger out," said Peregrine softly.

Saturday was way ahead of him. "What is it?"

"Brownies."

14

The Sea of Dead

RE THERE usually so many?" Saturday asked as the brownies advanced.

"No," said Peregrine. "Five or six in a pack at most." He'd killed them for food and fur only as often as they'd raided his supplies.

Their cloudy eyes, reflecting the torchlight, glowed like wicked fireflies in the darkness. The initial pair of eyes had become two pairs, and then six, and then too many to count. Peregrine had stopped moving forward again, but Saturday did not scold him this time.

"Animals don't swarm like that to attack," said Saturday. "They're fleeing something."

"Or some*one*," said Peregrine. Most likely the witch and

her spell preparations, particularly if she wanted brownie teeth for her cauldron. "Run."

They turned together and sped back down the tunnel.

Saturday stayed close behind him, keeping her head down. Peregrine heard her grunt and curse as the brownies caught up with her on their scrambling legs. Some ran past him. He shook his skirt when it grew heavy, shaking loose the one or two brownies trying to hitch a ride. They scratched his legs and nipped at his ankles with those pesky, pointy teeth.

"Is it safe to lead them back to the mirrors?" Saturday called up to him.

He didn't want to, but he wasn't convinced they were leading this unstoppable flock of brownies anywhere. "I don't see that we have a choice."

"Where do we go from there?" she asked.

That was the next problem. If there was another way out of the mirror cave, Peregrine had yet to find it. "We'll figure that out when we get there."

Saturday muttered something about "stupid boys" as a brownie went sailing past Peregrine's head. It landed with a squeak before him and scurried onward, disappearing into the wall of the tunnel.

Peregrine stopped and turned, catching an armful of Saturday. It was not unpleasant, especially now that she'd bathed, though he was mindful of her dagger.

"What?"

"Look. There." Peregrine waited until she saw what he saw. Before them lay the cave of mirrors, but there were no brownies inside it. No more of the rodents ran ahead of them. Peregrine lifted a squirming brownie from Saturday's shoulder and set it on the ground. It ran away from the cave, back down the tunnel to his brethren.

Peregrine lifted his lantern and scanned the wall of the tunnel, into which scores of brownies seemed to be disappearing. There wasn't an exit; he'd been down this way and back a thousand times with as many mirrors in tow. But he had never noticed that the natural spacing between the two pillarstones here was actually a fissure in the wall to a chamber beyond.

Without disturbing the swarming brownies, Peregrine leaned into the crack. He could feel a draft—only a slight one, but a draft nonetheless. It smelled of warm metal and water and musk; he didn't sense any sharp brimstone or dangerous gasses. The pillarstones and wall were thick and white with calcite, so the layers upon layers of scratches that the brownies had worn deep into the stones had never stood out.

"We could wait here until they're gone," said Peregrine, but he worried about the wisdom of keeping Saturday too close to the mirrors. Her desire to try the looking glasses again would quickly overpower his desire to keep her conscious.

"Or we can find out where they're going," said Saturday. She indicated the runesword at his side. "May I?"

Peregrine brightened. "Oh no. Me first this time." He handed her the lantern and loosed the sword. Its length was awkward in the confines of the tunnel. Silver runes began to creep up his wrists and forearms. "You may want to step back." Surprisingly, she did exactly as he suggested.

The pillarstones were old and thick, but their age worked in his favor. Years of brownie tracks had worn down the stones enough so that it took only a handful of swings before the white calcite icing of stone shattered. The stragglers of the brownie herd squeaked their displeasure at the mess, hissing and spitting at him as he continued forward.

The wall beyond was a different story. Peregrine pushed the larger remnants of the pillarstones out of the way while Saturday kicked the wall with her booted foot. Peregrine would have warned her about the futility of such a gesture, but this wall proved surprisingly thin. The fissure widened and the wall began to give way. They made short work of the hole, stopping as soon as it was large enough for them to squeeze through.

Saturday barreled ahead, but Peregrine had experienced too many close calls to venture forth into parts unknown without a light. A brownie with a notched ear jumped atop his lantern's lid as Peregrine pulled it awkwardly through the fissure.

"Peregrine, there are stars here!" Saturday called out to him. "Hurry up and see!"

He couldn't help but smile to himself as he extracted arm, lantern, and brownie from the fissure. He enjoyed hearing her say his name without malice.

She met him on the other side. The brownie launched itself off the lantern and scurried off to rejoin his pack.

"No, no, douse the light," said Saturday. She pulled at his skirt, wrapping the material around the iron cage. "Look."

Above them twinkled thousands of bright golden lights,

glittering metals shining their hearts out. But these specks were not reflecting light; they were *emitting* it.

"I can't remember the last time I saw a sky like this," said Saturday. "Can you?"

He avoided the question. "It's wonderful," he said, and it was the truth. Peregrine gently lifted Saturday's hand away and removed his skirt from around the lantern. He held the light high, revealing a large and complex calcite formation glistening white as the driven snow.

"Do you recognize this cave?" Saturday asked him.

"Yes." Peregrine lowered his voice, out of reverence more than necessity.

"You have names for everything." Saturday pointed at the massive rock formation. "So what do you call that?"

"The dragon," answered Peregrine.

Saturday examined the formation more closely, trying to make head and tail of it. It was a little difficult to picture at first glance. Most artists' renditions showed dragons rearing back while attacking, or in mid-fire-breathing flight, not curled up in peaceful rest. Saturday's mind began to unravel the sculpture. "Oh," she said. And then, "*Oh.*" And then after another longer pause, "Really?"

"Really," said Peregrine. "Saturday Woodcutter, please allow me to introduce you to the dragon."

"I'm at a bit of a loss. What does one say when one meets one's death?" Saturday bowed politely to the dragon. "Enchanted."

"Very much so," said Peregrine. "Unlike my father's plight, the spell on the dragon is a sleeping death. This mountain has been his tomb."

"A prisoner, like us." Saturday stepped forward. "May I touch it?" She had already stretched her arm out, but her hand hovered over the glowing stone. "Do we have time?"

"The ceiling of the witch's lair caved in," he told her. "It happened right before you arrived. We are currently on the other side of it. It will take the witch a very long while to find us here. Watch your step." Just as white rock had dripped and crept over the dragon's body, so too had it grown over the bones of the dragon's victims.

Saturday lifted a boot and walked precariously through the sea of dead, trailing her fingers along the dragon's contours. Thankfully, whatever godstuff slept within her remained dormant, as did the dragon. Peregrine let out a breath he didn't know he was holding. He watched her pat the dragon's beak, and what was either a short horn or a pillarstone the cave had grown atop the dragon's skull.

"I should stay here," said Peregrine. "Perhaps I can kill the dragon before it fully wakes. You and Betwixt might have a chance then."

"No," Saturday said flatly. "If anyone stays on this mountain, it will be me. I will leave no one behind. That's final."

Peregrine hoped the spirits of the warriors on whose bones he stood could see the headstrong young woman who walked that last footstep that they could not. "Where have you been all my life?" he asked.

"Cutting down trees," she said. "Now come on. Cave-in or no, I mean to find the witch before she finds me. And I am not leaving here without my sword." Saturday paused and turned away from the dragon. "Wait, a real cave-in? You mean, where the ceiling collapses and there's a giant gaping hole to the outside world?"

"That's exactly what I mean," said Peregrine.

Saturday jumped; stone skulls shattered beneath her boots. "Then that's our way off the mountain!" She grabbed him by the cheeks and kissed him heartily.

His pleasure at her vigor was tempered as he realized the flaw in this plan. Like she, he hoped they would survive, against all odds, so that they might experience the rest of their lives together. But if they did survive, he still had a promise to keep. To Elodie.

Damn the gods and their sense of humor.

Peregrine sighed and reluctantly led Saturday into the caves of the witch's lair. It was a short distance from the dragon's chamber, under a small archway and through a tunnel with only one turn. At that turn the air grew freezing.

Saturday, flushed with energy, gave no indication that the chill affected her. She slowly crawled up the enormous pile of rubble, all the while staring at the sky. "I wasn't sure when I would ever see daylight again," she whispered.

Peregrine found purchase on a nearby boulder and climbed to the top to see the sky for himself. Rife with deadly frost or not, there was nothing like fresh air after breathing in a cave. "I hate to disappoint you, but that's not daylight," he said.

"It's too bright to be starlight," said Saturday. "What, then? Dusk? Dawn?"

Peregrine motioned for her to join him at the top of the boulder. "In the far north, especially during the White Months, the skies fill with ice clouds shot through with color. We call them the Northern Lights."

"I see that now . . . look at all the colors! It's like a strange rainbow." Her raised chin revealed the graceful lines of her neck and the cords of muscles that ran down into her broad shoulders. "It's so beautiful. I've never seen anything like it."

Peregrine might have said the same thing to her. But he didn't. Nor did he take her hand again, despite the nagging, incessant need to do so. It was enough for him to sit beside her, shoulder to shoulder, and share the moment.

Like most moments, it didn't last long.

In a blue flash, the giant fallen pillars and rubble blocking the old entrance glowed brightly before dissolving into ash. A flame-yellow Cwyn flew through the newly opened space and circled over Saturday's head, presumably speaking to her the same way Betwixt spoke while in fully animalian aspects.

"Don't apologize," Saturday told the bird. "She was going to find me eventually." Saturday brought her gaze back to the hole in the ceiling. "I need wings."

"And a thicker skin," said Peregrine. Slowly he stood up, reluctant to go. "I must leave. It will only be worse for you if she discovers me here." He rolled off the boulder with practiced grace and landed on the opposite side of the pile, near the entrance to the witch's bedchambers.

Saturday leaned down to him. "I'll try to keep her distracted as long as I can. Find my sword. Please."

Peregrine curtseyed. He would have given her his heart had she not already possessed it. "As you wish." The raven descended and beat her wings in his face to hurry him along.

"JACK WOODCUTTER!" he heard the lorelei shriek. Cwyn disappeared; she did not want her mistress seeing what should not be seen.

Needing no further prompting, Peregrine crept stealthily back to the far wall, disappearing down a tunnel similar to the one that led to the dragon. The rubble caught his feet but he stumbled only once. Thankfully, the racket the lorelei was making hid his missteps. He only hoped he found Saturday's sword before the lorelei rendered her unable to wield it.

"Congratulations," he heard Saturday reply calmly. "You've found me."

The lorelei's answer to Saturday's question was muffled as Peregrine quickly and quietly crawled his way to the witch's bedchambers.

He needed to hurry, but it wasn't easy. The caves were in a state of chaos. They had not looked this bad when he and Betwixt had pulled Cwyn and the witch from the wreckage. Every artifact had been swept off every shelf, leaving only a fur-covered bed surrounded by piles of broken rubbish.

Logically, the bed was the only place here that could conceal something as large as Saturday's sword. Peregrine kicked through the piles gently, so as not to injure himself, but as quickly as he could manage. He stepped over an array of broken vials; his footsteps smeared their contents across the floor. With a giant shove he flipped the witch's bed over, fur sheets, pallet, and all. There was one deep clang followed by many other higher-pitched ones as the pile on the far side of the bed spilled and scattered. Peregrine ripped the covers away to reveal something he expected and something he didn't. The first was Saturday's sword. The second was a small golden cup.

He bent down and gingerly lifted the cup from the furs. It seemed so innocent, this instrument of his demise. He'd assumed it had been left beside the stream where he'd disappeared. His fingers remembered clutching it in his frozen hand. The dim lantern light drained the color from the gold, but he could tell it still shone. The gems along the edge matched the gems in the ornamental dagger at his hip. These were the only artifacts left from his life before, and both were stamped with the arms of Starburn.

He slipped the golden cup into the pocket of his skirt. Then he bent and retrieved Saturday's sword.

His temples throbbed mightily. The sword sizzled in his hand, though it did not burn. "No!" he cried. In his haste he had forgotten to cover the sword before touching it.

There was a new smell in the air, a burning not of flesh but of spices he'd forgotten how to name. The image of the sword in his hand wavered and shrank, shifting into something else. He only hoped that Saturday would be able to change it back into a sword. He also knew that, whatever object the sword became, it would be inextricably tied to Saturday's destiny, as the ax had been, as he now was.

The lantern began to flicker. In that dying light, Peregrine watched Saturday's once-majestic sword solidify into a ring.

He closed his fist around the golden band and held it to his chest, to the other ring there. "She's going to kill me."

Beneath his feet, the mountain began to tremble.

15

Wicked and Whole

"JACK WOODCUTTER!" shrieked the witch. She stood, glorious, triumphant, and almost naked amidst a sea of dust as vivid blue as her skin. Cwyn, her feathers a sunset fire of orange, hovered above her like a flame above a fairy candle.

Saturday forced herself to remain calm. She needed to stall as long as possible so that Peregrine had a chance to search for her sword. "Congratulations," she said. "You've found me."

"You should know by now you can never hide from me." The witch sniffed the freezing chamber air. Her tongue darted out to taste it. The powerful magic with which she was suffused emanated from her in waves. Around her, the cold, wet air turned to snow, falling in fat white flakes to the blue cave floor.

"Stealing your eyes hindered you for a while," Saturday guessed.

"But not for long," said the witch. "Never for long. Just as it will not be long now before I finish my Grand Spell. Do you have the ingredients I asked for?"

Saturday raised the sack. "Spiced moss and mushrooms, as requested."

"And the seeds?"

A cold gust whipped down her back and froze her feet inside her boots, but Saturday maintained her balance atop the boulder. She had forgotten about the seeds . . . but Peregrine had not. She hadn't eaten all the tomatoes, and she knew there was at least one pomegranate left from the small harvest he'd picked for her in the garden.

"Seeds, too," she announced proudly. But she did not budge.

"Excellent! Now, are you coming down from there, or will I have to send my familiar to fetch you again?"

Saturday tossed the sack into the drifts of snow piling up around the lorelei's bare feet. "There you go. All yours. You don't need me."

"Your second visit has entertained me far less than your first," said the witch. "You will come down here right now, and you will take this sack to the cauldron in the kitchen."

Saturday put her hands on her hips. "And if I don't?"

The witch lifted a finger, and Saturday's muscles stiffened again, but not from exhaustion. Her hands and feet were drawn into the air, one after another, marching her like one of Peter's wooden puppets down the pile of rocks to the cavern floor before the witch. Her boots slipped on the snow-covered ground but she did not fall, buoyed as she was by magic. She fought against the pull, breaking into a sweat as she struggled, but her body's will was no longer her own.

Guided by the raven's eyes, the witch captured Saturday's chin in her cerulean claws.

"No more games, Jack." The lorelei sucked her pointy, yellowed teeth. She took a deep breath of the steam that rose from Saturday's skin into the frozen air between them. "I will bathe in your blood," she whispered. "I will strip the skin from your flesh, fill my stomach with the meat from your bones, and then grind those bones to make my bread. I will consume every part of you, and when I have done so, all your strength will be *mine*. Together, we will open the portal back to my home, and my brethren will fall to their knees in despair at my power."

"I will fight you with every ounce of my being," Saturday said through her teeth.

The witch grinned again, lashing out with her free hand and slicing the swordbelt from Saturday's waist with her claws. Saturday felt the weight fall from her hips as her dagger, empty scabbard, and Peregrine's hairbrush clattered to the ash-strewn cavern floor.

"Come," said the witch. "I've made you a cage."

The lorelei released Saturday's face to grasp the front of her shirt. With preternatural strength, the witch pulled her along the clear path she had created in the fallen stone — away from her bedchambers. Saturday's dragging feet kicked up the blue dust and she sneezed mightily. The longer Saturday kept the witch occupied, the longer Peregrine would be safe.

The witch stomped unceasingly up through the tunnels, up and up some more, the caverns around them lit only by the light of her stone bracelet. Eventually, Saturday began to recognize rock formations that led to the kitchen.

As they turned the corner, the witch threw Saturday sideways across the room, as if she weighed no more than a sack of potatoes. Saturday got barely a glimpse of the cage before her face hit the far wall of it. Catching her breath, she sat up and put a hand to her cheek. It came away bloody.

Dozens of short swords and long swords and maces and daggers made up the bars of Saturday's cage. She recognized both the flaming sword and the ruby-bladed one — she grabbed at the latter's handle and tried to pull it away, but to no avail. A fine blue sheen ran along the metal and bound all the pieces, one to another, like magical glue. Weapons that might have meant her escape had become the very instruments of her capture.

"Clever," said Saturday, because it was. "The cleverest thing would have been for your bird to kill me the minute it found me instead of bringing me back here."

"But I couldn't have done all this without you, Jack," said the preening lorelei. "I didn't recognize the power surrounding you the first time you visited. I will not make that mistake again."

Saturday's hands searched for a loose weapon in the cage's makeup. Failing that, she began to feel along the smooth floor for a pebble, a spoon, a bit of ice, anything she might use as a weapon.

The witch tossed a skull into the cauldron, followed by what looked like several shards of calcite and the tip of a waxen fingerstone. The thick liquid swallowed it all, each bubble emitting the stench of rancid flesh. Clouds of deep purple gathered above the cauldron, snapping and churning with lightning and thunder. The fingerstones overhead sparked and glowed with power.

"Stone of Memory, hear my plea,
From worlds away I call to thee."

She danced as she sang the couplet over the fire; the rags of her dress waved as she swayed backwards and forward. With each word she spoke, her skin turned a deeper and deeper blue. The knobby horns on her head seemed to grow.

Saturday grabbed the hilt of every sword in the cage, pushing and pulling them one by one in another effort to free them from the bars and attack the lorelei or turn over the cauldron or destroy the ingredients. She needed to stop the spell!

Out of the corner of her eye, she spotted a small pile of rocks that had been shoved to the side, the discarded remnants of a fallen fingerstone. Saturday moved slowly to the far end of the cage, careful not to catch Cwyn's attention. She stretched her right arm out behind her, as far as she could, praying to reach a stone sizeable enough to hide in her hand, or sharp enough to pierce skin.

The blades of the swords bit into her shoulders as she pressed against them, splitting the fabric of her shirt and dotting the tears with blood. Thankfully, the overwhelming presence of magic in the room healed the shallower cuts almost as quickly as she acquired them.

"Basselure, hear my call,
Jinni, pyrrhi, lilim, all."

Saturday never thought there would come a moment in her life when she wished she were taller, but a few inches would have been quite the mercy. The clouds over the cauldron spun faster. Lightning shot out from its center and cracked against the cage of swords. She felt the jolt, but she continued to stretch with all her might.

The witch held spears of icerock above the cauldron and melted them in her hands. Saturday's fingertips collected only pebbles. She risked a rather deep slice in her forearm to reach a slightly larger rock, but she only managed to nudge it aside. *There!*

Beneath the rock, slipped into a crack in the floor, was the broken blade of a small dagger. Saturday scooted the blade gently to her and slipped it inside her palm, giving no hint that she had discovered anything at all. Cwyn watched her with traitorous raven eyes.

The witch tossed a few more small skulls into the cauldron, along with the fresh heads of several brownies and a generous portion of the spiced moss Saturday and Peregrine had collected. The clouds above the cauldron spun and popped and grew; Saturday gagged at the new stench that filled the kitchen.

The witch's voice deepened.

"Teeth for taste as scent is sown . . ."

Cold . . . taste . . . scent . . . The witch had used her ingredients to represent every physical sense inside her cauldron. The colorful mushrooms could be for sight, but how did one put sound into a stew?

The answer came quickly. The geis seized Saturday's muscles once more and compelled her back to the witch's side of the cage. Saturday squeezed the broken dagger blade inside her fist. Blood slowly dripped from cuts in her palm that opened, healed, and reopened again.

The witch now held a dagger of her own, wicked and whole. With it she sliced off Saturday's left ear and dropped it in the cauldron.

" . . . the snip and snap of blood and bone."

Saturday dropped the blade and clapped her hand to the side of her head where her ear had been. It had not been a neat slice; she could feel a jagged tear of skin and sinew left behind. She would not scream for the witch's satisfaction. Instead, she growled through her clenched teeth and concentrated on slowing the blood and healing herself. This scar would never fade — the ear was lost. Even if she'd had her sword, the appendage couldn't have regrown in the time she had left. The witch needed to die *now*.

As Saturday suspected, the mushrooms were next into the pot.

"Though I lack the eyes to see,
Doorway show yourself to me!"

The mist above the cauldron swirled with a myriad of colors, as if each was fighting the others. The clouds grew up to the high ceiling, encompassing the chimney and the large pillars on either side of it. The fingerstones in the ceiling glowed like the moon.

Saturday needed to shift the lorelei's focus. Biting back the pain, she forced herself to keep on her feet and address the witch.

"Your daughter should be here to witness your triumph," Saturday screamed over the howl of the wind generated by the churning cauldron-clouds.

"I was just about to call her," said the witch. With that, she tossed the fruit and the remnants of a half-charred book into the fire.

"From seed of birth to page of death,
I hail the daughter of my breath."

As the book burned, the acrid cauldron stench was replaced by one of charred cinnamon. An image appeared in the clouds above the cauldron of a woman with pale olive skin, long dark hair, sculpted lips, and eyes of starless night. The vision even gave a sense of the palace behind her. She was standing in the bedroom of a queen, addressing her looking glass.

"Hello, Mother. Miss me?"

So this was Leila.

Cwyn croaked, but Saturday could not tell if the animal's exclamation was one of joy or frustration.

"How can you be in the fire, child? You are right here."

"Silly Mother. I haven't been with you for a very long time, and you never even noticed. I should be wounded, but how can I be? You seem to have misplaced your eyes. Here. Let me help you with that."

The image of Leila waved her hand. Green lightning shot out of the cauldron-clouds. The witch blinked.

No, said Cwyn. *She can see!*

The witch still had no eyes to speak of, but somehow the empty sockets were doing the job anyway. She raised a thin blue claw to the vision in the clouds. "Daughter? Is that you?"

"Yes, Mother," Leila said impatiently.

"Then who is here with me?" asked the witch. "Who is the daughter I know, the daughter who keeps my house, the daughter who inspired this spell?"

"An imposter," said Leila.

The witch instantly whipped her head around to the cage. "Jack Woodcutter, this is all your fault!"

"Use your eyes, Mother," said Leila. "That can't be Jack Woodcutter. She's a girl."

Saturday wanted to reach through those magical clouds and wring Leila's neck. If she managed to make it off this mountain alive, she vowed to someday perform that task.

"Not Jack Woodcutter?" asked the witch calmly. And then, "NOT JACK WOODCUTTER?"

"Goodbye, Mother," Leila said passively. "Much love. Have fun destroying the world." And with that, the vision was gone.

The lorelei didn't seem to care. She stretched out a hand and Saturday slammed forward against the cage bars, slicing her arms again and jarring her bad ear. The lorelei took her by the shirt collar and shook her mightily. "NOT JACK WOODCUT-TER!"

"Saturday Woodcutter, at your service." Saturday clasped the hand the lorelei had on her collar, locking the demon's thin fingers inside her own large and bloody ones. "You rescued me from a ship full of bloodthirsty pirates! I'm so glad this ruse is over so I can finally thank you properly."

"You were in this together," said the witch. "You and the imposter."

"If you say so," said Saturday. "But you will not be harming him today. Or ever again."

The pronoun had the desired effect. "Him?" The lorelei's skin swirled black and blue. The clouds shot lightning into her claws and the cage and Cwyn's scarlet wings. Saturday swore she heard a crack in the very ether itself.

"FILTHY HUMAN! I WILL KILL HIM!"

"I can't let you do that." Saturday threw her weight back, pulling the lorelei's arm. This time the witch slammed against the blade-bars of the sword cage. Her demon skin split into even lines where the blades bit into her face, and blood dripped down to her chin. Saturday only wished she'd gotten an ear.

Cwyn fluttered frantically, like a silk scarf tossed in a sea of lightning. Her crimson wings began to swirl with black as well.

The lorelei stared Saturday down with her empty, bloody eye sockets. Every inch of the witch was blue-black now, even the tips of her hair and the pointed horns at her temples. The air in the kitchen crackled with power.

"I WILL KILL YOU ALL." The lorelei's unearthly voice echoed throughout the chamber. Faint voices from the world beyond the cauldron answered her cry.

"Not if I kill you first," said Saturday.

She moved one hand to the demon's struggling wrist, braced the other against the handle of the stuck fire sword, and slammed the lorelei against the bars again. The enchanted sword began to glow, but Saturday had no time to wait for its magic to manifest. Throwing her head back, she called out a rhyme of her own to the gods.

"Fire from earth's hallowed ground,
Help me take this demon down!"

Saturday inhaled and felt the power from the cauldron-clouds enter her body. Her bones became iron in the heat of the forge. Lightning shot from her fingers. The blue-green bracelet at her wrist burned with an inner fire . . . and the sword in her hand burned with an outer one. Flames erupted along the blade of the sword and then the lorelei, pressed against it. Saturday's clothes and Cwyn's feathers caught fire too, but Saturday held the demon against the burning bars with all her might.

The lorelei gasped as she took her last breath of this life, but she did not scream. "Thank you," she said. Her body seemed to melt at the edges, and then disappeared in a puff of brilliant blue steam.

Behind her, the raven fell into a pile of crimson ash.

The flames engulfing Saturday and the cage vanished, though the blade-bars still glowed red with heat. The swarming clouds of colors shrank to the size of pebbles before exploding in one last great burst of sound and light. The explosion cracked the cauldron and spilled its corrosive contents to the floor. The liquid quickly burned its way down through the icerock, down and down to the Earthfire far below.

The hungry screams from the world beyond had been silenced. In the aftermath, Saturday heard only her ragged breaths and the stubborn beat of her defiant heart. She was glad there was no one to witness her tears.

A bright red glow filled the cave. Saturday raised her head. It was not the bars emitting the light, but the pile of Cwyn's ashes. From those ashes rose the silhouette of a young woman. As the shadow solidified into radiant flesh, the beautiful woman grew old and round. "Well done, child," was all she said before she vanished completely in a puff of black smoke.

Two-faced witch. Saturday was not sorry to see her go. She only lamented that Vasilisa had not freed her from the cage of swords first.

Alone again, Saturday blinked into the quiet darkness. If the witch's geis on Vasilisa had broken with her death, then why hadn't the cage fallen to pieces? Saturday leaned back and kicked her boot against the bars. They didn't budge. She tried again, the force of the blow resonating in her bones. She might as well have been kicking the wall of the cave. Carefully, she reached out and felt along the bars with her fingers.

The blades of the swords were no longer sharp. The heat of the fire she'd summoned had melted the weapons together, solidifying the bonds the demon had created with her magic. Grasping the bars with both hands, she tried to lift the cage, but its weight was beyond her strength. Stubbornly she tried again. And again.

Sweating with the effort now, Saturday fell back into the middle of the cage. She had defeated the lorelei, and in doing so had imprisoned herself even further.

Beneath her, the ground rumbled. Saturday had felt this sort of tremor before, on the day she'd broken the earth and called the ocean. The rumble came again.

As predicted, the mountain was waking up, and the dragon with it. And if she had truly fulfilled her destiny, then she could die now and would, here in this cage of her own making at the Top of the World.

"NO!" The screech Saturday let loose would have made the witch proud. She railed at the bars. She pulled and lifted and kicked and strained. She made up nonsense rhymes and cried them into the darkness, one after another, but the magic in the walls did not answer her. She screamed at the ceiling in fear and

frustration, her shrieks turning to hysterical laughter at her predicament.

"I thought you'd killed the lorelei, but I could swear I still hear her."

The voice that split the darkness was not Peregrine's. "Betwixt?"

"To the rescue," said the chimera. "Though to be fair, you rescued me first."

In the blackness Saturday could not see what new form Betwixt had taken, but the sound of the bars creaking apart was a blessing in her ears. She stood to face the noise, and was subsequently embraced by a pair of very large and very fuzzy arms.

"My hero," Saturday said into the musky fur of the chimera's shoulder.

"*My* hero." Betwixt returned the greeting. The mountain shivered and rocked. "We need to get out of here."

"Do you have a light?"

"There's no time," said Betwixt.

"I'm naked," said Saturday. "And unlike you, I can't see in the dark."

"Ah." Saturday stood still while Betwixt rummaged in the dark. A bundle of cloth hit her in the midsection. "Put those on. I'll see to a light."

One of the items Betwixt had tossed her was a shirt. She quickly put it on. The other was a skirt, but she could not tell the top from the bottom. Eventually, she discovered a drawstring in the thing and pulled it tightly around her waist. Though she was covered in yards of cloth, she still felt naked, but there was little time to care. She heard flint strike steel and waited. And waited. Her ruined ear throbbed. She pushed her muddy hair over the ragged lump of flesh. The mountain bucked and chuckled at her predicament, tickling the dust between her toes.

She heard the unmistakable crack of a fingerstone before it plummeted to the floor behind her. It was nothing like the crack of the portal to the demon world the witch had almost made. Those inhuman cries would haunt her for a long time.

A spark burst into life, and within moments Saturday could see the torch. It was held by a hulking, ugly minotaur. Dark fur bristled over his wide chest and bare human feet. Dark horns sprouted from either side of his head. His well-muscled arms and legs radiated pure brute strength.

He was the most beautiful thing Saturday had ever seen.

Betwixt handed her the torch. "Let's go."

"Is Peregrine with you? Is he safe?"

"He's fine. I'll take you to him. But we must hurry."

Saturday followed the chimera's lead through the caves. Around them, boulders trembled and fingerstones fell. The blasted skirt continued to tangle in her legs, catch on protrusions, and trip her up. When the floor became too steep for her to climb and hold the torch and her skirt at once, Betwixt grabbed the back of her shirt and hauled her up the rest of the way.

Saturday's torchlight fell on the walls of the small cave they had entered. "These rocks are unfamiliar to me."

"Peregrine would not have brought you to this place. But

this is the faster path. And I thought you should see this before it crumbles into legend."

On every wall there was a picture of her. In shadows and colors Peregrine had captured her wide smile and bright eyes. There were axes and swords and trees and her, over and over again. "Peregrine did all this?"

"Yes."

"When did he have the time?" As the words left her mouth, Saturday felt a fool for asking.

"He has been dreaming of you his whole life," said Betwixt.

"He told me as much, but I never . . . I guess I never realized what that meant."

"I thought you should know."

Saturday touched the closest cave painting, wondering how it felt to love someone so completely, for so long. The sheer grandeur of his passion made her feel small. She wasn't sure her own meager feelings would ever measure up to this obsession.

"Come," said Betwixt, and in a heartbeat he had morphed into a lizard with batwings. Saturday followed him through a gap where the ceiling dipped low, tossing her torch to the other side before crawling under to retrieve it. Betwixt had changed back into the minotaur; he held the torch aloft to light her passage.

This chamber's walls held no paintings, only hash marks. "Peregrine began marking his days here. Eventually he gave up."

Betwixt blew softly on the torch, and the flame rose. With it, Saturday could see more marks, so many that they completely blackened the calcite, as far up as a human hand could climb or reach.

"How long *has* he been here?"

"Too long," said Betwixt. He blew on the torch again, this time extinguishing it completely. As her eyes adjusted to the darkness, Saturday saw a glow coming from a hole in the space before them.

"It is a slide to the witch's lair," said Betwixt. "I will go first, so I can catch you when you fall."

A shadow moved across the hole, and Saturday heard Betwixt's mass barrel down it. She counted slowly to five, giving him a moment to land. The mountain groaned, and Saturday felt a blast of air from the aperture behind her as the back half of the cave collapsed.

She blew a kiss to the dark walls around her, crossed her arms over her chest, and jumped.

16

Wings of Ice and Stone

PEREGRINE HAD just crossed the moat outside the witch's lair when a minotaur dropped
from the sky. The beast landed well, but hard, and then turned
his snout back up to the ceiling as if he were waiting for something. The mountain groaned.

"Betwixt! Is that you?"

"Yes, my friend." The chimera's gravelly voice came from
deep inside his hefty bull chest.

"What about Saturday?" Peregrine lost his footing and fell
backwards into the moat. The water was hot. The Earthfire was
rising up the mountain to meet them.

"Close behind me," said Betwixt. "The witch is dead."

Peregrine considered the mountain's revolt. "So we are free now? Truly free?"

"As free as any band of misfits trapped on top of the highest mountain in the world as it begins to crumble."

A cascade of pebbles and dust fell from the hole onto the minotaur's outstretched arms. He roared mightily. The mountain roared and shook in answer. Another shower of rocks fell and Saturday came immediately after. Betwixt caught the large bundle of blond hair and rags easily in his brawny arms.

Saturday smiled at the minotaur. "No one's been able to catch me like that since I was a girl."

"You still *are* a girl," said Betwixt.

"We must go," said Peregrine.

Betwixt set Saturday down gently. Peregrine let her gain her footing before catching her up into an embrace of his own. "You did it."

"Yes. I did."

Peregrine tried to examine her face, but her hair was a wet mess again, caked with either red dirt . . . or dried blood. "Are you all right?"

He moved to cup her head in his hands, but she leaned in and kissed him instead. This was no kiss of exuberance or companionship; it was one of relief and hope. In the brief moment that she held him, he let himself hope as well.

"Any sign of the dragon?" she asked.

"Not yet." Peregrine caught her arm as she tripped over the uneven floor. She was wearing one of his old kitchen skirts. "You really *are* a girl!"

Saturday rolled her eyes. "It was either this, or stay naked."

Peregrine raised his eyebrows.

Saturday punched him in the shoulder. "I could still take lessons from you."

"You never know," said Peregrine. "One day you may need them."

They ran back into the witch's lair and stopped at the base of the cave-in. Saturday sifted through the ash and rubble to find her savaged belt and scabbard. "Where's my sword?"

He could put off her disappointment no longer. Peregrine pulled the transformed ring from his skirt pocket and placed it in Saturday's hand. "I'm sorry."

There was no singing in the air as she touched it — it simply stayed the ring that it was. Saturday stared into her palm, snapping her fingers into a fist around it when she felt the mountain buck and lost her footing again. "You have got to be kidding me." She closed her eyes and held her closed fist to the cold sky. "Change, damn you! I command it!"

The incredible magic she'd been able to perform now abandoned her. Try as she might, the ring would not transform. Their only decent weapon was the runesword at Peregrine's waist. "Take this," he said.

Saturday stopped him. "There's no time. We need to go." She raised her arm as if to throw the ring across the cavern. "Stupid, useless magical—"

Peregrine caught her hand. "Never lose hope. The gods have ways of returning such items to their owners."

"The gods also have ways of forcing unwilling humans into

destinies," she said. "Here. You take it. I'll just lose it." With a nod, Peregrine dipped his head to remove the chain that held his father's wedding band. Saturday recovered a dagger from the ground near where her sliced swordbelt lay. She also found the wooden hairbrush Peregrine had given her. He expected her to toss the useless item away, but instead, she tucked it in the pocket of her skirt. The gesture warmed him.

Meanwhile, the rest of the cave began to warm by other means. Molten Earthfire poured through the hole in the ceiling from which Saturday had dropped, turning the moat to steam as it slid across the floor.

Peregrine scrambled higher on the pile of rock and tilted his head back at the night sky. Pillows of steam venting from the mountain blotted out the stars. The hole in the ceiling had widened as the mountain shuddered. "We need a rope," he called down to his friends.

"I need wings," Saturday said.

"I can give you those," said Betwixt. The air crackled with magic and a song much like the one Peregrine had heard when Saturday's sword had changed in his hands. Betwixt was swallowed inside a ball of golden light.

Peregrine caught her by the neck and kissed her hard. "In case we never get this chance again."

She kissed him back. "We will. We have to."

"Because you're going to save us."

Saturday smiled. "We're going to save each other."

Betwixt whinnied. The chimera stood proudly before them, a great stallion of white and gray and silver like a well-muscled cloud on a summer's day. From his haunches unfurled wings, each almost as large again as he was from tip to tail. The feathers shimmered in the hot air like new-fallen snow and hope.

"Pegasus! Brilliant!" Peregrine whooped at his friend. He scrambled down from their perch, dragging Saturday after him.

"I'm a woodcutter," she said. "I'm no good on a horse."

"I'm the son of an earl," he shot back. "I was born on one. Hop on."

"I'm wearing a skirt."

Peregrine reached down between her feet and pulled the back hem of her skirt forward and up, tucking it securely in the front of her waistband. "Voilà, pantaloons. Now, up!" He knelt, and she used his leg to launch herself onto Betwixt's back.

Peregrine rested one hand on Betwixt's back and vaulted himself up after her. "Let's fly!" he announced.

"Wait!" yelled Saturday.

The mountain rumbled and roared again. More bits of the ceiling crumbled down into the lair. Earthfire crept slowly across the floor. A few fist-sized rocks rolled under Betwixt's hooves and Peregrine worried about his friend breaking a leg. One of the rocks leapt onto Peregrine's skirt and crawled into his lap. It shook off the dust to reveal the ginger fur beneath.

"A brownie?"

"Just let it come," said Saturday.

There was little time to argue over the wisdom of saving a rodent. Peregrine urged the notch-eared brownie into his pocket and signaled to Betwixt that they were ready.

The pegasus broke into a solid gallop across the lair and up the pile of fallen rubble. Peregrine worried about their speed, the weight of them on the chimera's back, and the sword at his side banging into Saturday's leg. Then Saturday wrapped her arms around his waist, Betwixt spread his wings, and Peregrine worried about nothing at all.

Hot steam and the cold night stung his cheeks; he opened his mouth and breathed them in together. They tasted like freedom. Betwixt's wing beats came slow and even, each one carrying them farther and farther away from the prison that had been their home.

Peregrine turned to look back at the mountain. It looked so peaceful at this distance, like a cake dusted with sugar on a midnight-velvet table. The vents of steam might have been birthday candles, just blown out. Ice crystals twinkled on the peak like the stars above would have, had they not been hidden beneath row upon row of brilliant ice clouds that shone down upon them, all the colors of the rainbow.

"The Northern Lights!" Peregrine called to Saturday, and she followed his pointing finger up to the heavens. He took in their beauty, closed his eyes, and memorized the view. When he opened them back up he saw Saturday smiling at him with those bright eyes he had loved for so long. He leaned into her slightly, hoping to steal one more kiss without throwing Betwixt off balance.

Behind them, the mountain erupted.

Earthfire spilled down the mountainside. Shards of ice flew past them, biting into their legs and Betwixt's flanks. Despite the danger, the chimera spread his wings wide and rode the drafts of air, refusing to let them force him to the ground. They spun and spun, jumping from one draft to another until Betwixt found suitable purchase.

Peregrine's stomach rolled over. Saturday's arms tightened around his chest. Peregrine folded his arms on top of hers and curled into the wind, squeezing his legs against Betwixt and praying for them to stay balanced and airborne. He wished for a saddle, and then chuckled at the idea of wasting a wish on something so ridiculous.

They spun around again, and Peregrine watched as the tip of the mountain was blown high into the air. As if in slow motion, the giant crystal pyramid hovered before splintering into a million pieces. Those splinters didn't fly out; instead, the pyramid expanded, growing wider and wider before it threw its head back and roared.

The dragon awoke from its sleeping death and took to the skies.

In his youth, Peregrine had heard stories about Lord Death and his angels with their wings of feathers and fire. This Death rode the chaotic currents on wings of ice and stone. The beast was alive, and it was not happy.

Saturday's arms locked around Peregrine. Had he been able to manage it he would have told her not to look, not to turn her head and risk the dragonfear, but what mortal could resist gazing upon such a legend of dangerous beauty? The beast was magnificent; having slumbered so long inside the mountain, it was now truly a part of it. Its white horn and beak stood out prominently, but they were decorated with more small peaks where there should have been none, all across the dragon's face and wing coverts. Its claws and primaries looked to be carved of pure, clear crystal, as did its eyes, though they burned red with rage and flame.

The dragon opened its mouth again. The belly of the beast rumbled like the mountain. Earthfire shot from its mouth and spewed across the distance in their direction. The flame glowed pink through the vanes of Betwixt's translucent wings, outlining the quills and revealing just how little kept them all from tumbling to their deaths. Peregrine felt the heat of the blast on his face. Betwixt caught the updraft and let it carry them farther away from the mountain.

The chimera's wing beats came faster. The dragon screeched after its prey. In his pocket, Peregrine felt the brownie's claws against his skin as they seized up in fear. The weight of the rodent moved up his leg; Peregrine thought it might fall out of his pocket, but only a whiskered nose and two very pointed teeth poked through to witness the majesty of their hunter.

His hands twisted deeply into Betwixt's soft mane, Peregrine turned to look back again. The dragon's wings scooped the air and thrust it back, propelling it forward at a speed that cut the distance between them in half. This time, the dragonfear took him. His lungs turned to ice and his breath left him. The dragon was close, so close that Peregrine could make out the rows of its hungry teeth. The next fiery breath would consume them. His eyes wide, Peregrine gasped for air that would not come.

Saturday's face moved in to interrupt his view of the

dragon. Peregrine blinked. She planted a quick kiss on his lips that melted the dragonfear that gripped him, and he shuddered as he drew in a cold, misty lungful of life. Her eyes twinkled. They were about to die. Why was she smiling?

Between them, she held up her dagger, seized a handful of his long hair, and sawed it off. She muttered something into the dark bundle and threw it up into the air above her head, releasing it directly into the dragon's path. The blue-green band on her wrist sparkled like her bright eyes. Peregrine watched as the hair floated peacefully on the wind, waiting. When the dragon was but a breath away, the strands turned into crystal-wings. The mad black and blue flock of them flew into the face of the beast, attacking and confusing it. Peregrine thought he could smell blood on the currents as the sharp crystalwings bit into the dragon's thick skin.

"DIVE!" Saturday yelled to Betwixt. Peregrine leaned forward and pressed his face into Betwixt's mane, summoning the strength to hold on. The pegasus folded his wings, bent his head forward, and they plummeted through the atmosphere.

Peregrine could feel Saturday's scream of excitement into his back. He cried out too, letting loose into the freezing night air all the frustration he'd been holding inside himself for so many years. The freedom was intoxicating.

Now that they were low enough, Betwixt played hide-and-seek through the clouds as they flew farther south, descending all the time over the peaks and valleys of pure white snow. The dragon fell back but did not tire, trumpeting in triumph every time it spotted them again and regained pursuit.

They might make it. Dear gods in the heavens, they might actually survive this!

To his left, Peregrine saw the morning sun peek over the horizon. But as the fingers of dawn rose to greet them, they also revealed another peril: what Peregrine had thought were snowy plains below them were waves on a vast ocean, whitecapped, beautiful, and deadly.

Peregrine had seen hundreds of maps, and at no point did he remember the ocean rising to meet the mountains. Worse still, there were naught but wispy, rainbow-hued clouds to hide them from the dragon. Nor was there any place to land once Betwixt grew too tired to fly.

Saturday's arm moved from around his waist once again; this time, she removed the wood-handled brush from her skirt pocket. She closed her eyes, as if saying a small prayer, and threw the brush behind them. It tumbled ungracefully through the air before being swallowed by the ocean.

This time, nothing happened.

Peregrine bowed into Betwixt's mane again, shielding his raw cheeks from the continued onslaught of wind. Saturday curled into Peregrine as well, muttering something into his back. A prayer, an apology, a declaration of love, a curse — Lord Death would let him know which, but he bet on the latter.

A new roar echoed in his ears, but it was not the dragon. Colored lightning fell from the chaotic clouds around them to snap against the breaking waves. Betwixt ascended as the waves rose up to meet them. The valleys began revealing houses, fences, and trees. Faster and faster the ocean fled, and from that drying earth grew the forest.

As soon as Betwixt found a suitable stretch of solid ground, he landed. The chimera's breaths came heavy and his straining muscles were hot beneath Peregrine's hands. He folded his great wings and continued to gallop, dodging back and forth as massive oaks and evergreens shot up around them.

The dragon shrieked in frustration at the loss of its quarry. Peregrine heard the rumble and blast that came with its fire, but the wet, new wood of this forest blessedly caught no flame. Betwixt slowed under the cover of a copse of ash and chestnut, the monoliths' leaves taking on autumn hues even as they budded and grew.

The dragon shrieked again, but this time it sounded farther away. Peregrine could no longer distinguish its wing beats. Betwixt stopped to let them dismount. Peregrine collapsed to the damp ground, for his legs did not have the strength to hold him. Saturday hugged the nearest tree trunk before sinking down to the forest floor beside him.

A lump in his skirt squeaked, and Saturday shook the fabric in an effort to free the frightened brownie. The rodent bit her fingertip before disappearing into the wood.

"Ungrateful scamp," Peregrine called after it, but he had no strength for bluster.

"It's only a scratch," said Saturday.

"Shame," said Peregrine. "Now you cannot tell the world you escaped a dragon unscathed."

Saturday bowed her head so that the longer strands of her hair occluded her face. "I need to get to the abbey," she said. "My mother will be waiting for me there."

"Then we go to the abbey," said Peregrine. His skin itched mightily. He scratched at his chin. Now that the witch was dead, Leila's curse seemed to be running its course, slow bit by slow bit.

"Which abbey?" asked Betwixt.

"I . . . I don't know. From our house it was north and east, on the plains between the mountains and the sea. My aunt is the abbess there."

"What is your aunt's name?" asked the pegasus.

"Six," answered Saturday. "Or, rather, Rose Red."

"Rose Abbey," said Betwixt. "I know the place. When we've rested, we'll make our way there."

Saturday nodded and leaned back against the tree. Betwixt shook out his wings and grazed on a patch of newbirthed grass.

Peregrine lay back on the solid ground, dug his fingers into the soft dirt, and breathed in the sweet, fresh forest air. He knew that living to see the end of this day had consequences. For the moment, he simply wanted to enjoy his freedom.

17

Fate's Playthings

IT TOOK the trio about a day to get to Rose Abbey. When they tired of walking, Betwixt flew, when he tired of flying, they walked, and when exhaustion overwhelmed them all, they collapsed on the forest floor, slept awhile, awoke, and started again. Betwixt gorged himself on sweet, wet grass and Saturday remembered enough of her skill to bring down a small rabbit with her dagger, but they were still filthy and half starved when they reached their destination.

They found the road to the abbey from the air. Upon it rode a wide, flat wagon with a single driver who appeared intent on the same destination.

Betwixt landed before the great walled entrance to the

abbey just as the wagon arrived. The climbing roses that covered the bricks reminded Saturday of the roses surrounding the Woodcutter house. To the left of the grand archway, crimson petals bloomed like bloodstains. The roses to the right of the archway bore petals of the purest white.

The large mahogany doors of the abbey opened before the party was halfway through the courtyard. A slip of a woman with a mop of red-gold curls burst out onto the stone porch and flew down one side of the split stair, while another woman in stately burgundy robes gracefully descended the other. Peregrine dismounted and helped Saturday down from Betwixt's back. She locked her unsteady knees, bracing herself for the impact of Thursday's embrace.

"Saturday." Her sister breathed her name into the skin of her neck opposite her ragged ear. "You have no idea how good it is to see you." Thursday backed up to hold her at arm's length. "You look like hell."

Saturday shook her hair into her face to hide the worst of the damage.

Erik, not to be outdone by the Pirate Queen, caught Saturday up in a quick hug. "Missed you, Giantess."

"Back at you, Hero."

"Perhaps I should be calling *you* that."

"Some strays have followed you home." Thursday nodded to Peregrine and Betwixt. "Spoils of war?"

Peregrine swept his skirt back in a half-bow, half-curtsey, as if he wore royal robes instead of ancient rags. "Peregrine of Starburn. This is my companion, Betwixt."

Betwixt stepped one foot forward, spread his wings to either side, and bowed his head low. The effect was incredibly impressive.

"You've got stories," said Erik.

"We all have stories," said the abbess.

Saturday bowed to her aunt. "Hello, Aunt Rose."

"I'd say 'well met,' dear niece, but I suspect none of us has glad tidings this day."

"Don't hug her," warned Thursday. "She smells like the devil's stable."

The driver dismounted from the wagon's seat and removed his hat. He was a scruffy, hirsute man with eyes like the storm they'd flown through to escape the dragon.

"Wolf." The abbess held her hands out to greet him.

He kissed both her cheeks and then knelt to kiss her ring of office. "My beloved Rose Red."

"I had not foreseen that this day would bring such a bounty." Rose Red shot a glance at Thursday. Thursday, who possibly knew all of this from her spyglass, looked away. "I believe it would be best if Saturday and her companions were properly bathed and clothed before we go any further. Erik, would you see Betwixt to the stables?"

"No need, Your Eminence." In a flash of light, the pegasus was replaced by a scruffy young boy with stubby horns, a short beard, and goat's feet. Betwixt, in his new form, bowed again to the abbess.

If this act surprised Rose Red at all, she did not show it. "All children of earth are welcome in the home of their Mother

Goddess. Shall we?" As they entered through the large doors, the abbess waved her hand and several acolytes appeared.

Thursday grabbed Saturday's hand and pulled her along. "Come on, Miss Molasses," she said. Of all the Woodcutter sisters, it was no surprise that she and Saturday most often repeated this particular phrase of Mama's.

Erik led Peregrine and Betwixt in the opposite direction. Saturday hadn't realized until that moment that she wasn't truly comfortable leaving her companions. Peregrine's eyes met hers across the foyer and he nodded that he would be all right. Saturday hoped that was true. Everything was changing so fast.

"Where's Mama?" she asked.

"Inside," Rose Red said calmly. "I'll see to her. You may join us in the chapel when you're ready."

"Thank you," she told her aunt. If Mama saw her like this, who knew what conclusions she'd jump to. She let Thursday drag her to the women's chambers.

The acolytes filled two tubs for Saturday. She'd need them. This bath was a far cry from the crystal lake with its hot springs, but it came with large cakes of soap. Saturday stripped quickly and jumped in, eager to scrub the curses and weariness out of her skin.

Thursday spoke to the waiting acolytes and they left quickly with the dirty things. "I had them fetch you some proper clothes," she said, and Saturday thanked the Earth Goddess (whose house she currently stank up) that her companion was the sensible sister. "Do you know you've been missing for more than a month?"

Had she really? "It felt like only days," said Saturday. "But time passed strangely on the mountain where we were held. Where is your ship?"

"I was dubious of your fickle ocean," said Thursday. "I told Simon Silk to leave at the slightest inkling of magic, with or without me onboard. At the first sign of green lightning, he was gone."

"So you're stuck here?"

"I've been landlocked before," said Thursday. "Don't worry. I'll find my ship. If she doesn't find me first."

"Trix is alive," said Saturday. "I saw him in a magic mirror. But you already knew that."

"I knew the lingworm had saved him, but I do not know his plight. My spyglass has spotted him only once since then. Speaking of . . . where's your sword?"

Saturday sank beneath the surface of the water to put off answering. "Lost," she said when she came back up for air. She lathered the soap into her hair a third time for good measure. It smelled of lavender and rosemary, sweet and green and alive.

"I wouldn't worry about it. Things have a way of turning up again in the strangest of places. Unfortunately, the same can't be said about your ear. May I have a look?"

Saturday only acquiesced because Thursday didn't make a big deal about it. Friday would have fainted dead away. It wasn't painful anymore, but Saturday was genuinely curious as to how the stump of it had healed.

"It's not bad, actually." She felt Thursday trace the scalloped edges where her lobe had been, and the cauterized scar tissue beneath it. "It looks rough, but you'll be able to hide it well enough with your hair until the color fades. I've seen worse on my ship."

"I imagine so."

"Men who fight trolls regularly learn not to get too attached to their limbs," said Thursday. "The price of adventuring."

"It was a witch," explained Saturday. "Of the evil demon variety."

"Ugly breed."

"She locked me in a cage and used my ear as an ingredient for a terrible spell that would have torn the world apart. I had to stop her."

"Did you kill her?"

Saturday could have said a thousand things. She'd had no choice; they had to escape; she was saving the world. But the only answer she gave her sister was "Yes."

"Did you stop the spell?"

Among other things. "After breaking the world, I felt I had no choice."

"Fitting, then, that your flesh and blood were part of the equation. Fortune favors the blood, you know. I fully believe Luck has always smiled upon our family because of all the Woodcutter blood Jack has spilled into the ether." Thursday's lips curved into one of those wry smiles that hid secrets, but Saturday was too tired to let it frustrate her. "Do you feel different, having killed someone?"

"She was a beast," said Saturday. "I've hunted beasts before."

"Not like this, you haven't, and you know it."

Saturday stood up from the warm bath and dunked herself

into the cool one. Soap and herbs and dust remnants merged into a film on the surface. "Killing the witch set us all free, including the dragon that slept in the mountain. I should have tried to kill it, too, while it slept, but I didn't." And now every bit of damage it did to the countryside would be on her head.

"You are a warrior," said Thursday, "not a killer."

"The price of adventuring," said Saturday, mocking her sister. She held her breath and sank beneath the surface of the water again, wishing a part of her soul clean that would never again be pure.

"So, do you love him?" Thursday asked when she surfaced.

"The wagon driver?" said Saturday. "We've only just met."

Thursday reached into the bath and flicked water at her. "Peregrine, you dolt."

"I might," she told her sister. "I haven't had much time to think about it. We've certainly been through a lot together. The place we were kept, the things we've seen . . ."

"Hard to explain to anyone who wasn't there?"

Saturday nodded.

"I know what you mean. The three of you have a special bond now, no matter what your future holds."

Saturday nodded again. Thursday no doubt had the same sort of bond with her crew.

"It's just . . ."

"Spit it out," said Saturday.

"He was a prisoner up there for how long?"

"I don't know," said Saturday. "Years, probably a decade at least. A long time."

"And the first time he's offered a bath and clean clothes, his only response is to never take his eyes off you," said Thursday. "Most girls would make a big deal out of that."

"I'm not most girls," said Saturday.

"Preaching to the choir, sister dearest," said Thursday. "I just wanted to make sure you knew. Special breeds of stubborn idiots like you and me tend to miss these not-so-subtle clues."

Saturday laughed then, because she knew it was true. Peter and Papa teased her enough about her hard head. The memory made her heart ache. Pain shot through her chest. She slipped in the tub and Thursday reached out to her, but she'd already grasped the sides and caught herself.

"You're bleeding," Thursday noted.

Saturday followed her sister's gaze to the tip of her finger. Her tight grasp on the lip of the tub had reopened the wound where the brownie had bitten her. She stared at the small droplets of blood welling up out of her unhealed skin. She was no longer indestructible. She'd fulfilled her grand destiny. What was she supposed to do with the rest of her life?

Thursday tossed a hand towel over the finger and pinched it. "Welcome to the mortal world."

The acolytes returned with fresh clothes: shirt, vest, and trousers. They located some ointment and a bandage scrap to knot around Saturday's finger to stop the bleeding. A new belt was provided, but it felt cheap and empty without a scabbard. She slid the dagger underneath the leather strap on her left side, but it didn't have the heft of the sword, or her ax. She felt unbalanced.

"I have a present for you," said Thursday. Saturday hoped it wasn't a sword. It wasn't. What Thursday held out to Saturday was her old messenger bag. She opened it up and checked the contents: a change of clothes, some rags, a small sewing kit, a ball of twine, a canteen, some fishing hooks, three stones Sunday had given her for good luck, and Thursday's ebony-handled brush . . . little of which would have been much good to her up on the mountain, but all of which set her mind more at ease now. The bag even smelled like her old room.

"I took the liberty of tossing out all the old hardtack and replacing it."

Saturday put the strap over her head and felt the reassuring weight at her side. "Thank you."

Thursday winked.

The Woodcutter sisters followed the acolytes down several hallways and through a garden to the chapel behind the main building. Sunlight spilled in through the stained-glass windows. It fell in patterns of color on the marble floor, like the Northern Lights on the eve of their escape.

They were the first to arrive in the nave of the chapel, with its intricately carved pews and columns shaped in stone likenesses of the animals dedicated to the Earth Mother. Bear, Cat, Wolf, Serpent: at their heart, they were just pretty rock formations. It was a pity so few had witnessed the natural temple at the Top of the World, so much more organically magnificent than this fabricated, orderly chapel. Saturday felt sure the Earth Goddess would agree.

The chapel door opened again and Betwixt entered,

wearing trousers this time, and naught else but a gleaming pelt of russet fur. Beside Erik was a man who could only have been Peregrine, dressed in hose and a long, double-breasted coat that flared out around his knees, much like the skirts he favored. Saturday might not have known him but for the thinning shock of silver-blue in his shorn hair and the determined look in his eyes as he made his way across the room. Those eyes seemed more greenish-gray than black now. Unlike her, he didn't give a second thought to the chapel.

"Is it really you?" she asked softly. Mama had taught her to always whisper on sacred ground. His nose seemed larger, his chin and shoulders seemed squarer, and he wore the runesword at his side with the ease of . . . well . . . an earl's son. Without saying a word he held his right hand out to her, palm up, revealing the line of blue scar on his wrist that Cwyn had given him. The skin around it was darker than it had been in the mountains, and significantly less green in hue.

The hand continued up past her cheek to touch her hair. "It's curly," he said. The words came from a larger chest, in thicker air, and held no falsetto of pretense. Part of Saturday missed the strange boy who'd teamed up with her in the White Mountains, but the rest of her began to realize how easy it would be to fall in love with the man who stood before her now. She wondered how much more he still had left to change; wondered if the man he'd become could still love a warrior who'd shed blood and unleashed terror on the world.

She heard the catch in his breath as he discovered her damaged ear, but he said nothing in front of her family.

"Thank you all for coming," Rose Red said from the altar. Wolf, who had removed only his hat, stood patiently by her side. "If you would please join me in the sacristy."

Saturday scanned the pews once more. Where was Mama?

They followed the abbess back behind the altar, through a small doorway and into a room few but the most blessed had ever seen. A tall, hooded monk awaited them there.

Unlike the chapel, the sacristy was plain. Only a few of the gray cinderblocks bore patterns or runes. The windows here were little more than narrow slits; dust played in the shafts of sunlight that sliced through the dusk to the unadorned floor. In the center of the room was an oaken table.

On the table lay the body of her mother.

"No!" Saturday tried to run to her mother's side, but Erik stopped her.

"Please," said Rose Red. "Let me explain."

Peregrine put a hand on Saturday's shoulder, and she steeled her nerves. He removed it quickly enough that no one would assume she needed his strength, but he did not move from her side. Betwixt stood before them both, the perfect picture of ease and innocence. Saturday knew better.

"I put her to bed in my cabin on the ship," said Thursday. "She never woke. She was probably already gone before you were taken."

Knowing that didn't make Saturday feel better.

"I've seen this before," said Peregrine. He turned to Saturday. "So have you."

And so she had. She had seen a body trapped in a similar

likeness of death, though it had not been human, nor so well preserved. "She's under a spell," said Saturday. "The sleeping death."

"She is not the only one," said Rose Red. "Trix's mother was the first. Then Teresa, our third sister. Their bodies are being watched over in the vaults." The hooded monk nodded a silent affirmation.

"Your twin has fallen as well," Wolf said gruffly. "Her husband, the Bear Prince, keeps her in a glass coffin at his palace in Faerie."

Rose Red clenched a fist but did not break her composure. "Not Snow White."

Wolf bowed his head. "Bear bade me come to you and fetch you back to her side."

"Wait." Saturday held up a hand. Her blue-green bracelet caught a ray of sunlight. "The witch on the mountain captured the dragon in order to siphon its power," she said to her aunt. "Who would want to siphon power from your sisters?"

The answer was obvious, but Rose Red said it aloud anyway. "Sorrow."

"My eldest aunt," Saturday explained to Peregrine.

"Your family has a lot of very powerful women," he replied, and Saturday smiled. She had lamented the same fact many a time.

"I cannot go back to Faerie," said Rose Red. "It will be just what Sorrow wants. My strength is here, on this sacred ground, surrounded by the gods to whom I have dedicated my life. If my sister wants to take my power, she will have to come here to get it."

Wolf was not happy about her answer, but he accepted it. "I will pass along your condolences."

"We will go with you to Faerie," said Saturday. "We will find this Bear, and collect Wednesday and Aunt Joy, and join forces with them. Sorrow must be stopped." Saturday had finally found a purpose beyond her destiny. "But first I would like to say good-bye. I didn't have the chance to before."

At Rose Red's nod, Erik let Saturday cross to Mama's side. She knelt beside the wooden table and took Mama's small hand in her large one. The skin was soft, neither warm with life nor cold with death.

"I'm so sorry, Mama." There were no tears on Saturday's cheeks, only the flush of shame.

She felt a large hand on her shoulder that she did not recognize. She turned her head and noticed the brown sleeve of the monk who stood guard over her mother. "Those of us who are Fate's playthings often have little choice where our path takes us," he said. "It's not your fault, Saturday."

The brother's familiarity annoyed her. How could he assume to know her pain? She stood up and spun around with dagger in hand, not caring a fig for the sacredness of this space. "Who are you?" she demanded.

"Answer her." Peregrine's tone was that of an earl and not a simpering witch's daughter. Beside him, Betwixt smiled with a mouthful of feral teeth. Saturday's heart welled with pride.

The monk laughed. "Well, now. Don't you make quite the trio?"

Saturday pulled back the cowl to reveal a rugged man with ruddy cheeks, hair like sunshine, and bright blue eyes that twinkled mischievously. Saturday had seen those eyes before.

In a mirror.

"Jack?" Peregrine stepped forward. "Is it really you?"

"Hello, Ladyboy. Good to see you, too." The two men chuckled into an enthusiastic embrace.

Saturday sheathed her dagger and put her hands on her hips. So this was the infamous, legendary Jack, sung about in a hundred kingdoms and known in every corner of the world. This was the man she had been mistaken for, the reason she'd been imprisoned and forced to unleash chaos upon the world. The resemblance *was* oddly striking: it was as if someone had painted a portrait of herself and one of Papa and then muddled them together.

"No hug for your long-lost brother?"

Saturday imagined that handsome face wasn't used to disappointment. She punched the smile right off his chin.

"That's my girl!" cried Thursday.

"I told you we should have introduced them properly," Erik said to Thursday.

"Oh no," said the Pirate Queen. "This is *much* better."

"I was captured because of you!" Saturday yelled at the legend that was her eldest brother. "I almost died because of you! I killed a witch, woke a dragon, lost my sword and my ear, and cut my finger . . . AND IT'S ALL YOUR FAULT." Saturday punctuated each sentence with a fist on his tree trunk of a chest, so like their father's. Jack took every blow in stride until Saturday ran out of accusations, and then he hugged her anyway. Saturday's feet actually left the ground.

"You've been busy," he said into her hair.

"It's nothing you haven't done," she said when he set her back down.

"I may have vanquished a sorceress or two in my time, but I can't say I've ever bested a demon witch like the lorelei."

"You took her eyes," said Saturday. "I'm sure that was difficult enough."

"But I didn't rescue the damsel or wake a dragon," he said. "That must have been something to see." Saturday was secretly pleased to have accomplished something her infamous, back-from-the-dead brother had not.

"What happened to the eyes?" asked Peregrine.

"They . . . melted," said Jack. "It's how I knew she'd been defeated." He noticed Saturday's hand drop back to Mama's shoulder. "She would be proud of you."

"After she gave me a severe tongue-lashing for abandoning her, perhaps. Jack"—addressing her brother by his name still felt strange—"I promised Peter that I would protect Mama. I promised. And I failed." She had also promised him a wealth of gold and a pretty girl, but Peter would not hold those things against her.

"I'm sure Mama forgives you for not being there when she fell ill. You were too busy saving the world." He winked at her. "These things happen."

"But what about the dragon?"

"The price of adventuring."

Saturday moved to smack him again. He deflected her arm and kissed her cheek. "Let me worry about the dragon," he said. "You've got other things to do."

"So you're not coming to Faerie with us?" It wasn't fair to have to leave the legend so soon after having reunited with him. There were so many things to ask!

"I have to go find my ship," said Thursday.

"I should return to Arilland and bring this news to the king," said Erik. "And someone needs to tell Jack Woodcutter about his wife."

And Peter, thought Saturday. Poor, sweet Peter. At least Papa would not have to bear the news alone. "All right, then Peregrine and Betwixt and I will go to Faerie. If that's all right with you?" she asked Wolf.

Wolf bowed his head. "It would be my honor."

"Saturday," said Peregrine.

"Don't argue. It's a good plan," she told him.

"Saturday, stop. Please."

It was the "please" that shut her up.

"There's something I have to do."

"I know," she said. "You want to return to Starburn. And we will, in time. But this may be another matter of life and death."

From beneath his linen shirt, Peregrine pulled the chain around his neck that held both her ring . . . and another's. It was then that she realized exactly what he was trying to say to her.

Peregrine slid her ring-that-was-a-sword off and then refastened the chain around his neck. "I wasn't supposed to survive."

"But you did," said Saturday. "I saved you."

"We saved each other," he said.

Those words, the ones she had spoken at the Top of the World before the mountain had exploded, shredded her heart like crystalwings.

"I would love nothing more than to kneel at your feet right now, put that ring on your finger, and bind my destiny to yours, whatever that may be. But I cannot." Peregrine placed the ring in Saturday's hand and curled her fingers closed around it. "I must keep my promise to Elodie."

Saturday could say nothing to this; she would not have respected him if he were the sort of person who did not keep his promises. Peregrine had to leave, and she had to let him. "What if she did not wait for you?"

"Then I will catch you on the road to Faerie."

"And if she did?"

Peregrine reached out a hand to touch her but let it fall short. "I do not want to say goodbye."

"Nor do I," said Saturday.

"I will return," Betwixt told her. "Either way, I will return to you with word."

It was the best Saturday could hope for. "Thank you."

With polite nods to the rest of the sacristy and a pained look at Jack, Peregrine and Betwixt made their exit.

Saturday stared at her palm and tried to summon power to

her like she had in the mountain. "Change back into a sword!" She willed magic into the ring with every fiber of her being. "Change, damn you!" But the stubborn metal would not budge.

A small, cool hand slipped into her free one, and Saturday turned to see Thursday at her side. "Men are bastards," said her sister. "Amazing, wonderful, fabulous, heartbreaking bastards."

"I couldn't agree more," said Jack.

"Come now," said Rose Red. "Let's get you all fed before you set out on your respective journeys."

Saturday, Thursday, and Jack all planted a kiss on Mama's forehead and the company slowly filed out of the sacristy.

"I think I missed something," Erik said to Jack as they crossed the threshold back into the chapel. "Who's Elodie?"

18

The Bitter End

PEREGRINE HATED himself for leaving Saturday, but he'd have hated himself more for staying. No matter who he had been — sheltered earl's son or demon witch's daughter — he was a man of his word. He would not dishonor Elodie or the legacy of his father. Saturday deserved no less. Neither did he.

"Where do we go first?" asked Betwixt. "Starburn?"

Peregrine nodded and put a hand on Betwixt's scruffy shoulder. In his other hand was a small satchel that contained his worldly possessions: a shard of mirror, a vial of gryphon's tears, and a golden cup. He had left the runesword with Jack, and the wish that it had better luck besting the dragon a second time around. Saturday had given him no token to take with him, nor had he asked her for one.

"Before you set out on this journey with me, my friend, I must ask you one question."

"I promise to give you the straightest answer I can," said Betwixt.

"Is there a home you need to visit? A family to which you need to return? A quest of your own to finish?"

Betwixt scratched at his stubby faun horns, like the witches', only furrier. "Whatever home or family I was born into I left by choice long ago. I'm a useless sack of trouble on my own. You're stuck with me."

"It's a burden I'm prepared to bear."

"And you are a burden I'm prepared to bear," replied Betwixt. In a flash of golden light, he was the pegasus again, silver coat, white mane, angel wings, and all.

As he galloped to speed and took flight, Peregrine looked back down on the gardens of Rose Abbey. But for a few hooded acolytes, no one had come to see him off.

It was just as well.

From the air he looked north, to the White Mountains, but nothing stood out against the jagged horizon. No plumes of smoke and Earthfire spewed from the Top of the World, no hued clouds shot down colorful lightning, no dragon spun on lofty breezes.

More terror and tragedy would come, in time, and he would do his part to remedy the damage he'd had a hand in, but today the world was peaceful. Today, the sun would trek across the sky and march time onward. There would be a tonight, and then another today, and soon he would be back where he belonged. He only hoped that place was at Saturday's side.

Selfishly, he prayed once more that Elodie had forgotten him and gone on to live a full life.

~eeeee~

It had been so long since he'd seen the castle at Starburn that he didn't recognize it the first time they flew over. He motioned with his hands and legs for Betwixt to circle around and land in the woods, just outside the gates. Hidden in the brush, Betwixt changed from his regal pegasus form into that of a tri-horned mule. And so the long-lost son of Starburn returned to his castle at sunset, on the back of a humble pack animal.

No one seemed to care.

In fact, there seemed to be no one there at all. No soldiers looked down from the towers. No market stalls populated the bailey. There was no smell of horses or hearth fires or children, fresh fruit or rotted meat. There were no sounds but for that of a few empty pennant poles, rusted and banging about in the wind.

"Do you think it's a spell?" Peregrine whispered into the silence. "That they're all asleep somewhere?"

Betwixt snuffled warily in reply. "Or dead."

Peregrine dismounted at the front of the keep, walked up the steps, and banged on the door. The knock echoed through the empty bailey. He knocked a second time, and a third. He'd just about given up when the grilled porthole in the door opened.

"Go away! We've nothing to give!" The woman's voice was common; the top of her kerchiefed head barely reached the porthole.

"Not even scraps for a beggar?" asked Peregrine.

"We've barely any scraps for ourselves. Go on, then, and leave us in peace."

"I have a message for your master."

"Bah. You mean the mistress."

Mistress? "Yes, she will do." Perhaps he should have asked for Hadris straight off.

"She's not here." It sounded like the woman spat at the door. "And thank the gods. We've nothing left to give her, either."

"What on earth is going on here?" Peregrine asked. Betwixt snuffled again. The chimera was right. It was time to get to the point.

"I am Peregrine of Starburn," he declared to the porthole, "and I have come to reclaim my lands." Not that there appeared to be much to reclaim.

There was a riot of giggles and the porthole slammed shut. There was a dragging, a rattle of chains, and then the door opened. Two small people stood before him, a man and a woman, both middle-aged, and both flushed with repressed amusement. Peregrine could tell from their complexions that they were not dwarves from the mountains but petelkin, a rare diminutive breed of human.

"Pleased to meet you, Your Lordship," said the female

petelkin. "I'm the Queen of the Troll Kingdom, and this here's my brother, God of the North Wind."

At that announcement, the two of them collapsed in laughter.

"I actually am Peregrine of Starburn," he repeated. He simply had no idea what else to say.

"Bah," said the woman. "Peregrine of Starburn is a myth. Peregrine of Starburn is a wish young girls make on stars."

The man, who indeed could have been her brother, eyed Peregrine. "Did you come from the stars?"

"Very near there," he said. "Look, I can prove it. I have items in my possession that bear the Starburn coat of arms."

"You and half the countryside," said the woman. "Everything was sold to pay the mistress's debts before she got herself married off."

"When she ran out of furniture, she sold the people," said the man. "We only got to stay because of the contract." The woman gave her brother a good smack before he could say anything else on that particular matter.

"Out of curiosity," said the woman, "what exactly is it you've got?"

"Only what I was wearing or holding when I was cursed. This dagger"—he held the piece out for examination—"and this cup."

The woman snatched the cup from his grasp. Peregrine let her take it. She poked at the scrollwork and prodded the gems to see if any were loose. She made what looked like a sign of the Thief God over the Starburn seal, and then spat upon it.

Peregrine waited patiently while she continued to find what he knew she would: nothing.

She did not return the cup to him. "Come inside," she said.

"May my companion come as well?" asked Peregrine, motioning to the odd mule.

"Just so long as he don't scat on the floors," said the man.

In a flash of light, Betwixt became a faun again. "I promise to leave your floors exactly as I find them," he said with a jaunty bow.

The woman raised her eyebrows at the magical display, or Betwixt's nakedness. Her brother stared at Betwixt in full, open-mouthed bewilderment. "You *did* come from the stars."

Peregrine followed the woman down the long hallway, straight through to the kitchens at the opposite end of the house.

He couldn't recall what the kitchens of Starburn had looked like before he left, but he marveled at them now. Floors that could be swept, a pantry for storing dry goods, and air that smelled of wood smoke — wood! — instead of brimstone. There would be chickens beyond that back door, and cows, for eggs, milk, butter, and cheese. Mixing bowls and dishtowels made of proper cloth, not something an ancient soldier had worn up the side of a mountain to meet his death.

The woman stood before a low cupboard that faced away from them, still holding his golden cup. "Never seen a kitchen before, great man?" she teased.

"The kitchen where we were kept was far more humble," Peregrine answered honestly. "We didn't have a lot of the luxuries this house affords." Like windows. Or daylight.

"It'd have to have been a fire pit and a stick broom to be less extravagant than this," said the man.

"No sticks at all," offered Betwixt. "May we sit?"

The woman nodded and gestured to the small table beside the chopping block.

"As I said before, I'm Peregrine —"

"If you like," said the man.

"— and this is my companion, Betwixt."

"Pleasure," said the woman. She opened the cupboard, examined the contents inside, and then joined them at the table with the cup. "I'm Gretel. This is my brother, Hansel."

"God of the North Wind," said Hansel, letting loose a rowdy fart in illustration.

"Impressive," said Betwixt.

"If you really are Peregrine of Starburn," said Gretel, "and I'm not saying you are, when did you leave these lands?"

"Right after my mother's funeral," said Peregrine. "My father was still lying in state when my mother died. The living death took everything he had, and then everything my mother had, in the end. I wasn't the bravest of sons; staying here was simply too much for me to bear. I collected a handful of men at the funeral and left after the first mass with an eye to embarking on the adventure that was to be my life."

"What was the name of your horse?"

Gretel had used the past tense; Peregrine gave up hope that his faithful steed might still be alive. "Scar. Ugly as his name, but the finest piece of horseflesh east of Arilland."

Hansel pounded a fist on the table, as if Peregrine had got the answer right (well, of course he had), but Gretel put out a hand to curb her brother's enthusiasm.

"And who did you leave in charge of accounts?"

"Hadris," Peregrine said without hesitation. The estate accounts were something Hadris, the earl's steward, did anyway, but Peregrine had made a formal announcement to the effect before he'd left, to allay any doubts.

Hansel pounded the table again.

"As I live and breathe," said Gretel.

Peregrine finished the story for them, one they could have only known from the perspective of the men in his party who'd lost him in that tiny grove of trees by the streambed that day. "We stopped at a creek to rest on the way to Cassot. A fairy found me there and offered me a wish and a drink. But she wasn't a fairy, she was the daughter of a witch—a demon—who lived high in the White Mountains, at the Top of the World. She cursed me to take her place there, in her guise, for as long as I lived . . . or until I escaped, which was only a few days ago."

Hansel eyed Peregrine's outfit dubiously. "In her guise? Skirts and all?"

"Skirts and all," answered Peregrine.

"The sinking ocean," said Hansel. "The rising forest. The chaos rain. That was you?"

"Afraid so," said Betwixt. "We woke a dragon on our way out. It's pretty angry."

"But I've come back to set things right," Peregrine said, before the rest of them got lost in the twisted tale of the escape. "I don't know what that witch has done to my lands, but I intend to fix it. I promise you both, I will fix this. But first, I need to make my amends to Elodie of Cassot."

Gretel sighed. "We've kept three frivolous things in all this time. We've sold off the rest of the estate, bit by bit, but even when the walls were bare and the well dried up we kept them. It was our uncle's dying wish." She hopped off the chair and went back to the low cupboard, from which she removed three pristine, jewel-encrusted golden goblets. His own goblet completed the set.

She returned to the table and put her hand over Peregrine's own. For such a small thing, it was exceedingly warm. Or he was just exceedingly cold. "You've been gone a hundred years, milord," said Gretel gently. "Elodie of Cassot is dead."

Peregrine stood up fast, knocking the stool over in his haste. Elodie waiting, he had been prepared for. Elodie forgetting him, he had been prepared for. A hundred years passed and Elodie dead and gone had never crossed his mind.

"Pour our master a drink, Hansel."

Betwixt righted the stool and Gretel guided Peregrine back to the table. Hansel handed him a glass — actual glass! — of a tawny brown liquid that burned his nostrils. Peregrine forced himself to take a swallow, and it scorched a path of Earthfire down his gullet. He handed the glass to Betwixt, who gulped the rest of the contents whole.

"Forgive me, but this is easier for me to tell as a story," said Gretel. "You've only ever been a story to me." Peregrine nodded for her to go on. "When Peregrine of Starburn vanished on the way to claim his bride, people across the country were devastated. Gossip began to spread that there was a curse on Starburn, that none who lived here would ever be able to find true happiness."

"They weren't far off," said Hansel.

Gretel ignored her brother's interruption. "Not long after, a young lady appeared at the castle, claiming to be a cousin of the Earl of Starburn, and thus its rightful heir. She was the most beautiful creature anyone had ever seen, possibly the most beautiful woman in the world. And because she was so beautiful, everyone believed her."

"What did she look like?" asked Peregrine, but he already knew.

"Hair and eyes as black as the midnight sky, skin a dusky olive hue, and everywhere she went, it smelled like cinnamon."

Leila, it seemed, had not simply cursed Peregrine to take her place at the Top of the World. She'd taken his place here in Starburn as well.

"She was not as kind as she was beautiful. She cared nothing for people, only power. She traveled the world in style, attending party after party, drowning herself in one extravagance or another until Starburn was bankrupt. When there was no blood left in these stones, she married a dark prince from a kingdom west of Arilland and was never heard from again."

"It is said she lives there still," added Hansel. "That her beauty never dies. Just like you."

"The witch's daughter," said Peregrine. "Leila. She had that kind of power."

"I would believe that now," said Gretel.

"She only ever had us call her Mistress," said Hansel.

"And how do you two fit into all of this?" asked Betwixt.

"Our birth was seen to be part of the curse on this estate," said Gretel. "I was the first petelkin, and then my brother. Our mother died in childbirth. No woman was brave enough to bear a child in Starburn after that."

"I'm sorry," said Peregrine. "But I am glad that Leila didn't force you to leave."

"She couldn't." Hansel smiled proudly. "Because of the contract."

Gretel explained. "Before Peregrine left these lands, he publicly gave power of his estates over to his steward."

"Hadris," said Peregrine.

"By virtue of that power, none could remove Hadris or his family from these lands, not even the dark mistress herself."

"He fought long and hard, Great-Uncle Hadris," said Hansel. "To the bitter end." He raised his own glass in a toast and drained it.

Poor Hadris. He'd been a good, strong man, kind but strict, so much like the earl. Peregrine clapped Hansel on the back.

"You're a credit to his memory. I can't think of two people I'd rather have in charge of Starburn."

"Don't you want to run the estate, now that you're back?" asked Gretel.

"Yes. And no," said Peregrine. "There are still some things I need to do first."

Hansel elbowed Gretel in the side. "It's a girl," he whispered.

"You are not wrong, my good man," Peregrine said proudly. "She saved me from a demon witch. I owe her my life."

"Same here," said Betwixt.

Hansel grimaced. "She'd have to be the sister of Jack Wood-cutter himself to be worthy of our Peregrine."

"Funny you should say that," said Betwixt.

"Her name is Saturday Woodcutter," said Peregrine.

Hansel stared at them.

Gretel smiled. "A fortunate name for a fortunate girl; I hope she is prepared to prove herself worthy. Peregrine's story has been told at children's bedsides for a century. Every pretty little thing for miles has fancied herself Elodie and dreamt that her own Peregrine, done with his adventures in the Vanishing Lands, would appear to sweep her off her feet and take her as his bride. You've been wished for upon more stars than years you've been gone, I'll wager. I wished for you a time or two myself as a girl, I'm not ashamed to say." Gretel's blush convinced him otherwise.

"I'm honored." Peregrine took her tiny hand in his and kissed the back of it.

"And here I am, no longer the pretty little thing I was, and here you are, Peregrine of Starburn, done with your adventuring and knocking at my doorstep. Who would believe it?"

"Not I," said Hansel.

"Nor I," said Betwixt. He snorted and magicked himself back into a pegasus, much to Hansel's delight.

"I will be back soon," said Peregrine. "We will refill the coffers and stock the cupboards and open the market and Starburn will live again."

"Thank you," said Gretel. "Thank you for coming back to us. To me."

Peregrine bowed to the woman. As much as he wanted to stay, he desperately needed to catch up with Saturday and stand by her side for as long as she'd have him. "Thank you for telling me the story. In a way, Elodie will live on forever."

"That she will," said Hansel.

Gretel put out her arms and Peregrine knelt to hug the little woman. "From what I know, the real Elodie did wait for you, long past her prime, but a wandering knight fell in love with her anyway and followed her day and night until she finally accepted him. I don't know how many they had, but there were children, and I believe her family still resides in Cassot."

"I look forward to meeting them," said Peregrine, "and sharing with them the rest of the story."

Hansel crooked a finger and Peregrine leaned over to hear him whisper, "You might want to leave out the part about being a girl for a hundred years."

19

A New Adventure

H E'LL BE BACK, love. Trust me on this one. I've seen enough besotted men to know."

Love. The very word rankled, no matter what its use.

"Who, Peregrine?" Saturday asked Wolf nonchalantly. "Whatever. He'll be back, or not. Who cares?" She glowered at the path in front of them. Even the trees of the forest they rode through didn't make her happy anymore.

"You care, that's who," said Wolf. "You've been scowling for the past ten miles."

"I always do that," said Saturday.

Wolf looked skeptical.

"I'm just tired. This wagon is bruising my backside. And it's too bright." She held up a hand to shield her eyes from the glowing red sun setting through the leaves ahead of them. After spending so long cooped up inside a mountain, she still hadn't acclimated to the light.

The wheels began to kick up sticks and stones. "Whoa, Sassy." Wolf snapped the reins and guided the old gray mare back onto the path. "From what I hear, you could make our journey a lot shorter if you wanted to."

It was true enough; her knapsack still held the ebony-handled brush Thursday had given her. She could throw it like the one she had thrown from the back of Betwixt, calling the Wood to them and Faerie with it. Assuming that the power would do as she willed. So far, there was no evidence that she could harness anything from the ether outside the mountain.

"I've had enough of magic shortcuts," she said. In the back of her mind, Velius crossed his arms over his chest proudly. She wanted to slap that vision. She spun the ring-that-used-to-be-a-sword on her finger: once, twice, thrice. Stupid teachers. Stupid ax. Stupid sword. Stupid witches. Stupid gods.

"Suit yourself." Wolf directed his attention to the road. It was a small comfort. "They call you Earthbreaker, you know."

"They *who?*"

"Bards, minstrels, the usual folk. They all come to Faerie to play for the queen." Wolf risked a glance at Saturday from the corner of his eye. "I knew Jack wouldn't be able to lord his legendary status over his sisters forever."

This time Saturday did smile. "I suppose not. So what is it they say?"

"Just verses about mirrors and swords and oceans, for now,

bits about you taking over a pirate ship before trapping a giant bird that you rode to the Top of the World." Wolf tilted his hat back. His sideburns covered most of his face; those and his long, wavy locks were almost every color Saturday had ever seen on a head of hair. Tufts peeked out from his tall collar and beneath the long sleeves of his coat. His hands were weathered and his nails were thick. His eyes were yellow shadows beneath bushy brows.

"I look forward to hearing the new tales, once word gets out about the witch and the mountain and all," he went on. "Instead of batting their eyes at idiots, young girls will start taking up stick swords to slay a dragon and save the prince." He chuckled at the idea. "Yes, I do look forward to that."

"He's not a prince," Saturday grumbled. "He's the son of an earl." And unlike in Jack's tales, Saturday hadn't gotten to keep her prize in the end.

" 'Prince' is more romantic," said Wolf. "Give it a fortnight, *Hero.* He'll be a prince. Mark my words."

"If you say so." Saturday took up the scowling again in earnest. It had been so hard to let Peregrine leave the abbey. Too hard. She had stolen an acolyte's robes and watched him fly off with Betwixt. She spun the ring on her finger again: once, twice, thrice. She would not beg the gods to let him come back to her. She was done asking for anything, in rhyme or otherwise.

"Wolves mate for life, you know," he said, apropos of nothing.

"Yes. So?"

"So I know love when I see it. No two people who love

each other as much as you and that boy do will ever be apart for very long, so there's no sense in you wasting life worrying. Besides"—he pulled his hat back down—"your sour face is ruining my evening."

Saturday had half a mind to jump off the wagon and walk to Faerie. Everything Wolf said was gods-meddling rubbish. How could he be so sure that Saturday loved Peregrine if she didn't even know it herself? All she knew was the hollowness in her chest and the ache in her head. Her mind didn't seem to be able to focus on anything. She felt angry and empty and overly warm and slightly ill. Perhaps she'd caught a chill in their rush from the mountain, or the abbey's rich food had disagreed with her. There was a madness inside her that wanted nothing more than to scream and cry its way out.

Oh no. Saturday sat up. This was no malady. Wolf was right: this was *love.* She loved Peregrine, so much that it actually hurt.

Saturday stood in the wagon, raised her face to the gods, and vented all her frustration at the sky.

Old Sassy startled, and Wolf snapped the reins again to keep her in check. "Worked it out, did you?"

"Why?" Saturday cried.

"Love works in mysterious ways," said Wolf.

"No, why did he leave me?"

Wolf reached up and pulled her back into the moving wagon before she toppled out. "Look," he said. "Some things you have to go out and do to prove to everyone else that you're good enough, right?"

Saturday had worked hard the whole of her life to be as

special as the rest of her family. The fey-unblessed sister had longed for years to leave the confines of her quiet, mundane life, until the day she finally did . . . wrecking half the countryside and blowing up a mountain to boot.

"Well, sometimes a man needs to go out and do something to prove that very same thing to himself." Wolf drew Old Sassy to a halt. "We know just how amazing you are — in a month every child from Faerie to the Troll Kingdom will know too. This is not about you, love. It's about Peregrine proving to himself that he deserves you."

Wolf clicked his tongue to set the mare going again while Saturday brooded in the twilight. "That's stupid," she said finally.

Wolf shrugged. "I don't make the rules," he said. "You don't think he'd actually go back to a betrothal after all you've been through, do you?"

"Yes, I do," said Saturday. That was the trouble. Peregrine was stubbornly honorable enough to keep a promise made by someone else.

"Then let's hope this Elodie is smarter than he is."

~ellee~

Saturday and Wolf passed the next two days in companionable silence. They let the horse graze at intervals while they hunted for their dinner, and they slept under the stars. Saturday rested, letting the soul of the forest nourish her from the inside out, bringing her back to herself.

On the third day they stopped at a creek outside the borders of Faerie, and Saturday decided to test her magic once more. She took the ring from her finger and placed it in the palm of her right hand. The tiny circle of metal mocked her pain, symbolizing the loss of a sword she'd always wanted and a man she hadn't, but loved all the same. Unbidden, a single tear fell from her cheek and landed in her palm.

Weight forced her hand to the ground. Saturday smiled down at her sword. "Hello, stranger."

"Probably not wise to go flashing that around the halls of the Fairy Queen," Wolf said from over her shoulder.

Saturday picked up the sword and examined it. Other than a dull sheen to the blade, it didn't look worse for the wear. "I just wanted to see if I could still . . . if I was still . . ."

Wolf tossed down the bundle of firewood he'd been collecting. "You're not going to get any less special, if that's what you're afraid of. You've burned that bridge. There's no going back."

There was a rustle of white feathers in the trees across the stream.

Saturday remained calm. She'd been jumping at birds the whole journey, and Wolf had teased her for it every time. None of them had been the pegasus. There was no reason to think this was either, until a silver-white horse emerged from the brush on angel wings.

She took her sword in both hands and forced the stupid look off her face. Her fingers and toes tingled. She told herself it was an aftereffect of the magic. Her heart knew this was a lie.

"Took you long enough," she said as Peregrine dismounted.

"I see you got your sword back."

"It wasn't easy."

"Come on," Wolf said to Betwixt. "There's a lovely meadow full of nice, peaceful buttercups this way."

Saturday let them go and tried concentrating on the sword. Swing. Block. Parry. Thrust. "How's the old homestead?"

"Not the trip down memory lane I thought it would be." He'd crossed the stream now. "A lot changes in a hundred years."

Saturday dropped both the sword and the pretense. They hadn't survived two witches, an exploding mountain, and a dragon just so Peregrine could lose everything.

"A hundred years?" It was bad enough having no family left to speak of; after a hundred years, every bit of the world he'd known would have vanished completely. Saturday couldn't imagine the loneliness.

"About that, yes. I told you time passed differently up there."

Saturday remembered the hash marks on the cave walls. He must have had some inkling, but every time she'd asked about it, he'd evaded the question. She wondered how long a person had to be a prisoner before he stopped thinking of time altogether in order to stay sane.

"Peregrine, I'm so sorry." She touched his jaw, dark with beard stubble. Only a few strands remained of the silver-blue streak in his dark hair. His eyes were truly green now, without a trace of black. "Leila's curse. It's broken? Even though she's still alive?"

"The curse has been fulfilled," he said. "I lived a long and fruitful life. And now I'm dying." He turned his face in toward the palm of her hand, taking a deep breath of her scent.

"What?!" Saturday swore. "What happened in Starburn?"

"This happened long before Starburn. It started happening even before we left the mountain. Leila cursed me to die, so I am dying."

"But you're not ill!" cried Saturday. "And the part about losing a vital organ? We all came down from that mountain in one piece. You're not sick, and you certainly haven't lost your mind." She shook her head. "I have, maybe. But not you. Never you."

"I lost my heart," he said, looking straight into her eyes. "That's pretty vital."

"Over me? No. No one should have to die for me. You can't die, Peregrine. You can't. I just got handed the rest of my life and I have no idea what to do with it, but I knew at least I had you. You and Betwixt and me, we all have each other. Now what do I do?" She pounded his chest with her fists. "What do I do?!"

"You're the strongest woman I've ever met—"

"I'm one of the only women you've ever met," said Saturday.

"—and your life will be full of amazing things. You don't need me for that."

Saturday couldn't look at him anymore. She stared at her feet instead, at the toes of boots that had seen the Top of the

World and the edge of an ocean. "But I want you there," she said to the ground. "I just want you, period. I love you." She took a deep breath, inhaling as slowly as she exhaled. Damn the gods. Damn Fate. Damn everyone. "How long do you have?"

"Until I die?"

Saturday turned on him with the full force of her anger. "No, until the moon dances, you idiot."

"Right." Peregrine pressed his lips together. "I suspect I have only as many years left as any other mortal man."

It took a beat for his words to register. "Why, you——"

Saturday raised her fists to punch him again, but couldn't bring herself to do it. Laughter erupted from the other side of the bush that hid Wolf and Betwixt from sight.

"That's enough from you!" she yelled at the shrubbery. She pushed Peregrine hard enough to topple him over, turned on her heel, and went back for her sword.

"Calm down," said Peregrine. "It's not like I'm dying to-morrow."

"Keep it up and you might be." Saturday picked up her sword.

"Saturday, you can push me away all you want, but I'll have you know that I plan to fight for you. I will fight to stand beside you, and I mean to die beside you."

"I could run you through right now," she offered.

"I wish you'd wait. We're desperately low on gryphon's tears."

Peregrine regained his footing all too quickly, and when he turned her back around to face him, he noticed the tears she didn't want him to see. He wiped them away for her. "We should bottle these instead," he said. "They're far more rare." He held her then, like he hadn't held her since that first cold night on the mountain after Cwyn had captured her, like she wished he'd hold her every day from now on until the end of their adventures.

"So," he said finally. "You love me."

"You loved me first."

He hugged her tighter. "And don't you forget it."

There was a smattering of applause at Peregrine's declaration. From the shadows and the fireflies stepped the figure of a thin young man with a quiver of arrows at his back and a bow slung across his chest.

"Trix!" Saturday ran and embraced her little brother, bow and all.

"Watch it, sister, you're armed."

She let her sword fall to the ground again. "I'm sorry," she said.

Trix reached up, took her face in his hands, and kissed both cheeks. "I'm sorry too," he said. "Will you ever forgive me?"

"Hmm." Saturday scrunched up her face in thought. "Well, I'd make you promise to do the washing up for a month, but since I don't think either one of us is going to see the tower-house for a while, how about you just owe me one?"

"Deal," said Trix. He spat in his hand and they shook on it.

"It is so good to see your face," said Saturday. "I missed you."

"Really?" asked Trix. "I didn't miss you. You were with me the whole time."

"Was I?"

"Oh yes. Every time I needed to be strong, I thought of you, and you gave me your strength." He pointed to the blue-green band at her wrist. "And every time you needed my strength, I gave it to you. Didn't you notice?"

Saturday ran her finger across the strip of fabric with her siblings' hair inside it — even Jack's, now. She had thought it was the magic of the mountain funneling through her the whole time she was imprisoned — and maybe it was — but it was her family's strength, too. That strength and love had let her shift the ring back into a sword, once the Top of the World was a distant memory behind them. "I did," she said. "Thank you."

"Once or twice I swore I could even hear your voice," said Trix.

Peregrine and Saturday exchanged glances, remembering what had happened in the cave of mirrors. It was probably best that particular room had been consumed by Earthfire.

"Amazing thing, magic," said Peregrine. "I'm Peregrine, by the way."

"Trix," he said as they shook hands. "I'm the reason Saturday got into all this mess."

"I fell in love with your sister in the middle of this mess," Peregrine replied.

"Really?" said Trix. "Which sister? I have seven, you know." Saturday grabbed Trix before he could get away and tickled him mercilessly, as they had done back home, before she'd broken the world. She didn't know how much she'd needed that until just then. Who'd have ever thought that one day she'd long for a moment of normal life?

"How did you find us?" Saturday asked when they'd caught their breaths.

"A brownie told me," said Trix. "A wild one, from a tribe I'd never heard of. He showed up at the Hill spouting all sorts of wild tales about dragons and witches and falling off a mountain. Said he was rescued by a bad-tempered giant in a skirt. I can only assume he meant you." Trix examined Saturday from head to toe, and then Peregrine, in his long, full coat. "Then again, maybe he meant you," he said to Peregrine. "Either way, I'm here. We need your help, Saturday."

"I'm here to give it," said Saturday. "Who's 'we'?"

"I come to you as the emissary of the Queen of Faerie," Trix said in his noblest voice.

"Do you, now?" asked Saturday.

"I speak to the animals," he said. "And for the animals."

"So it's the animals who need help?" asked Saturday.

"Yes. And the Queen of Faerie, too. And . . . well . . . pretty much everybody in the whole world."

"Again?" said Peregrine.

Saturday sighed melodramatically. "Typical. You in?" she asked Peregrine.

"Always," he answered.

"Same here," said Betwixt as he emerged from the bushes.

"I'm headed in that direction anyway," said Wolf.

"Saturday," Trix whispered, "why didn't you tell me you have a *pegasus?*"

Saturday planted a kiss on her brother's cheek before he could cringe away. "Trixie, dear, I have a lot of new surprises. Do we need to leave now?"

Trix looked up at the clear night sky. "We can wait until dawn."

Wolf's eyes flashed yellow in the darkness. "Sassy and I don't mind traveling through the night if you don't."

"Then let's go!" cried Saturday.

Peregrine tugged at her elbow. "One quick thing."

"Make it snappy."

He pulled Saturday into his arms and kissed her soundly.

Somewhere on the forest floor, a sword shifted back into a ring. Somewhere above them, a silver moon danced among the clouds. Somewhere on a peak in the White Mountains, a dragon drifted lazily through the air. And somewhere on the borders of Faerie, Saturday Woodcutter embarked on a new adventure.

As their lips parted, Saturday smiled up at the gods. Those troublesome bards could sing all they pleased — she'd won her prince after all. She tossed her short hair in the forest breeze and laughed until two strong hands captured her head and turned it to the side.

"Ah . . . beloved?"

"Yes, dearest?"

"What on earth happened to your ear?"

ALETHEA KONTIS

is the author of many shiny books and stories for children of all ages, including *Enchanted,* the acclaimed previous book about the Woodcutter family. A student of science fiction greats Andre Norton and Orson Scott Card, Alethea lives and writes in Virginia.

Visit her at www.aletheakontis.com.